SKYLAR

ALSO BY GREGORY MCDONALD:

Gregory Mcdonald

SKYLAR

William Morrow and Company, Inc.

New York

It is the policy of William Morrow and Company, Inc., and its imprints and affiliates, recognizing the importance of preserving what has been written, to print the books we publish on acid-free paper, and we exert our best efforts to that end.

Library of Congress Cataloging-in-Publication Data

Mcdonald, Gregory, 1937–
   Skylar / Gregory Mcdonald.
     p.   cm.
   ISBN 0-688-14163-3
   I. Title.
  PS3563.A278S54 1995
  813'.54—dc20   94-39543
                                                  CIP

Printed in the United States of America

First Edition

1 2 3 4 5 6 7 8 9 10

BOOK DESIGN BY JUDITH STAGNITTO-ABBATE

For Ray Fraley, Jr., Dot and Don King,
Mary Elizabeth Abernathy, Cheryle Higgins Johnson,
and Mr. Tommy Gordon

". . . in real life, mysteries occur to real persons with their individual humors, and mysterious circumstances are apt to be complicated by the comic."

—ISRAEL ZANGWILL (1864–1926)

SKYLAR

1

"Where's Skylar?" his mother asked, seated in front of the vanity mirror, brushing her hair.

Leaning over her to straighten his bow tie in the mirror, his father asked, "Where the hell is Skylar? Where the hell is Skylar ever?"

"Damn you, Skylar, I hope the skeeters get you!"

"There ain't no skeeters in Greendowns County."

Naked in the dusk, Skylar and Tandy were playing in the river.

She grabbed the hair on his forehead and forced his head under water.

He lowered his head even more. He put his head between her legs. Straightening his legs, hands behind her knees, he made her belly flop onto his back.

"Oof!" Heels of her hands against the muscles of his buttocks, she arched her back, tried to hold herself off him, keep her face out of the water.

Water swirling around his chest, he turned and turned, his feet stirring up mud. Tandy's hands slipped off him. Her shoulders and face revolved around his waist below water.

At the edge of the river, the brown dog, Julep, barked and danced, wanting to take part in the playing but not wanting to get wet.

Reins free, the horse, Runaway, munched along the top of the riverbank.

Skylar let go of Tandy's legs. They slipped over his shoulders and down his back. Free in the water, she rolled onto her back.

Looking up at his wet shoulders, dripping hair, then into his eyes, she smiled. She opened her legs.

With one strong backward stroke of her arms, she came to him. She put her legs around his waist and gripped him as hard as she could.

He leaned forward from his waist and lifted his feet off the mud. Falling onto her, he put his arms around her chest and his face against her throat.

They sank. As he kissed her, she coughed into his mouth.

He put his hand against the river bottom and sprang them both back toward the surface.

Standing, the skin of her shoulders and upper arms gleaming in that light, her breasts firm and pointing up, she sputtered water into her hands. "I guess if you haven't drowned me yet, you're prolly not goin' to."

He took her hands away from her face. Not otherwise touching her, he put the tip of his tongue on the skin of her cheekbone, just below her left eye. Gently, slowly, his tongue made circles on her wet skin.

She raised her chin and closed her eyes.

Skylar ran his tongue to her ear and then down her jawline. She lifted her chin more. He kissed her throat.

He ran the tip of his tongue down between her breasts. Without lifting his tongue from her skin, he circled the nipple of her right breast.

He knelt in the river-bottom mud. He ran his tongue down between her ribs and into her navel.

Tandy put her hands on his shoulders and stepped forward. She placed her feet on the river bottom either side of and behind his hips. Crouching a little, she fit her knees into his armpits and squeezed, making his breast muscles bunch forward. She cupped her hands against his breasts and, pressing firmly, revolved them in different directions.

She took a deep breath. Then, looking up the riverbank, she said, "You recognize you're payin' your cousin no mind, Skylar?"

Kneeling, he looked up at her, smiling. "But ain't sex fun?"

"You're right about that, Skylar."

"Yeah. I'm right about that." Underwater, he pressed his nose against the forward base of her pubic hair.

Face raised to the sky, Tandy said, "You're too right!"

Underwater, he could not hear her.

He stood up and took her hand and began to lead her toward the riverbank.

"We've always had sex fun," he said.

"You always surprise me, no matter what we're doin'. You know that?"

At the edge of the water, she slipped a little.

He put his arm around her waist and lowered her onto the mud. His chest on hers, his waist flat on the ground, his penis in the cool mud, he ran his tongue around her lips, then put it into her mouth. He opened his mouth to circumscribe her lips. Then he thrust his tongue toward her throat.

"Yeow," she finally said, softly.

Putting more of his weight on his left hipbone, he slid his leg up her thigh. She rolled more onto her side.

He put the muscles just above his knee against her crotch and began rubbing. He put his hands onto her shoulders and pressed down firmly but gently.

Her hands were flat against the muscles below his shoulder blades. She pulled him more toward her.

"Oh," she said.

Julep was nibbling Skylar's toes.

Skylar put his right hand under Tandy's left arm, ran it quickly down her side, grabbed her left cheek, and lifted it.

Riding Skylar's bucking, rubbing thigh muscle, Tandy came.

They stretched on their backs in the mud.

"You've got to go meet your cousin. Your parents—"

"You just knew I wasn't gonna meet him straight out."

"He arrived at your house hours ago."

"I didn't happen to be at home just then, did I?" With his fingers, Skylar plopped mud onto Tandy's stomach. "I'm a dirt dauber."

"Your parents are giving a dress-up lawn party for him." Her left hand smeared the cool mud around on her skin.

"And I'm still not there."

Tandy sat halfway up. "We've got to wash off."

"Yes."

"I hate to put on jeans when I'm wet."

"No hurry." Skylar stepped back into the river.

Following him, she said, "It's getting right late. Let me do your back."

Standing waist deep in the river, they cupped water in their hands and rubbed each other down. "Making love for hours," Tandy said. "Making love all day. It's been nice growing up with you."

"Are we grown up?" Skylar asked.

They ducked their heads below water and shook the mud out of their hair with their fingers.

On the riverbank, still wet, still erect, Skylar pulled on his jeans and his socks and his boots. He raised his fly zipper carefully.

Tandy shook her jeans as if they instead of herself were wet. Holding them at her side, she looked at Skylar.

She said, "You ride Runaway thataway and you might just break it off. Where's my shirt?"

"You don't need a shirt. It's almost dark." Skylar jumped onto the saddleless horse. He had not carried a shirt with him all day. "Let's go."

While wriggling into her jeans, Tandy picked up her shirt. She climbed on to the horse behind Skylar, with his help, without putting her shirt on. She put her arms around his chest and her face against his back.

After they started off, Julep trotting behind them, she said, "Whoa. You're taking the long way."

Skylar said, "I know."

She said, "You ought to hurry."

"I know."

"Skylar," she said, "this is the way to the back of Whitfield."

"I know."

"Skylar, what're you doin' now?"

"Goin' to scope out my cousin."

Still shirtless, Skylar and Tandy lay on their stomachs in the dark on the hill overlooking the lit back lawn of the main house at Whitfield Farm.

They had left Runaway down the far side of the hill, this time tethered to a tree. They had climbed the hill quietly.

Julep lay under a bush near them, snoring from his long day keeping up with Skylar and Tandy.

The back lawn had been rigged out in the Whitfields' usual way for a party. Besides the permanent electric security lights at the back of the house, jack-o'-lanterns had been hung from the trees and the dog run. Rustic serving tables covered with white cloths, a dozen card tables, four folding chairs at each, had been set out.

On the clipped lawn, drinks of one sort or another and paper plates of hors d'oeuvres in their hands, dressed in summer finery, were many of Skylar and Tandy's classmates, their brothers and sisters, younger and older friends, their parents, older people who were friends of Skylar's parents, and of his.

"I'll bet your parents are boilin' like tea water," Tandy had said as they dismounted Runaway. "Your not being there to greet your cousin and all."

"Style," Skylar had answered. "Gotta have style."

"What do you mean, 'style'?"

"Philosophy of living."

"Is that the same thing as being contrary?" Tandy asked.

Now, lying on her belly looking down the hill, Tandy said, "Look at your daddy. You couldn't slip a sardine through his lips. Your mama looks like she's tryin' not to fart."

Skylar laughed. "My mama's never been known to fart."

"There's Jon Than," Tandy said. "Standin' significantly close to the iced shrimp. 'Spose the ice reminds him of home?"

Skylar had already focused on his cousin. "Probably standin' next to the ice in case he needs a transfusion, sudden like."

In their world of Greendowns County, any stranger stood out like a thistle in a field of cow flaps.

"Looks like you, Skylar."

"No, he don't."

"Sure does. I'd know him for a Whitfield anywhere, even at a distance."

"To me, he looks like afterbirth."

"Better lookin' than you, proly. Smarter, too."

With the heel of his hand, Skylar pressed down between her shoulder blades.

"Quit that! I'm layin' on a stob." Tandy grabbed a twig from under her ribs and flung it aside. "I think I like your cousin better'n I like you already."

"Go kiss him up. You know he's got mono."

"He doesn't stand sexy like you, always sort of on one hip. He stands more like a soldier. Or a Stop sign."

"You'll love mono."

"The kissin' disease," Tandy said.

"Har-vard," Skylar drawled. "My cousin goes to Har-vard."

Tandy said nothing.

"He's here to rest," Skylar said. "And to goad me, I 'spect. He can take to the bed and stay there, all I care."

"You know, Skylar, you might just like him, give him a chance."

"My daddy says people from Boston are so intolerant they can't even tolerate the intolerance of others."

"You notice something else about him?"

"Proly smells like fish."

"Look at all the faces down there and then look at his face."

Skylar scanned the faces at the party and then refocused on his cousin's face. "He's paler than even the women."

"He's the only one on that whole lawn not smiling—'cept for Mr. Simes, of course. Don't people in Boston get taught to do nice and smile polite-like?"

"I've never met anyone from Boston before."

"You still haven't, Skylar."

"Wish I'd never."

"Mary Lou's been talkin' to Jon Than a long time now. He hasn't smiled at her once. She must think she's got her mouth on crooked."

"Battin' her eyelashes at him fast enough to give him a week of sneezes."

"She sure is showin' out," Tandy said. "Drawlin' all down her dress, ah do declare."

"I bet that Yankee boy would no more think of reachin' out and touchin' her skin than he would of belchin' durin' a sermon."

"He's backed up twice. When they started talkin', they were at the middle of the table with the iced shrimp, and now they're down at his end."

"Yardage definitely goes to Mary Lou."

"Watch out, Mary Lou!" Tandy mock-shouted. "That boy's got the kissin' disease!"

"Poor Mary Lou. She's confrontin' her first damnyankee. Hope she remembers her great-great-granny shot one of 'em in the foot."

Tandy drawled, "She'll proly consider herself insulted the rest of her natural life."

"Her daddy don't seem too happy with her charmin' a Yankee. He looks like he's about to thunder."

"You ever in your life seen Mr. Simes look happy?"

"Never once. My daddy says it's because he travels so much for business he's all the time constipated."

"Watch Dufus. He's comin' up behind Jon Than. I'll bet he—damn it, he did! Skylar, did you see what that boy did?

He poured beer down the back of Jon Than's pantleg on purpose! Did you see that?"

"I don't expect anyone else saw it."

"Now Dufus is comin' across all apologetic. Tryin' to wipe down Jon Than's pants with his smelly old bar rag!"

Skylar laughed. "Good old Dufus!"

"Look! Jon Than's makin' like it never happened!"

"Dufus is deliberately messin' up Jon Than's white pants, and Jon Than hasn't looked directly at Dufus yet! Why, he's brushin' off ol' Dufus instead of his pants."

"Jon Than damned well better recognize Dufus, or Dufus will go for his head, next."

"Dufus is sayin' he's real sorry, but he's talkin' into empty air."

"Skylar, don't you think you'd better get down to that party, right quick?"

"Good ol' Dufus."

"Dufus is mad, now. He's so mad he's serving ol' Mr. Pendergast. He always ignores ol' Mr. Pendergast." Tandy giggled. "Mary Lou Simes is turned off, too. Suddenly, she's real interested in the shrimp."

"Mary Lou hates shrimp, unless it's popcorned."

"Here comes your mama to rescue Jon Than."

"O, Lordy Lord," Skylar said. "That Jon Than hasn't done anything right yet! He's as insultin' as a catfish served up cold."

"Skylar, what are we doin' layin' up here on the hill when you're supposed to be down there helpin' your mama and meetin' your cousin?"

"Reconnoiterin'."

"Spying."

"Enjoyin' the party. We can see better from up here."

"They need your help."

"That's one thing I'm seein'."

"Skylar, you're afraid you're goin' to feel inferior next to your Boston cousin. Say that's the truth."

"No way."

"You're as ascared to meet up with him as a bunny with a rattler."

"Just wanted to have first look at him."

"Skylar, you're bad!"

"I need you to do me."

"Now? You serious?"

"Sure enough."

"Skylar, you really are bad!"

On the terrace, Monica Whitfield approached Jon.

"Warm," Jon said.

Monica noticed the sweat on Jon's forehead. "Trust all this isn't too much for you, Jonathan, on your first night here."

"I'm fine. Just not used to this heat."

Monica looked at the air wondering just how warm it was. "I love the heat," she said. "What happened to your trousers?"

"Nothing." Jon took a small step back and sideways. "Nothing happened. Nothing important."

Monica looked at her nephew, wondering just how foreign he felt. "That Skylar," she finally said. "I could just pinch his head off."

"Not here yet?" Jon smiled.

Her eyes swept the dark hills of the farm. "He must be somewhere."

"I'm sure he couldn't help being late," Jon said, wondering what there could be to do around here to make anyone late for anything.

"How nice of you to defend your cousin, Jonathan. Your cousin as yet unknown to you."

"Are you worried about him?"

"No. Not specifically. Only generally."

"Did Uncle Dan say Skylar is out on a horse?"

"Skylar's horse is missing. So is his dog. So is Skylar."

"Undoubtedly, he had something better to do."

"Do you suspect he's avoiding you?"

For just an instant, Jon frowned. He could not think how to evade such a truthful question.

Monica said, "I'm sure he'll show up with some fanciful excuse. How someone desperately needed his help at fixing the innards of a tractor, or something."

"Is Skylar good that way? I mean, at fixing tractors?"

"Not especially. He's good at fanciful excuses. I saw you talking with the Simes girl."

"Mary Lou."

"Simes. She graduates next year. The Simes children are the perfect example of how two dolts can marry and produce nice children. You'd almost think they aren't related. That bullet-headed man over there is her father, John Simes, and that twittery little sparrow helping herself to the spiked punch is her mother, the original M.L."

"M.L. for Mary Lou?"

"Jonathan, you'll have to do your best to get used to the way we talk around here . . . and otherwise relate to each other. Her brother, Jack, is that big bruiser over there. Halfback at the state university. And her little brother, Andy Divan, is that cute boy over there in shorts."

"Why do you call him Andy Divan?"

"We don't. We call him Andy-Dandy."

"Of course."

"His middle name is Divan."

"Why?"

"Must be a family name, somewhere," Monica answered. "I doubt he's named after the conceptual couch. John and M.L. are dreadful people partly because they have so little humor."

"I see," said Jon, feeling really very warm.

"Anyway, Mary Lou is our county's Teen Queen."

"Teen Queen?"

"Yes. She regularly wins beauty contests. She won in the six-and-under and the twelve-and-under categories, too, and every contest since. Homecoming Queen. Soybean Queen."

Jon looked across the lawn at Mary Lou, now talking to a group of five young men. "She enters beauty pageants?"

"I forgot. Such are much bigger in the South than in the North. We have every hope Mary Lou will win the state championship."

"Beauty contests?" Jon wanted to say, *cattle shows?* "I've never met a girl before who had been in a beauty contest." *Nor have I ever wanted to.*

"Yes," said Monica, watching two more young men join the group around Mary Lou. "Mary Lou is very popular."

Jon cleared his throat. "I looked in Skylar's room. The door was open from the bathroom. Skylar plays the trumpet?"

Monica smiled. Her nephew was embarrassed by talk of beauty contests. "In the South, Jonathan, we admit it when someone is good-looking, or ugly; tall, short, fat; black, brown, white; male, female. . . . It's the differences among people we love. Equality is admired as something toward which we strive. Homogeneity is disdained as something admittedly impossible and very likely intolerable. As your aunt, I feel I should tell you these things."

In the soft light and the warm night air, Jonathan Whitfield blinked at his aunt as he listened to her slow, quiet but jarringly direct speech.

Monica put her hand on her nephew's arm. "What I mean, Jonathan, is that it's all right to be a man here. It would have been all right for you to have openly admired Mary Lou while she was paying attention to you. And to have slugged Dufus when he purposely poured beer down your pantleg, or at least looked like you were considering slugging him. They both then would have known where they stood with you, you see."

Jon blinked. "Dufus?"

"Yes." Monica smiled. "Dufus never seems to mind getting slugged."

"I've never understood why I like this," Tandy said. "What it does to me."

In the woods at the top of the hill overlooking the party on the lit back lawn of Whitfield Farm, Tandy pulled Skylar's jeans down his legs as far as his boots would allow.

"Neither have I." On his back Skylar raised and spread his knees. "I know why I like it."

Kneeling, Tandy ducked beneath Skylar's jeans-hobbled feet. She squeezed her head and arms and shoulders between his thighs. Then she stretched her legs flat on the ground.

Skylar crossed his boots at the ankles and embraced Tandy's chest with his upper legs.

Tandy's left hand played with Skylar's stomach muscles.

Her right hand held him like an ice-cream cone, which she licked.

In a moment, Skylar was quivering, vibrating uncontrollably, releasing the sexual tensions they had built for hours.

"Yee—ow!"

Below, on the terrace, Monica said to Jonathan, "Here comes Skylar now."

2

"Ha, Jon Than. I'm Skylar."

Eyes widening, Jon rose from the large, cushioned wicker chair where he had been sitting alone on the side porch of Whitfield Farm.

Skylar shook his hand.

"What does 'Ha' mean?" Jon asked.

"Ha," Skylar answered. "How're ya doin'?"

" 'Ha'?" Jon repeated. " 'Jon Than'?"

Skylar craned his neck to look onto the back lawn. "Where my parents at?"

"Are you human, vegetable, or mineral? You *look* relatively human," Jon said. "Shirt, necktie, jacket, creased slacks, shoes—no, boots—hair combed. Perhaps you were assembled at the local emporium. You don't *sound* human. 'Ha? Jon Than? Where my parents at?' Has no one ever shared with you any of the rules of pronunciation, or of grammar? What's all that noise supposed to mean?"

Skylar looked Jon square in the eye. "Can you possibly elucidate the precise location of my parents, please, asshole?"

In the semidark of the porch, Jon's eyes were stretched wide. "I assume they still are in the backyard."

"Thanks," Skylar said. "Tell me, Jon Than, can you catch mono from a guy?"

"You'll never know."

Skylar laughed. "Not 'less you tell me."

Most of the people at the party were now sitting at the little tables eating barbecue, slaw, and beans.

At her table, Monica Whitfield was apologizing for Skylar's tardiness. "I suppose Skylar feels shy with his cousin. They're the same age, look somewhat alike, but they've never met, you know. Jonathan is at Harvard. Of course, he went to a very good prep school. Skylar applied to Vanderbilt, Duke, and the state university. . . ." Monica sighed.

"And?" asked Jeneen Wilmot.

"Not even the state university."

"What did they say?" Tom Wilmot asked. "Did they give any encouragement at all?"

"They didn't even deign to answer. Unless Skylar just swallowed the rejection letters, didn't let us know they arrived. It would be typical of him."

"But Skylar's a bright boy," said Tom. "Always trucking off to state math contests and spelling bees."

"That was when he was ten years old, Tom, before he discovered such things matter," Monica said. "I suppose college admission officers are not too impressed by our local school system. And of course Skylar never played sports."

"Why didn't he?" Tom Wilmot stirred his remaining slaw and beans together. "Tall, slim, muscular. I should think any coach would want him for any sport."

"Our fault, I guess," Monica answered. "Skylar's always been content to work around the farm. Lord knows he's been needed. Together, he and Dufus have done all the essential muscle work around here. Still, we should have insisted Skylar do the right things to impress college admissions officers. You know: break his head playing football; write editorials for the school newspaper entitled 'My Country 'Tis of Me.' That sort of thing."

"Best way for him not to be accepted," Tom said, "is if he

never really applied. Some younguns are afraid to leave jeep country, you know."

Rose Holman said, "Skylar will do just fine."

Monica noticed there were seven people sitting at one small table: Mary Lou Simes and six young men.

Monica said, "I suppose Skylar's not getting into college will ruin his chances with Mary Lou."

Tom snorted. "You expect her to be admitted to Vanderbilt?"

"No, but I expect her husband will have been."

Rose Holman commented, "Certainly the Simes children can go to Vanderbilt University, or anywhere else they want, with all the money their grandmother left them."

Jeneen Wilmot said, "Nonsense, Monica. Everyone knows Skylar and Mary Lou have been an item since they were born. Skylar's been her escort at all the beauty contests since they were three years old. Mary Lou put a nose ring on Skylar while they were still in diapers."

Tom said, softly, "Is that why you've put up with the Simeses all these years?"

"They're neighbors," Monica said.

Rose Holman said, "Why worry about who Skylar's going to marry, Monica? I've never heard marriage is the point of a college education."

Monica looked at Rose through lowered eyelids. "It's just that one thinks of the future in a certain way, Rose. If Skylar and Mary Lou married, they'd probably stay around here. Parents have to think that way, in Greendowns County."

Rose said abruptly, "That Skylar's the sexiest boy in several counties."

Monica choked. "Sexiest?"

"Yes, Lord, yes." Rose Holman had turned eighty-three her last birthday. She never married. "His eyes go all over you, wrap you up, and grab you in. Hug you. Stand near Skylar, you feel like you're fallin' into him, bein' sucked up inside him, somehow. I call that sexy. I don't know any other word for it."

"My, my," Monica said. "The things a mother hears."

"I don't know what else that boy of yours has, Monica, but he has more sex than a cathedral organ."

Monica said, "Whatever it is you're talking about, Rose, I don't think it leads to a recognized profession."

Jon trailing well behind him, Skylar entered the party on the lawn obliquely, almost backing into the lit area, trying to give the impression he had been there awhile. He backed among some people more or less his own age, still standing by the bar table.

"How're you doin', Dufus?"

"You want a beer, Skylar?"

"Sure. Only don't spill it."

Dufus glanced at Skylar in surprise and then laughed.

"Holler later?" Dufus asked.

"Sure enough."

Jack Simes said, "Skylar, what are your intentions regarding my sister?" and smiled.

It was a joke that had started between them when Jack was a high school junior, the Big Man On Campus, and Skylar a lowly freshman.

"Screw your sister," Skylar answered.

The first time he had answered that, Jack seriously had considered crunching Skylar with his hands. Then he had laughed.

Skylar's father rose from a table and crossed the lawn to him.

Dan Whitfield said to his son, "A quiet word with you, please, Skylar."

"Yes, sir."

Beer can in hand, Skylar found himself back in the shadows at the fringe of the party confronting his father.

"Skylar, where you been?"

"Just fuckin' around, sir."

"Skylar . . ." Dan Whitfield seemed to writhe with exasperation.

"Sir?"

"Must you always be so crass?"

Skylar considered his answer. "Sometimes I'm not so crass."

"Your mother could have used your help."

"I mowed the lawn." Skylar looked down at the lawn. "Dufus and I strung the lights." He looked around the terrace at the hanging lanterns. "We set up the tables and chairs." He looked at each table and chair.

"Skylar, your cousin arrived at four o'clock this afternoon."

Skylar looked at Jon standing near them in the dark. "You want me to be that boy's companion, you're gonna have to pay me. And not just minimum wage."

"You could have been here to greet him. That would have been polite."

"Polite. Shoot." Skylar pretended to study his cousin at a distance. "Looks to me like that boy's dirtied his pants already. I expect too much excitement at one time isn't good for a Yankee."

Skylar's mother joined them at the fringe of the party. "You have an excuse?"

"No, ma'am, but I can make one up real fast."

"Skylar, I've talked to you about this."

Skylar looked around at the party on the lit part of the terrace. "Hell, it looks to people like you two grabbed me into the dark and are really beatin' up on me."

"Jonathan's going to have to take it easy," Monica said. "Rest. He's been ill."

"I might cry out."

"Can't you make it easy for him, Skylar?"

"Sure. I've been lettin' him rest. Do I have to watch him rest?"

"Skylar, don't you want to be invited North to visit his family?"

"No, ma'am, I surely don't. That cold weather just might make my blood freeze up. I expect bits of frozen blood would sound just awful clatterin' around inside my head."

Turning, Dan said, "Jonathan, come here a moment, will you?"

Jon stepped forward.

Dan Whitfield put his arm around his nephew's shoulders. "Jonathan, I'd like you to meet my son, Skylar."

"Ha, Jon Than." Skylar shook hands with him. "How're ya doin'?"

Jaw clenched, Jonathan said, "Pleased to make your acquaintance."

"Wet your pants?"

"Skylar!" Dan said.

Monica said to Jon, "I know you've met almost everyone here, Jonathan, but Skylar will bring you around and introduce you to his special friends."

"Sure," Skylar said. "Come on in the house and meet my dog, Julep."

"Here's Mary Lou now," Monica said. "Mary Lou, how pretty you are tonight."

Mary Lou held a half-full wineglass in her hand. "Real nice party, Miz Whitfield."

"Ha, Mary Lou." Skylar kissed her cheek. "This here's my cousin, Jon Than. Don't kiss him."

"We've met," Jon said hastily.

"How you like Greendowns County so far, Jon Than?"

It was clear from his eyes Jon was confused by the presence of a girl who deliberately entered beauty contests. " 'Grendon'?"

Skylar said, "The county's pronounced that way."

" 'Pernounced'?"

Dan said to his wife, "We have other guests to attend to. Thank God."

Monica said, "I'm sure you three will get along splendidly."

Skylar watched his parents cross the lawn and separate.

"Skylar, you bastard," Mary Lou said.

"What did I do now?"

"You haven't called me all week."

Skylar cupped his hand around one side of his mouth and called, "Mary Lou! Mary Lou!"

"Stop that!"

Everyone at the party was looking at them.

With his index finger, Skylar beckoned Mary Lou forward.

He brushed back her hair. He cupped his hand around her ear as if to tell her a secret. He put his lips around her ear and squeezed its base gently. Then he thrust his tongue into her ear.

"Skylar!" Mary Lou shrieked.

Everyone was looking at them again.

"You can always trust Mary Lou to shower thoroughly," Skylar advised his cousin. "Guaranteed: no earwax. Want a drink?"

"Skylar, you give me goose bumps," Mary Lou said. "Or you make my flesh crawl, one."

"Bourbon? Ever had any good bourbon, Jon Than?"

"I can't drink."

"Or you could do what Mary Lou is doin': Walk around with a wineglass with vodka in it."

"Skylar! Damn you!"

"One isn't supposed to drink while suffering mono," Jon said.

"Skylar, I don't even know why I come talk with you," Mary Lou said, "pay you any mind at all."

" 'Cause I have the cutest knees you ever saw. That's what you said."

"When we were four years old!"

"I never forget a compliment," Skylar said. "Are you sufferin', Jon Than?"

"Only from embarrassment."

"That's right." Mary Lou said to Skylar. "You're embarrassing me in front of your cousin."

"Shoot," Skylar said. "I doubt I could embarrass either one of you if I took it on as a paid job."

"I didn't ask you," Mary Lou said to Jon. "How long you going to be here, Jon Than?"

"I hope to leave tomorrow."

"Sure enough?"

"No way," Skylar said. "He's going to be here until he's

sick no more, which will probably be the same day we plant him."

"Which doesn't change my statement that I hope to leave tomorrow."

"He's going to rest. He's going to sit on the veranda with a blanket over his knees and sip iced tea while Dufus and I sweat ourselves dry workin' the farm. That right, Jon Than?"

"Sounds good to me. Can you sing work songs while you broil in the sun?"

"Go to bed early every night, too," Skylar said. "No later than seven o'clock, I hope."

"Don't you like it here, Jon Than?" Mary Lou asked.

"Aunt Monica is very nice," Jon said. "Uncle Dan." He glanced at Skylar. "It's a pretty place. Hot."

"You'll get used to the heat," Mary Lou said. "You met my little brother, Andy-Dandy?" The twelve-year-old boy had arrived sweating and breathing hard. "Andy, this here is Jon Than Whitfield."

"Pleased to meet you." The boy shook hands.

"Are you a kitchen implement?"

"Sir?"

"Why do you let them call you Andy-Dandy? You want to grow up to be something that peels carrots?"

Andy smiled at Skylar. "Is he speaking any language I'm acquainted with?"

"Yeah." Skylar sipped his beer. "It's a dialect called nasal."

"Skylar, you stop insulting your cousin right now," Mary Lou scolded, "or I won't speak to you anymore! Why are you being so rude to your cousin?"

"He's a carpetbagger."

Still grinning, Andy said, "Oh, Skylar! You're scared all the girls are goin' to like Jon Than more'n you!"

"That may be right," Skylar said.

With a wooden serving tray, Dufus was bringing the remaining barbecue around to the tables to offer replenishment to those who had already been to the buffet, served themselves, and eaten.

While Skylar watched, Dufus tripped over something that wasn't there, turned, and glared accusingly at the ground.

"Dufus has got some bourbon just below the surface of his skin," Skylar said.

"Well, I do like Jon Than more'n I like you," Mary Lou said. "I surely do."

"So do I," said Andy, smiling. "We don't need you around here no more, Skylar. You been replaced. By a gentleman."

Skylar said, "He's a no-good, rich, good-lookin', northern preppy."

"Skylar's jealous," Andy said.

"Sent here to goad me."

"Goad you?" Jon asked.

"You haven't heard I'm not going to college?"

Jon said, "I heard."

"And you mean to tell me you're not here to mortify me to death?"

Jon looked Skylar in the eyes. "That wasn't my personal plan. . . ."

"What is your personal plan, Jon Than?"

Jon shrugged. "Now that I think of it, goading you to death, to use your dubious expression, would give me something interesting to do." Again his eyes scanned the dark hills behind Whitfield Farm. "Can't imagine what else there is to do around here, I mean, after one has observed the various stages of baking cow flaps. . . ."

Andy tugged at Skylar's sleeve. "Where's the dog?"

Jon said, " 'Whar's the dawg?' " and shrugged.

With the serving tray still more than half-filled, carried showily on the palm of one hand at shoulder height, Dufus was about to walk behind Mary Lou on his way back to the serving table.

When he tripped this time, Dufus fell forward.

The serving tray hit Mary Lou on the back of the neck.

Barbecue meat and sauce went on her hair, down her bare shoulders and back, onto her party dress.

It also went on Dufus's face as he had tried to break his fall by flinging his arms around Mary Lou's waist. His face was flat against the small of her back.

Mary Lou fell a step or two forward. She dropped her wine-glass on the lawn.

She pulled Dufus's arms from around her waist and stepped out of his embrace as she would an ugly skirt.

When she turned around, Dufus, barbecue on his head, sauce dribbling down his face, was on his stomach. Raising himself onto his elbows, he looked up at her like a guilty puppy. The black bow tie on his white shirt was askew.

"Goddamn you, Dufus!" Mary Lou rubbed the back of her neck. "You ruined my goddamned dress!"

"Mary Lou . . ." Dufus took a deep breath.

"I was gonna wear this dress—"

"Mary Lou, he really did trip." Skylar started to help Dufus to his feet. "Really, really did. I mean, he did. Really."

"Why, Mary Lou!" said Andy-Dandy in a falsetto. "You look good enough to eat!"

Barbecue sauce and grass sticking to his face and white shirt, Dufus stood hunched before Mary Lou as if before a firing squad.

"I'm sorry, Mary Lou. I do apologize."

"Goddamn you," Mary Lou said into his face. "Dufus, I do declare the best part of you ran down your daddy's leg."

" 'Laig'?" asked Jon.

Skylar said to his cousin, "Mary Lou's mighty popular around here."

"Oh, you, Skylar!" Trying to brush off the back of her dress, Mary Lou turned toward the house.

"You stay right there, Mary Lou," Skylar said as she stomped away. "I'll get the garden hose. Have you cleaned off in no time at all."

"Skylar?" Dufus looked as confused as a puppy who finds himself suddenly put outside in the rain. "Don't you think it's time we convinced everyone 'round here they're nearsighted with laryngitis and can't neither see us nor call us?"

"I do." Skylar put his hand on Dufus's shoulder. "I think

we've done real well at this party, Dufus. Worked hard. Spread the charm around. You and I have given everybody a wonderful time, wouldn't you say?"

"Wonderful," said Jon, glancing down at the back of his own trousers. "Just wonderful."

Dufus said, "Skylar, if we done any better, they might just elect us to a hanging."

"Right." Skylar looked uneasily at Jon. "Time to call it a day, Dufus."

Beaming, Dufus held his hands out, palms up, to be slapped. "Time to call it *night!*"

3

Monica answered her husband. "I don't know where Skylar went. Dufus is gone, too."

"Well, they might have stayed around to help clear up."

Monica Whitfield looked at the party debris around the terrace. "I suppose there's nothing here that can't wait until morning. Mrs. McJane brought all the usable leftovers, the salads, inside. The animals can have anything they find."

"I suppose so." Dan Whitfield was putting liquor bottles from the bar table into a box. "Is Jonathan gone, too?"

"I suppose Jonathan's gone to bed," Monica said. "He's supposed to rest. He must be tired from the trip, the party."

"And Skylar seems to like him about as much as a sore throat."

"I don't know," Monica said.

"Come on. Skylar didn't show up until the party was nearly over. Then he stood over there by the bar table and generated shrieks, shouts, and snarls like a loose cougar."

Monica said, "I'm just not sure I'll ever get used to a young man who doesn't say 'ma'am.' Did you notice?"

"Jonathan?"

"Basic respect for elders, in fact, for other people, whatever they are, I'm pretty sure is one of the rails on which any society runs."

Lifting the heavy box into the house, Dan Whitfield said over his shoulder to his wife, "Turn off the lights, will you?"

Julep preceded Jon into Skylar's bedroom from the bathroom.

"Is this your dog?" Jon asked. He pronounced it "dawg."

"Yes." Skylar sat on his bed pulling on fresh jeans.

"He was in my room."

"That's not your room," Skylar said. "That's a guest room."

Jon was dressed in a white bathrobe.

"What's his name?"

"Julep."

"Are mint juleps brown?"

"Yes."

"You seem to be getting dressed."

"Yes."

On the floor beside the bed were two pairs of boots. One pair, which Skylar had worn to the party, was black, ornate, and clean. The other was brown, plain, and dirty.

"Are you going out to do something on the farm?" Hands in the pockets of his robe, Jon stood in the middle of Skylar's bedroom, looking around at the bookshelves, the stereo, the bugle, and two trumpets on their shelf. "I mean, if there's some job that needs doing on the farm at this hour of the night." Jon glanced at his wristwatch. "Eleven-thirty, I could go with you, help you. Try to help you."

Sitting on the edge of his bed, Skylar watched his cousin closely. "Hain't you tied?"

Thinking, Jon looked across the room. " 'Hain't you tied . . .' " he repeated. "Am I tired? No, I'm all right." Jon surveyed the books on the shelves. "You read these books?"

"Books?" Skylar asked. "Shoot. I thought they was thick wallpaper."

For a moment, the cousins looked at each other wordlessly.

Skylar asked, "You'd help me on the farm this hour of the night?"

"Sure. Not sure I'd be much help, but I could try."

"Okay." Skylar began pulling on the dirty boots. "Go pull on some jeans and let's go."

"Jeans? I haven't any jeans."

"You came to a farm without any jeans?"

"I have shorts." More quietly, Jon said, "Designer jeans. Not like yours."

"All God's chillun got shorts." Stamping his feet into his boots, Skylar crossed the bedroom and opened a louvered closet door. Inside were several shelves of folded blue jeans. "Take a pair of mine."

Jon snorted. "You have a lot of jeans."

"I seem to mess up two, three pairs a day. Mess 'em up terrible. One way or the other." Skylar tossed a pair of folded jeans at his cousin. "Nothin' you can do to 'em that hasn't been done already, I'm pretty sure."

Skylar picked up his trumpet. "Let's go."

Jon smiled. "You take your trumpet to work on the farm at midnight?"

"Cattle farm," Skylar said. "Got to show these critturs who's got the biggest horn 'round here."

"Is this truck homemade?" Jon asked through the open passenger window.

"Customized." Skylar climbed in behind the driving wheel. "I customized it."

Climbing in the passenger side, Jon said, "What color is it? I can't tell in the dark."

"Red. Mostly. After it rains." Skylar started the motor. Without turning on headlights, he started down the moonlit gravel drive to the barn area. "Mostly I guess you could say it's dirt brown. With fly-speck ornamentation. I'll bet you thought they were decals."

"God," Jon said. "You have a gun rack."

Skylar said, "I have a gun, too."

Slowly, but without fully stopping, Skylar turned the truck in a tight circle between the barns.

There was a thump and a clatter from the truck bed.

"What's that?" Jon looked through the rear window.

"Dufus."

"I never saw him."

"He would have gotten in front, except he saw you're there."

Skylar's trumpet was on the seat between them.

"There's plenty of room in front."

"That's okay." Skylar looked through the rearview mirror. "I suspect Dufus needs an airing."

"Where does Dufus live?"

"In one of the sheds." Skylar turned right onto the road through the farm. Then he turned on his headlights. "Been saving power."

"Tell me about Dufus."

"He helps out on the farm. Does whatever needs doing. Doesn't much like helping out at parties though, in case you didn't notice."

"Does he go to school?"

"He did. He went to school a lot. He attended sixth grade for years and years, right up until he was sixteen. Then he got discouraged and quit. Said he honestly couldn't face sixth grade again without worrying he might lose his composure."

The truck was roaring uphill on the narrow, curving road.

His face in the breeze from the wing window, abruptly Jon asked, "Why aren't you going to college?"

"I'm an underachiever," Skylar answered. "Like Dufus."

"Your father is my father's brother," Jon said. "Your mother, besides being a gorgeous and gracious lady, may be brilliant, I'd say from the few words I've had with her."

"My daddy took over my mother's family's insurance brokerage. My mama's a housewife who helps out in the local library. Together we work the farm mainly as a means of keeping the land. I don't expect anyone in my family is drafting a Nobel Prize acceptance speech. Maybe your daddy is. Or your mama. Your daddy is an investment banker?"

"Yes."

"What does that mean?"

"It means he makes money go in decentric circles until there's a profit."

"You mean, he stuffs paper money in a hole?"

"In his pocket."

"What does he produce?"

"Money."

"He left the South just for that? Just to make money?"

"And he's never been back."

"Uh," Skylar said. "Different value systems, I guess."

"He says he broke his back working on Whitfield Farm when he was a boy and never held enough paper money to blow his nose on until he went North."

"Uh. He learned workin' this farm that all you need to blow your nose is to know which way the wind is blowin'."

"Skylar?" Jon used both hands to adjust the wing window. "Skylar, I suspect you're a phony."

The truck's right tires hit the soft shoulder and raised dust. "Sorry, Dufus."

"Those books in your room have been read."

"They're secondhand."

"You're talking differently now than you were before."

Skylar sang a few bars of "Mary Lou."

"What happened to your accent, Skylar? Your southern drawl? Your twang?"

"You bound and determined to bother me?"

"Yes. It's my best ticket home. You have this pasted-together truck, your gun rack, your *dawg*, your little Miss Beauty Queen contestant, cow shit on your boots, yet you just used the words 'value systems,' and, without blinking."

"You really think ill of the South, and Southerners, don't you, Jon Than?"

"My father does. My mother thought my coming here would be 'an interesting cultural experience' for me, quote, unquote."

"A broken jaw is your best ticket home?"

"Your jaw; my ticket."

"Shoot, Jon Than, I suspect your daddy sent you here to show you how well he's done to raise himself out of our pile of cow shit."

"At first, I thought you were confirmation of everything I ever thought about you."

"Well, I am," Skylar said. "A hick you can be right proud to snub."

"Skylar, your accent keeps shifting back and forth."

"The way I'm talking now, Jon Than, that's accent." Skylar turned the truck onto a dusty parking lot. From the bed of the truck came a rebel yell. "Sometimes, when I feel like it, I also speak dialect. You ever hear of dialect, Jon Than?"

Looking through the fly-specked windshield, Jon said, "This is a dive."

"This is the Holler."

Skylar parked the truck facing a long, low red building with neon beer signs in its few windows. The unlit sign over the door saying THE HOLLER was fan-shaped. Music twanged through the roof and walls of the place.

Twenty feet from the front door, a man was on his knees vomiting onto the dirt.

Skylar shut off the engine.

"Shit," Jon said. "I'm not going in there."

"Then stay here, damn it. Or walk home. I don't care, Jon Than."

"I don't know where I am."

"You're at the Holler."

"I'll get killed in there."

"You might just get your ticket home, boy." Skylar picked up his trumpet.

Dufus was clattering around on the truck bed, yelling happily at the vomiting man.

"Skylar?"

"It might just be 'an interesting cultural experience' for you, fool."

"Skylar, what you just said about accent and dialect—did you read that in a book?"

"No." Skylar slammed the door of the truck. "I just made it up."

"This place smells of barf."

Slowly, not looking around much, not meeting people Skylar and Dufus greeted, Jon had followed them into the Holler and sat with them at a stained, knife-scarred table in a corner.

"Ha, Skylar." The waitress was wearing thigh-high boots, high cut-off jeans, a T-shirt that did not reach to the top of her jeans. She carried a round tin tray.

"How're doin', Marlene?"

"What you-all want tonight?"

"Dufus?" Skylar asked. "You want B and B?"

" 'B and B'?" Jon's eyebrows shot up as he looked at Dufus. "Brandy and Benedictine?"

"Bourbon and beer," Skylar said. "I'll just have beer. And a cup of tea for my cousin here."

"Coca-Cola," Jon said.

"We ain't got no coffee."

"He said, 'Coca-Cola,' " Skylar said.

"Oh." Marlene asked, "How many beers you need before you start playin' your horn, Skylar?"

At the other end of the room, a few people were dancing to music from a jukebox. The song playing was "Damnit, She's My Woman."

"None at all."

The three young men watched Marlene walk through the crowd to the bar.

"How old is she?" Jon asked.

"Old enough to find her way to the bar and back," Dufus said.

"I doubt she's fifteen," Jon said.

"Pretty legs," Skylar said. "You saw that."

"Comes from all that walkin'!" Dufus said. "Fetchin' and carryin'."

"Right." Jon grinned. "She's fetchin'." Jon noticed there

were more women in the room than men. A few women sat singly at the bar. Two tables had two or three women without men at them. While he watched, one woman left a table and sat at the bar by herself. He said, "This place is a whore-house."

"Why you say that?" Skylar asked.

Jon shrugged. "Tell me it isn't."

Dufus said, "The whole world's a whorehouse. Tell me it isn't."

Skylar said, "Jon Than, you're the only one at this table with a social disease."

Marlene returned with the drinks. Stepping deliberately, she placed her leg between Skylar's. While she placed the drinks on the table, Skylar closed his legs and squeezed hers. He ran his fingertips down the side of her thigh.

After she left, Jon said, "That was disgusting."

"Mostly, I only do what people want," Skylar answered. "And what I want, too, of course, to speak the absolute truth."

Skylar sat forward. "Jon Than," he said through the clatter and din of the music and loud talk, "Dufus and I sure hope you can see your way clear to attending church with us this Sunday."

"What? Oh, my God!"

"We'd be right pleased if you would."

"My God, Skylar. You bring me to a whorehouse in the middle of the night to invite me to attend church?"

Tandy, in jeans and a red-checked shirt, entered the Holler with her brother and a male cousin. She looked into the corner away from the jukebox. She waved at Skylar. The three went to stand at the bar.

"The trouble is," Jon said, watching Skylar's eyes roam the room, "I believe you're serious."

"Dead serious," Skylar said.

"He's serious." Dufus's eyes were not focusing all that well. "He's dead serious."

The music changed. From the dance floor came the noise of buck dancing. The male dancers raised their feet to their knees and stomped their boots on the floor rhythmically. There were a few whoops and hollers.

Jon turned around. "What are they doing?" He seemed angry.

"Enjoyin' themselves." Skylar sat back in his chair. "You ever enjoy yourself, Jon Than?"

A heavy, older woman in a voluminous black dress came through the crowd to their table. She looked under full sail and carried her glass as a prow.

Skylar rose and pulled out the fourth chair. "Here. Sit down."

"Skylar, honey." Gracefully, she lowered herself onto the chair. "You always look as good as a fresh peach." She knocked the knuckles of her right hand against Dufus's forehead. "You in there, honey?" She looked at Jon. "Hello, Jonathan Whitfield. How's your pa?" She waited for an answer.

"He's fine."

"That's good to hear."

Skylar said, "This is Mrs. Duffy, Jon Than."

"That's right," she said. "Mrs. Duffy. If you ever find out my first name and use it, you'll be thrown out of here by your ear onto your rear. If I can't have all that I want in this life, at least I'm not going to be called by my first name, especially by drinkin' people."

Evenly, Skylar said to Jon, "Mrs. Duffy runs this place."

"Do you own it?" Jon asked.

Skylar smiled at Mrs. Duffy. "Who owns the Holler anyway, Mrs. Duffy?"

She continued to stare at Jon. "Looks a lot like you, Skylar. Has he got any manners at all?"

"No."

"I'm sorry," Jon said. "Just seemed a natural question."

"What's a natural question for some is just plain rudeness for others," Mrs. Duffy said.

The woman and the young man continued to look at each other a long time.

Mary Lou Simes entered the Holler with three young men from the party at Whitfield Farm.

Going to the bar, Mary Lou bumped against two people. One of the men with her took her by her arm.

Softly, Skylar said, "Jon Than just suspicioned this here is a whorehouse."

Jon looked sharply at Skylar and turned red.

After watching Jon another moment, Mrs. Duffy handed Skylar her glass. "Would you mind getting that filled up for me, Skylar? I'm not sure you need to hear what I've got to say to this boy."

"Sure."

"Me, too." Dufus did not move either his bourbon glass or beer bottle.

After Skylar had given his drinks order to Father Jones at the bar, a man behind Skylar said, "Ha, buddy."

He was middle-aged with long, unkempt hair and beard.

"Ha."

Down the bar Tandy was talking to Mary Lou Simes.

"You doin' all right?"

"Just fine."

"Buy you a drink?"

"Taken care of, thanks."

Father Jones put a glass of soda water, a shot glass of bourbon, and a beer bottle on the bar.

"That girl down there, the one in the full white blouse, is that the Simes girl? Mary Lou Simes?"

"I don't know you."

"You need to, to answer a civil question?"

Skylar picked up the drinks off the bar. "Yeah."

The room was still noisy but weirdly quieter without the music, the noise of buck dancing.

Before sitting down, Skylar passed out the drinks. "What did you do with Jon Than?"

"Went to the men's room," Mrs. Duffy said, "after I notified him he was full of shit."

Tandy was steering Mary Lou to the women's room.

Mrs. Duffy put the trumpet in Skylar's lap. "Blow your horn, boy, heat my blood."

Skylar introduced the sound of the trumpet to the room with a few foolish noises before he really began to play anything.

While Skylar was playing his trumpet, he saw Mary Lou Simes walk out of the women's room, alone. Ignoring everyone, quickly she crossed the room and went through the front door, alone.

After finishing his second B and B, Dufus stood up from the table, hitched up his jeans, and ambled away.

Jon then appeared at the edge of the crowd near the bar. Standing still, facing away from the crowd, the bar, listening, he watched Skylar sitting in a corner next to Mrs. Duffy, playing his trumpet, a long moment. Then, slowly, he left the Holler through the front door.

4

"Mornin'."

"Mornin'."

Skylar had just pulled the shower curtain aside and was stepping out of the tub when Tandy entered the bathroom from his room.

When he reached for a bath towel, she put her arms around his neck and, standing more on the balls of her feet, nuzzled his nose and kissed him on the mouth. Holding his wet arms away from her T-shirt, he put one wet leg against her bare leg.

Instantly, he was aroused.

"I like you wet," Tandy said. "I like you wet with sweat. Also wet clean."

The door from the guest room to the bathroom opened.

Jon stood in the door, in his bathrobe.

Goggling, Jon said, "Good grief," and closed the door.

Tandy giggled. "Is that your cousin? 'Bout time I saw him up close."

She took the bath towel and began drying Skylar while he stood in the air.

Skylar began to sing "You Are My Sunshine."

If Jon had not been in the next room, Tandy would have

pulled off her T-shirt, and she and Skylar would have had their morning snuggle, either standing up or on the bed or both.

Sleepy at dawn, Julep came into the bathroom, stretched, yawned, and went back to his pillow in Skylar's room.

"What happened to Mary Lou last night?" Skylar asked.

"I don't know. Time she arrived at the Holler, she was a little sick with drink. Must be real tough bein' Ms. Perfect every livin' moment of your life, charmin' all the time, every hair in place."

"Mary Lou's not charmin' all the time. She's more real than that."

"It's gonna be a scorcher," Tandy said. "Wear shorts."

While Tandy stretched her arms and legs on the bed, Skylar rummaged through cabinet drawers beneath the bookcase for briefs and cutoffs.

"I took her into the john." Tandy yawned. "Seemed to me she needed a minute to catch up with herself. At the bar, she was flappin' her lips faster'n a hummin'bird flaps its wings."

"Did she say anything? I mean, in the john?"

"I don't think she even knew I was with her. She looked at herself real hard, in the mirror. Then she ran out like a goat had taken aim at her butt."

"She left the Holler by herself." Wearing shorts, Skylar was lacing his sneakers. "But she couldn't have."

"You two have me worried half to death." In the kitchen, Mrs. McJane brought the iron skillet to Tandy and Skylar at the small wood table by the window. With her spatula, she placed two fried eggs on each of their plates. "How close you-all are to each other."

Skylar grinned at her. "Why, ma'am, we're just like brother and sister." Beneath the kitchen table, his bare leg rested casually against Tandy's.

Mrs. McJane nodded. "That's what your parents think." From the sink, she said, "You're not brother and sister. I can guarantee that." Then she muttered, "Lordy, you two worry me some."

Skylar bit his toast. "Worry you 'bout what?"

Running the water into the frying pan, Mrs. McJane said, "Worry me 'bout what it's doing to you all. You ain't supposed to be so comfortable with each other, your age."

With her back perfectly straight, Tandy ate her breakfast.

Barefooted in his bathrobe, unshaven, unshowered, uncombed, Jon appeared in the doorway. He had come down the outside stairs from the second-story balcony off Skylar's and his bedrooms.

"Mornin', Jon Than," Skylar said. "I think you've met Tandy."

"Mornin'," Tandy said.

Mrs. McJane turned from the sink. "Lordy, I forgot all about the quiet cousin. You up?"

"No," Jon said, staring at Tandy. "Just looking for an unoccupied bathroom."

"Why, there's one right next to your room." Mrs. McJane looked at Skylar, glanced at Tandy, back at Skylar.

"That was occupied."

Skylar muttered, "Not now."

"Did Skylar lock you out of the bathroom?" Mrs. McJane asked. "If two boys can't use the same bathroom . . ."

"You look tired," Skylar said.

Only four or five hours earlier, Skylar, leaving the Holler with his trumpet, found Jon asleep in the passenger seat of the pickup truck.

Skylar had driven home, not waking him. He left both the truck and Jon in the barnyard.

"Get to bed late?" Skylar asked.

"I haven't gotten into bed yet." The expression on Jon's face as he watched Skylar eat his breakfast was curious.

"But you slept," Skylar said.

"Skylar." Jon hesitated. "The music you were playing on your trumpet last night in that godawful Holler place . . . was by Johann Nepomuk Hummel . . . and Telemann!"

"Hummelwhich?"

"Cousin, you're the biggest damned phony I've ever met."

"Ah'm jest a good ol' boy."

"Do people think you're making it up? I mean, the music? Is that what you tell them? And how do you know Hummel and Telemann anyway?"

"Must have heard it on the radio."

Mrs. McJane, heavy skillet still in hand, looked from Skylar to Jon, not knowing what the argument was about.

Tandy watched Jon with interest.

Skylar, sitting back in his chair, legs stretched straight out to the floor, fingers of his right hand playing with the handle of his empty coffee cup, said, very slowly, "Cousin? When you expect to see something? And you see something else? Don't describe what you see as phony?"

Tandy looked at Jon's legs below his robe. "You'd better be careful of the sun, Jon Than. You're as white as fresh milk."

"And the Recluse Spiders, too." Mrs. McJane, glad of something to say, put the skillet back into the sink. "Always shake out your boots before you put them on."

"And the copperheads, too," Tandy said. "Rattlers. Cottonmouths."

Skylar said, "And watch out for the wharupadangs."

Glancing at Tandy, Jon said, "I've got some other questions to ask you, too."

"Bathroom's free," Skylar said. "Why don't you get rid of your best stuff first?"

After Jon left, Mrs. McJane puzzled. "Ain't I here? Didn't I offer that boy breakfast?"

"Never mind him," Skylar said. "He's got the style of a groundhog."

"Each of these boys is more contrary than the other," Tandy muttered.

Mrs. McJane was looking through the window over the kitchen sink. "Anyway, that whole backyard's got to be cleaned up this morning, tables took down, chairs, lanterns, bits picked up. . . .''

"Not yet." Skylar stood. "Got to cruise the place first. See if that calf's dropped."

"Where's Dufus this morning?" Mrs. McJane asked. "Don't he want breakfast?"

"I don't know," Skylar said. "He didn't come home with me last night."

Shirt off, mouth open, jeans and boots muddy, Dufus was sitting on his Dr. Pepper box, back and head against the white cement-block wall of his shed, facing east, absorbing the early morning sun.

Sneaking up on him, Tandy drilled the middle finger of her right hand into his belly button, hard.

Dufus doubled over before he awoke.

"Mornin', Dufus," Skylar said. "You just gettin' home?"

Dufus rubbed the side of his head with the heel of his hand. "Yeah."

"You walk all the way from the Holler?"

"Yeah."

"What happened to you last night?"

Dufus considered for a full minute. "I went lookin' for Mary Lou."

"Why?"

Dufus arched his back in the sunlight and slapped his own belly with his hand. "Couldn't figure out where she'd gone. She left the Holler by herself. Boys she was with didn't even notice she was gone. Went out and checked the vehicles. She wasn't in any of 'em. Looked down the road. Couldn't see anybody movin'. Started circlin' in the woods around the place. Couldn't hear anything. Thought maybe she'd passed out. Looked for her for hours."

"Why?"

Dufus said, "Couldn't figure out where she done gone."

Tandy said, "She's probably home."

Chin in hand, Dufus studied dry soil. "How'd she get there?"

"You walked," Skylar said. "She's got two legs."

"I would've found her."

Skylar said, "Mary Lou doesn't love the dark—bein' alone in the dark." Tandy took Skylar's hand. "S'pose we ought to go lookin' for her, now that it's light?"

Dufus said, "S'pose."

"Call at her house, first," Tandy said.

"Get her in trouble with her old man," Skylar said. "If we did that, Mary Lou would come after us with her great-granddaddy's sword." Dufus nodded. "We know she was alone?"

"She left alone," Dufus said. "None of those boys she was with followed her. Mary Lou oughtn't be in the woods alone, at night."

Skylar frowned. "She wouldn't be."

Dufus rubbed his face. "This boy's goin' to sleep, no matter what."

"Something's not right." Monica Whitfield entered the bathroom where her husband was shaving and put a cup of coffee on the sink board. "It's past nine. The mess in the backyard hasn't been touched. Mrs. McJane says she hasn't seen Dufus yet this morning."

Shaving one corner of his mouth, Dan said, "Parties follow parties."

"Mrs. McJane said Skylar had breakfast early, and he and Tandy went down to the barns. Now his truck is gone."

Dan said something incomprehensible.

"And our invalid nephew appeared in the kitchen while Skylar was having breakfast saying he hadn't been to bed yet, looking like a piece of last month's bread, according to Mrs. McJane, and argued with Skylar about something Mrs. McJane didn't understand. Something about chipmunks."

"All sounds normal to me." Dan rinsed his razor.

"Why should Skylar and Jonathan argue about chip-munks?"

"So who's minding the phone?" Pepp was waiting for his coffee to cool.

"Just got a call."

From his counter stool in the coffee shop across the road from his office, Sheriff Culpepper studied his main office personnel, Adam Haddam, popularly known as Fleas.

"You suppose that's it for the day?" Pepp asked. "One call? The Sheriff's Office has had our call for the day, so you might as well come on over for coffee and leave the office empty?"

Fleas was referred to as "retired," but no one could recollect what he'd ever done consistently enough to be retired from. Apparently, he had approximated his Social Security payments sufficiently to supplement his income by manning the telephone at the Sheriff's Office.

"I didn't come over for coffee." Wiry and usually grumpy at age seventy-two, Fleas was known to consume enough coffee to keep the lawn around the jailhouse sprinkled in the worst drought. When the phone or the radio at the office did not answer, everyone in Greendowns County knew enough to wait until after Fleas finished relieving himself. "Tommy Barker?"

"Yes," Pepp answered. Tommy was a disabled, stiff-legged veteran who had all the considerable charm and energy of a boy just before hitting puberty. He had an income from the government. He worked for anyone in the county who had work to be done—or he or she couldn't do or afford to have done.

"Called." Fleas did not waste words. "Hunting woodchucks this morning. Discovered a mess in the woods." He paused. "Thinks it's human."

At first Pepp envisioned a pile of human excrement. "A human mess? What exactly does that mean, Fleas?"

"A mess that was human."

Pepp raised an eyebrow at his office personnel. "Tommy
Barker discovered a human corpse in the woods this morning?
Is that what you're saying?"

"Not sure. He didn't go up to it. Spotted it from a distance.
Realized he should leave the whole area undisturbed. Call us."

Good ol' Tommy Barker, Pepp thought. He would have that
kind of sense. "Where?"

"Near the crick, 'bout a quarter-mile down from the Holler."

The Holler. Saturday mornings follow Friday nights, even
as Sunday mornings follow Saturday nights. If there was going to be a time or a place for a corpse, a murdered corpse, to
be found in Greendowns County, this would be about the
time, and that would be about the place.

Pepp said, "I see."

Behind the counter, Fairer, who had been listening, said,
"What?"

"Where's Tommy now?" Pepp asked.

"Mrs. Duffy's trailer. She's still asleep, Tommy says. He
went in to use her phone without waking her up."

"Call Tommy back," Pepp instructed. "That will wake her
up." Pepp glanced up at the air-conditioning duct. "That's the
first thing. Tell him I'm on my way. That will give him plenty
enough time to visit with Mrs. Duffy. Then see if you can get
Handsome on the car horn and tell him to come pick me
up here. If you can't find Handsome"—Pepp checked his
wristwatch—"call Mrs. Hanson, his mother, I mean, and tell
her if she doesn't stop feedin' that boy a second breakfast
every day, his skinny little wife won't be able to bear his
weight anymore, and she's goin' to have to do without more
grandchildren. . . ."

By the time Pepp had finished talking, Fleas was gone, carrying a container of black coffee Fairer automatically had
handed him.

Calf down, cow down, goat down . . . a-moldering in the
woods by the riverbank, big dog, taken down by coyotes, natural enough . . . No. If Tommy Barker said he thought it was

a human mess, probably it was a human mess. Pepp expected Tommy had seen more than enough human messes, close up and from afar, while he was in that war that had stiffened his leg for him, to know one when he saw one.

"What do think it is, Pepp?"

Pepp resolved to remain calm, appear professionally competent, do, say nothing to excite the community.

He said, "Fairer, you know I'm a great detective."

"I do?"

"I've been crossin' the road to your coffee shop how many years now? Twelve years?"

"I do recollect the time you found my granddaddy's Ford in the quarry, after it'd gone missin' a month."

"Something I've never been able to figure out . . ."

"What's that, Pepp?"

"For twelve years I've been ordering black coffee from you nearly every day."

"That's true, Pepp."

Pepp picked up the tiny container of cream next to his coffee cup. "How come every time I've ordered black coffee in twelve years runnin', you've supplied me with one of these little containers of milk? To this very day?"

"Never know when you might change your mind, Pepp."

Between thumb and index finger, Pepp held the container at her eye level. "Tell me the truth, now, Fairer: Is this the very same container of milk you've been supplyin' me nearly every day and I've been takin' off my saucer and leavin' on the counter nearly every day, for twelve years, now, more or less? The very same container?"

Fairer grinned. "Sure is, Pepp. The very same. What you say, you just might be a great detective. A little slow, maybe . . ."

"And what would ever happen if one day I do change my mind, open this very same container, and pour this twelve-year-old glop into my coffee?"

"You wouldn't like it, Pepp. You'd change your mind again, I daresay. That way, I'd go on savin' cream on you."

At 11:20 that Saturday morning, John Simes looked through his front screen door at Sheriff Culpepper and Deputy Hanson.

John Simes said, "Mary Lou?"

Pepp said, "Yes, sir."

"Car wreck?"

"Need to talk to you, John."

"Mary Lou didn't sleep in her bed last night. Her girlfriends don't seem to know where she is. M.L. and I were just discussing calling you."

Sun-blinded, Pepp could not see John Simes's face well through the screen.

John Simes asked, "Is she dead?"

Pepp opened the screen door himself and stepped inside the cool foyer of the house. John Simes stepped back.

"Yes, sir." Of all the men Pepp had known, John Simes had the best control of his face. His face never gave away anything. Pepp had often thought John Simes would be a formidable poker player. Maybe his face had been permanently stiffened in that same war in which Tommy Barker got his leg stiffened.

"Someplace we can all sit down, John? You might consider askin' M.L. to join us. . . ."

5

Crossing the Simeses' front lawn to the police car, his hands at his sides in white knuckled fists, Deputy Sheriff Charles Hanson muttered, "Skylar . . ."

Sheriff Culpepper and Deputy Charles Hanson had done the best they could announcing the worst tragedy, the violent death of a young person, to her family.

"Skylar . . . Skylar G. D. Whitfield, S.O.B." Deputy Hanson slammed the car door. "I know I'm right." He turned the ignition key.

"Just go up the road and pull over," the sheriff instructed. "We need to think what we're doing next."

Sheriff Culpepper also needed a few moments to begin to recover from what he had already seen and felt that Saturday morning.

"We're going to Whitfield Farm," Hanson said, "to pick up Skylar Whitfield for murder."

M.L. and John Simes had just told them that Mary Lou had been with them at a party at Whitfield Farm the night before. They both assumed Mary Lou had then gone on to the Holler with Skylar Whitfield.

"That may be," Pepp said. "But let's just cogitate a moment before we do anything."

He pointed to the side of the road out of sight of the Simeses' home.

Deputy Hanson put the police car on the grassy shoulder of the dirt road and stopped. He did not turn off the engine.

Pepp said, "Say what you got to say, Handsome."

"Skylar's an asshole," Hanson said. "Drives around in that crazy red pickup truck of his, walks around with that crazy half-smile of his, you know, as if he's swimmin' in a bowl of turnip greens. He didn't do a damned thing for the high school, play sports, or even play that damned horn of his in the band, didn't even come to the games. He just came to school, went home, yet got his name published in the newspaper for highest marks every time report cards came out, always pictures of him every time that Mary Lou Simes decides to win another beauty contest, him always with that smile, came to school, went back to the farm, blasts the Holler sideways every time he goes there with his horn, and all the girls go 'Oo—ah!' every time he appears and flutter after him like a bunch of moths hot after a nekkid lightbulb."

"But I take it you have nothing personal against the boy?"

"Nothin' personal."

"Nothing personal at all," Pepp drawled. "Let's just consider a moment."

Hanson rested his arm on the windowsill of the car door and sighed.

Pepp considered what he had just heard about Skylar Whitfield, and considered the source.

Charles Hanson—'Chick,' as he preferred to be called—was called Handsome with rural humor, because he wasn't. He had been tight end on the high school football team, and had played hard and mean. As his best friend always seemed to be his mother, everyone was mildly surprised when Hanson married, without much advance warning, a girl built like a toothpick who had left school after the ninth grade and who produced a girl child three months after marriage.

Looking across the car at Hanson, thinking of Skylar, Pepp realized how much Hanson was running to fat for such a young, recently shelved athlete. Story was that Hanson's skinny young wife couldn't boil an egg without hatching a snake. So Hanson, alarmed at the perpetual possibility of imminent starvation, ate three or four meals at his mother's house a day, plus two or three at Fairer's Coffee Shop, preserved between times by stops at the pizza parlor and hamburger heaven. At twenty-one, the deputy's gut not only hung over his belt but rested on his thick thighs when he sat. After Hanson drove the car, Pepp always had to slide the driver's seat forward from the floor of the backseat.

Pepp had never had official business with Skylar Whitfield but had seen him around, driving that strange-looking red pickup truck, usually loaded with other kids and dogs, if not cattle or hay. When Pepp checked the Holler Friday or Saturday nights, Skylar would be there with a gang of kids, playin' his trumpet in the corner or jumping around to the jukebox. Pepp wasn't sure if Skylar was good-looking, but he had noticed the boy always moved and looked like a kid who had just been given a present. Pepp didn't understand it, but some people did feel that way about life.

"Nothing personal at all, Handsome. I can see that. Hasn't that boy had to work the family farm while he was goin' to school?"

"There's nothin' to workin' a cattle farm," said Hanson, who had hayed a few seasons.

"Oh," said Pepp, who knew differently.

"Not like milkin' or workin' row crops. Anyway, there's that other boy on the farm—Dufus. He does all the work."

"Dufus some kind of kin to the Whitfields?"

Hanson said, "Dufus dropped from the sky. And he's still bouncin'."

"Short-sheeted in the brain bed, was he?"

"Skylar could have played sports."

"Why didn't he?"

" 'Fraid of gettin' his pretty face broke."

"You're not afraid of gettin' your pretty face broke?" Pepp studied Hanson's nose, clearly broken several times.

Hanson shrugged. "Don't mind."

"I mind gettin' my pretty face broke," Pepp said.

Through his open window, Pepp scanned the rolling pasture the other side of the fence. He counted twelve heifers in the pasture. His mind went back to what he had seen two-and-a-half hours before, the human mess on the riverbank, the body of a pretty girl facedown in the mud, her head downhill of her body, her light skirt tossed up showing her panties, her slim, tanned legs soiled, her half-high-heeled shoes, thin straps around her ankles at odd angles to each other . . . her head had been beaten into a broken, raw, bleeding stump, probably by fists. He had left the crime scene in the hands of Deputy Aimes, county coroner Doc Murphy, and the county rescue squad. News travels so fast in small places Pepp had considered it his first priority to be the one to break the news to M.L. and John Simes personally, as soon as possible.

Mary Lou Simes. Voted time and again the county's most beautiful child, perfect body, perfect features, teeth, nose, eyes, always glowing, healthy, smooth skin, never a hair of head or eyebrow at a wrong set. Everyone had always loved looking at Mary Lou Simes. Greendowns County had been mighty proud of Mary Lou Simes and dreamed her future for her with enjoyment, pleasure.

Sheriff Culpepper had not loved looking at Mary Lou Simes this morning. His stomach heaved at the memory. He counted the cattle in the pasture again, this time from right to left.

Pepp said to Hanson, " 'Stead, Skylar got more attention from the girls than some of you guys who did get your pretty faces broken playing sports, that right?"

"Exactly right," Hanson said.

"Didn't need to extend himself." When Hanson didn't answer, Pepp realized he probably shouldn't have used the word "extend," that being doubtlessly beyond Hanson's vocabulary. "Sounds like a pretty cool guy to me."

"He's an asshole."

"Sounds to me like you've elected the Whitfield boy the murderer of Mary Lou Simes already, Handsome." Again,

Hanson did not answer. "Police work, though, police work has to do with evidence, not popularity or prejudice. Can you understand that?"

It took Pepp a moment to realize the wetness on Hanson's fat cheeks was not sweat but tears. Hanson, too, had seen the human mess that morning on the riverbank. He, too, either would have loved Mary Lou Simes or admired her mightily; the whole county did.

Pepp said, "Skylar might have murdered Mary Lou; then again he might not have. There's no knowin' until we get some evidence one way or the other. That's our job. So don't go actin', or even thinkin', as if you know something when you surely don't. You hear me, Chick?"

"Yes, sir."

"What you're tellin' me is, havin' Skylar around is like having someone around who doesn't do any work but gets more pay than anyone else." Suddenly, Hanson colored. He had been telling his mother, wife, friends, that he, Hanson, put in long hours patrolling in the police car, while the sheriff put in few. Of course, the sheriff was paid more than he. The sheriff must have heard he had said that.

"It's called resentment," Pepp said. "The other boys resent Skylar, too?"

After a moment, Hanson just repeated, "He's an asshole."

"He sounds like a private sort of guy to me."

"A private?"

Pepp found it difficult to remember that some of the people he had to associate with accepted only one meaning for some words that might have more than one. Having been ill-taught by underpaid, demoralized teachers in a land where declining mediocrity was idealized as the "normal," to which everyone ought to aspire, where almost half of the students never graduated from high school, never intended to—reading confused, embarrassed, and defeated them. So they did not read, did not expose themselves to the fullness of words. Pepp really couldn't understand anyone who did not read, any more than he could understand anyone who did not drink water on a hot day. Pepp knew that if he did not read, most likely he would lose his mind.

"Is Skylar joinin' the army?"

Pepp didn't answer. He had decided a long time ago it was not his job to instruct his associates in language. He smiled. He also knew this was how rumors started. By the end of the weekend, people around the county would hear that Skylar Whitfield was thinking of joining the army just because he, the sheriff, had laid the word "private" on someone who had never heard that use of the word. Ever afterward it would be wondered why Skylar hadn't joined the army. Thirty-five years from now the fact that Skylar Whitfield had once been rejected by the army would be referred to as a certainty, followed by the mythical addendum that no one had ever been sure why. . . .

Hanson held up two fingers intertwined. "He and Mary Lou Simes were like that. They were supposed to get married."

Pepp wrinkled his eyebrows at his deputy. " 'Supposed to'? The county voted them bride and groom, husband and wife?"

"I don't know what you're talkin' about," Hanson said. "You say 'Skylar' to anyone 'round here, and they'll say, 'Mary Lou Simes.' You say 'Mary Lou Simes,' and they'll say 'Skylar.' That's all there is to it."

"The county voted Mary Lou Simes and Skylar Whitfield bride and groom at birth, and now you've voted Skylar Whitfield the murderer of Mary Lou Simes before we know anything except somebody killed her."

"I'm not votin' nobody nothin'."

Pepp knew well enough that county people elected their successes and failures at birth. Whatever one did—declared successes fail, declared failures succeed—it was hard, if not impossible, to change people's birth opinion of one. Everyone was judged by the family name. Pepp wondered if this wasn't the main reason, not the poor economy, why more people, especially the young, still left the county than stayed. As a peace officer, Pepp had learned to be especially careful concerning the poor sods who had been elected criminals at birth by the county. He bent over backward to give them every fair chance. Too frequently, these people accepted the county's view of them and did, in fact, turn out to be criminals. The reverse was also true. And he had to be careful to consider those born with good family names as potentially criminal as anyone else.

"Well, you might be right, Handsome," Pepp drawled. "Whitfield Farm seems as good a place to start as any. Mary Lou and Skylar were friends and probably were together last night. And, it's close. Might as well stop by."

Dan Whitfield was holding the unfolded morning newspaper when he answered the door of Whitfield Farm to Sheriff Culpepper and Deputy Hanson. "Hi, Pepp. What's up? Come on in." He held the screen door open.

"I've got real bad news, Dan."

"You serious?" Dan Whitfield searched Pepp's eyes.

"Real serious. Is Skylar here?"

Dan Whitfield tried to read Deputy Hanson's face. "He was up early this morning, but I think he's gone back to bed. We all had a late night last night." Dan folded his newspaper. "God, Pepp! What are you on about?"

Pepp touched Dan's elbow. "Let's go into the living room. Is Monica about? Chick, would you please go wake Skylar up and bring him down here?"

"Is Skylar involved?" Dan asked. "In whatever's wrong?"

"Just need to talk to him. Come on in here, sit down," the sheriff said. "I'll tell you everything. But you need to sit down, Dan."

The door to Skylar's bedroom opened.

Without opening his eyes, naked on the bed, Skylar rolled over and stretched gloriously. He said, "Sleepy . . ." He smiled and braced his muscles, expecting Tandy to jump on him.

Standing over the bed, Chick folded his hands together, raised them above his head and, as if chopping wood, brought his joined fists down hard on Skylar's stomach.

Eyes snapping open in the semidark room, Skylar sat up involuntarily. Not knowing what was happening, he rolled away, off the far side of the bed, onto the floor, onto his hands and knees. He sucked in air. As soon as he could, he looked over the edge of the bed. At first all he recognized was the uniform of a sheriff's deputy. He sucked more breath. Then he crawled into the corner of the room.

Back against both walls in the corner of the room, breathing hard, one knee up, one hand to his stomach, Skylar focused on the bulk now standing at the foot of the bed.

"Chick! What the hell are you doing?"

"Get dressed, asshole." Chick surveyed the room, looking for something specific. "Where's the light?"

"Chick, are you out of your mind?"

"You're under arrest, asshole." Chick returned to the door of the room and fumbled with the light switch. He stuttered Skylar's rights.

"What time is it?"

" 'Bout three o'clock. Where's your pants?"

"Chick, what in God's name is going on?"

"Thought we wouldn't be on to you, uh? You're not goin' to get away with this one, boy."

"This one what?"

Hanson found the jeans Skylar had worn the night before tossed over a chair and threw them at Skylar still sitting on the floor. "Get dressed."

Holding his jeans with one hand, his stomach with the other, Skylar got up and went to the bureau. He took underpants from one drawer, socks from another. He moved slowly, trying to get his mind in gear.

Hanson snapped Skylar's underpants out of his hands and grabbed his rolled-up socks. He tossed them through the open door into the bathroom. "Just put your goddamned pants on!"

Skylar looked into Hanson's face. "Chick, will you please tell me what's goin' on? What's happened?"

"You're gonna tell us." Hanson yelled: "Put your pants on!"

Skylar stepped into his jeans. He was about to slip the empty scabbard off his belt when Hanson hit him hard on the side of his head, on his ear, knocking Skylar sideways, onto the bed.

Before Skylar began to recover from the blow, Hanson rolled him over on the bed onto his stomach. He put his knee into the small of Skylar's back and grabbed Skylar's hands behind him. Hanson pressed Skylar's hands up to his shoulder blades, held them there with one hand, and snapped hand-cuffs around both Skylar's wrists.

"Chick," Skylar said into the bedsheet. "What the hell . . . ?"

Job done, Hanson removed his knee from Skylar's back. He punched Skylar in the kidney.

"Chick! You son of a bitch!"

"Don't you swear at me, Skylar!" Hanson pulled Skylar off the bed by pulling the chain between his wrists. "I'm an officer of the goddamned law. Get up!"

Skylar, standing, still breathing somewhat hard, his left ear smarting, his right kidney hurting, said as calmly as he could, "Chick, please tell me what the hell is going on."

"I've recited you your rights. Get movin', Skylar. Down-stairs. We're takin' no shit from you. None at all."

"My belt ain't done."

Hanson pushed him by the shoulder. "Move it, sweetheart."

In the living room, Sheriff Culpepper sat forward in a soft chair. Dan Whitfield sat in his chair looking as if he had been dropped there from a great height. His face was ashen. He did not look up when Skylar entered. In her chair, Monica was crying quietly.

Hanson gave Skylar an extra push forward into the room.

"Mom . . . Dad?"

More tears came to Monica's eyes as she saw her son bare-foot and shirtless in jeans, his belt not buckled, his hands held by cuffs behind his back.

She stood up. "Really, Pepp . . ."

Pepp looked Skylar up and down and then looked at Hanson. "Handcuffs?"

"I recited him his rights," Hanson said.

Pepp snorted. "I just asked you to wake him up."

"He woke me up," Skylar said. "He beat me up." He tried to rub his left ear with his shoulder. "Will someone please tell me what all this is about?"

Monica sank back into her chair. In her hands was a tear-soaked handkerchief. "Mary Lou . . ."

"What happened to Mary Lou?" Skylar's heart was pounding. "Where is she?"

Dan said, "She's dead, Skylar. Somebody beat her to death down by the river not far from the Holler."

"That's enough." Pepp got up from his chair.

Without looking at anyone, Dan Whitfield, holding his stomach, got up and left the room.

"You were at the Holler last night, Skylar?"

"Yes, sir."

"What time did you leave?"

"About two o'clock. A little after."

"Mary Lou with you?"

"No, sir. I saw her there."

"You were there, she was there, but you weren't together?"

"She was with some other kids."

"Other boys?"

"Yes, sir."

"How did you like that?"

"Sir?"

"Who were you with?"

"Dufus . . . My cousin."

"Your cousin who?"

"Jon Than."

"Jon Than . . ." Pepp scanned his knowledge of county genealogy. "Who's that?"

"Jonathan Whitfield," Monica said. "Dan's brother's son. He arrived yesterday from Boston, Pepp."

"Wayne's son?"

"Yes," Monica answered.

Blood pounding in his ears, one ear ringing, kidney hurting, Skylar could not seem to get enough breath. Everything in the living room seemed soft, without edges.

Slowly, he sank. He sat cross-legged on the carpet, arms bound behind him.

Standing behind him, Hanson kicked Skylar's left kidney with the side of his boot.

"Quit that!" Skylar shouted. "Quit that, Chick, or I'll beat you to a bloody pulp! You'd better believe I will!"

After a moment, Pepp said, "Interesting you should say that, Skylar."

White-faced, Dan Whitfield reentered the room. He only glanced at his son sitting handcuffed on the floor. He fell heavily into his chair.

"Pepp," Dan said. "I don't see how you get off arresting Skylar, carryin' him off in handcuffs. . . ."

"That's not my intention," Pepp said. "I just want to ask him some questions. Deputy Hanson here has done his job with what you might call undue enthusiasm."

In a low voice, Dan said, "Take the handcuffs off him, Pepp."

Pepp crouched in front of Skylar. He touched the empty, rectangular, boxy leather scabbard dangling from Skylar's belt. He lifted the top back with his thumb to confirm the scabbard was empty.

"What's this for, Skylar?"

"My knife."

"What kind of a knife fits in here?"

"Swiss Army knife."

"A Swiss Army knife. What color is your Swiss Army knife, Skylar?"

"Red."

"You have a red Swiss Army knife. Skylar, can you tell me where your red Swiss Army knife is now?"

"It must be in my shorts."

"Why would it be in your shorts?"

"I was wearing my shorts this morning, cleaning up out back, from the party. I had my knife in my pocket."

"How come you'd carry your knife in your pocket? Why wouldn't you use this handsome leather scabbard?"

"No belt on my shorts."

"I see. You sure the knife was in the pockets of your shorts this morning?"

"Yes, sir."

"Skylar, you know anyone else around here with a red Swiss Army knife?"

"No, sir."

Pepp looked up at Hanson. "Do you?"

Hanson was smiling. "I do not. Never seen one in Greendowns County."

Monica said, "I got it for Skylar for Christmas several years ago, Pepp. I bought it in Charleston."

The corners of Dan's mouth lowered.

"Upstairs," Hanson said, "when Skylar was putting on his pants, he tried to slip the scabbard off his belt."

"Your shorts in your room, Skylar?"

"Yes, sir."

"And your red Swiss Army knife is still in the pocket of those shorts?"

"Yes, sir. I think so."

"You're sure?"

"Pretty sure."

Pepp stood up, his knees cracking. "Dan, would you mind coming upstairs with me to Skylar's bedroom? I'd like to look in the pockets of his shorts, and I sure would like for you to be with me."

Dan stood up. "What's this about, Pepp?"

"This morning, investigating the scene of the crime, we found a red Swiss Army knife about fifteen feet from Mary Lou's body. No rust on it at all. Right now, said red Swiss Army knife is in a Plasticine bag in the car."

With lowered shoulders, saying nothing, Dan Whitfield led the sheriff from the living room.

Skylar said to his mother, "That's where I went this morning. Tandy and I. We went looking for Mary Lou. We had the idea she'd gone missin' from the Holler last night. . . . We weren't sure."

Monica said, "No need to tell me you're innocent, Skylar."

So they waited in silence.

Pepp reentered the room ahead of Dan. "Guess we'll just leave those handcuffs on for now. There's no red Swiss Army jackknife in your shorts, Skylar—or anywhere else in your room that we can see."

Monica said, "Pepp, this is crazy, and you know it. Skylar never harmed Mary Lou."

"Monica, every murderer in the world has to be somebody's son or daughter. Frankly, this surprises the hell out of me, too. But a physical piece of evidence at the crime scene, namely one red Swiss Army knife, most likely belongs to your son. And Mary Lou and your son were at the same place at the same time last night. That gives me reason to take him in. Tell me what else to do." Begrudgingly, Pepp said, "You were right to recite him his rights, Chick."

Chick squared his shoulders.

"I was lookin' for Mary Lou this morning," Skylar said to the floor. "The knife must have slipped out of my pocket when I sat down."

Pepp's eyebrows wrinkled. "You tellin' me you knew this mornin' Mary Lou was missing?"

"She left the Holler alone last night. Dufus spent hours lookin' for her. I just assumed she was meeting someone outside, or went to sleep in a car. She was pretty drunk."

"Drunk, you say?" Pepp's eyebrows rose. "Mary Lou Simes?"

"That I don't believe," Monica said. "Mary Lou drunk. She'd never. She only had wine at the party."

"Her daddy would skin her alive," Pepp said.

"She was drunk," Skylar said. "Too drunk to go far. I didn't worry about her last night. She was with other people."

"And how did you know she was still missing this morning?" Pepp asked.

"Dufus hadn't found her."

"Tell me, Skylar, this morning before you went lookin' for Mary Lou in the woods, did you stop at her house?"

"No, sir."

"Why not? Isn't that the logical place to look for a teenaged girl early Saturday morning, her parents' house?"

Skylar said, "Her father . . . After looking for a while, we figured Mary Lou had made it home somehow."

"Who's 'we'?" Pepp asked.

"Tandy and I."

"Tandy McJane," Monica offered.

"So, according to you, Tandy and you went within fifteen feet of Mary Lou's body this morning, sat down in the woods fifteen feet from her mutilated corpse, and never saw her?"

Skylar said, "Must have."

Pepp said, "Skylar, isn't it more the truth that you went back to the woods this morning to look for your knife?" Pepp stared down at the boy sitting on the floor. "Isn't that the truth, son?"

6

Tandy was in a tree when she saw the sheriff's car pull into the driveway of Whitfield Farm. She had climbed the tree one-handed. In her other hand, wrapped in the hem of her T-shirt, was an unbroken robin's egg. She had found it on the ground where it had landed on a tuft of buck grass. She had spotted the nest in the tree, and decided she might as well put the egg back into the nest on the small chance a healthy robin acceptable to its mother could be born from it.

Sitting on a branch, legs dangling, after replacing the egg in the nest, she watched the activity at the Whitfields' house through the leaves. Sheriff Culpepper and Chick Hanson got out of the police car and, hitching up their gun belts, climbed the steps to the front door. After a moment, Mr. Whitfield let them into the house.

Tandy sat a long moment in the tree. Sheriff Culpepper wouldn't be running for reelection until the next year. He wouldn't win then, either, probably wouldn't even run, from the stories his wife was passing around about him. Why was he visiting Whitfield Farm? It was too early for him to be making courtesy calls, politely asking for campaign contributions.

The sheriff's car had come from up the road instead of from town.

After a while, Tandy scrambled down out of the tree, jumping from the last branch three feet off the ground.

Once she was on the road away from the Whitfield house, she began running at an easy jog.

She wasn't nearly out of breath when she came to the Simeses' house. She slowed to a walk. Hands in the back pockets of her cutoff jeans, she ambled by the Simeses' house not looking fully at it, just taking quick glances at it. The shades of the front rooms of the house, both upstairs and down, had been drawn closed. Tandy was sweating. Well beyond the house, she turned and ambled back.

Reverend Baker's little black Chevrolet was pulling into the driveway. Tandy knew the minister seldom made pastoral visits on Saturdays. Blood drained from Tandy's face.

Mr. Baker did not appear to see her walking by in the road. He was waiting for someone to open the front door when Tandy broke into a run again.

She stopped running when she came within sight of the Whitfield house.

She was abreast of the Whitfield house when the front door opened.

Shirtless, barefooted, in jeans, hands oddly behind his back, Skylar came through the front door, blinking in the strong sunlight. He stumbled slightly on the porch. Behind him, Chick Hanson pushed his shoulder.

Skylar nearly fell down the steps.

Sheriff Culpepper came through the front door, saying something to Mr. and Mrs. Whitfield. Then he crossed the porch and came down the steps.

Pushing Skylar head down with the flat of his hand, Hanson put Skylar into the backseat of the sheriff's car. Pepp got in back, too.

Through the open back window of the sheriff's car, Skylar nodded across the lawn at Tandy.

Hanson got into the driver's seat and started the car. It scrunched down the gravel driveway onto the road. He turned toward town.

Leaning forward in his seat, Skylar nodded at Tandy again.

Pepp barely glanced at her as the car passed her.

Tandy stood in the middle of the road and waved after the car.

"They cotched you, boy, without shoes." The voice from the jail cell next to Skylar was a deep rumble. "Or a shirt."

Sitting on the edge of his thin, smelly bunk mattress, Skylar saw with peripheral vision a bulky shadow moving slowly in the next cell.

He did not look directly at his jailmate, or answer him.

Checking him in, Fleas had taken Skylar's belt and knife scabbard.

Fleas had not needed to ask Skylar his name, address, or age. In the space allotted for criminal charge, Fleas had printed, neatly, *Murder.*

After Chick Hanson had shoved Skylar into the jail cell and slammed the barred door, Fleas also wordlessly had brought Skylar a pail of water, leaving it in a corner of the cell.

On hands and knees, Skylar had sniffed the water in the pail. With cupped hands, he drank. Then he put water on his face, neck, chest.

It was not only incredibly hot in the jail, it was airless.

The low voice from the next cell rumbled, "You use shit, boy?"

Elbows on knees, head on hands, Skylar did not answer.

"You floatin', boy, or crashin'? You skatin' on the ice right now?"

The bulky shadow, the low rumble, moved closer to Skylar.

"I'm one glad man they cotched me."

Still Skylar did not turn his head.

Skylar rubbed his sore ear. His stomach muscles, which Hanson had hit with both hands, felt more stiff than sore. Straightening his back, he rubbed both of his kidneys simultaneously.

Skylar put his feet against the edge of the mattress and his back against the jail-cell wall. "Mister, I'm sorry for your trouble and all, but I don't particularly want to listen to you. I just heard a friend is dead. I don't need any more grief just now."

During the silence from the other cell, Skylar scanned his own cell, the concrete floor, the cement-block walls, the narrow horizontal window above his head containing two metal slats. The bunk was metal. Besides the pail of fresh water in one corner there was a bucket in another corner. The odor from it was sharp.

Halfway across the ceiling of his cell there was a line, an indentation. Skylar looked up carefully at it.

It seemed that part of the ceiling of his cell was a heavy metal slab. It extended over the bars along the corridor of cells to his right. There were no cells to his left.

Skylar got off his bunk and climbed the bars of his cell.

Standing on the horizontal bar second from the top and the bottom, holding on to a vertical bar with his left hand, he pushed up on the metal slab with his right hand.

Straining, trying to use his whole body as a jack, Skylar pushed up on the metal slab again and again.

There was a rustle from the next cell. The shadow moved.

"What're you doin', boy?" There was a low, rumbling laugh. "I'm a good mite bigger'n you are, boy, and I can't move that piece of ceiling. I tried 'nough times. Yes, sir, I surely have."

Sweating heavily, hair soaked with sweat, Skylar returned to his bunk. "It's just that I want to get to church in the mornin'."

"Where do you stop your run?" Judge Hall called through his car window.

"Up there. Top of the hill," Pepp answered while trying to keep his breathing even.

"I'll wait for you there."

"Then I run back."

The judge pulled ahead slowly not to raise dust from the

dirt road. That caused more of his car's exhaust to hang in the air.

Continuing to run, Pepp coughed and waved his hands in front of his face.

Damn. Pepp had thought no one knew where he ran late afternoons. He drove to a sloped road well west of town, parked the police car out of sight on a timber road, and gave himself an easy three miles run up the road, three miles down. Every afternoon: It was his time of day to get away, run, be alone, out of sight, get rid of stress. Pepp had realized years before that his job usually wasn't that stressful, but his marriage was, always. Of course, a pickup truck or car occasionally passed him. The passengers would wave, and he would wave back. Still, Pepp had hoped this habit of his running six miles along a road every afternoon shirtless and in shorts had not become county news. Now he knew it had.

Judge Hiram Hall knew how to find him. If the judge knew, probably everybody knew. Again, as many times before, Pepp realized the county sheriff really couldn't do anything without everyone in the county knowing about it sooner or later.

What was so important to bring the judge out looking for him on a Saturday afternoon? The judge always played golf Saturday afternoons. The judge had let Pepp understand enough times that he was not to be disturbed from noontime Saturday until noontime Sunday, "not even if a Republican president of the United States tried to speed through the county," the judge had said. After golf, the judge was apt to lift a few with his cronies in the nine-hole golf club's locker room.

"Wish I were in your shape, Pepp." Judge Hall had parked his car in the shade of a tree. He sat sideways on the driver's seat, his feet on the dirt road. "You have almost indecent energy, Pepp, for a man in his mid-forties."

The judge's golf hat was green, his short-sleeved shirt powder blue, his slacks pink.

Stopped, Pepp put his hands on his knees and sucked in breath. He did not like stopping at the top of the hill. Usually, he turned and started the easy jog down the hill without pausing.

"You run six miles every day?"

"When I can," Pepp said. "Most days."

"Must have good habits," Hall said, "otherwise." Squinted, the judge's eyes looked into Pepp's face. The expression on the judge's face made Pepp curious.

"Pepp, it seems this county has let a rip-roarin' tragedy happen. Our little Miss Beauty Queen, Miss Mary Lou Simes, has gotten herself beaten to death. And the story that comes to me is that young Skylar Whitfield has been arrested and jailed as the star suspect."

Pepp nodded.

"Where's Skylar now?"

"In jail."

"Pepp, wouldn't you say the Simeses and the Whitfields are about the two most liked, if not admired, families in the county?"

John Simes's immobile face appeared in Pepp's imagination.

"Oh, I know," the judge said. "Ol' John's been quite the sourpuss since he returned from that war. We all understand that, or at least accept it. But, Pepp, this whole county, the whole state, admires his kids. Jack plays first-string football for the state university. Mary Lou was determined to let the world know how pretty Greendowns County's women can be. And Skylar, Pepp. Skylar Whitfield somehow can't get through town, I've noticed, without all the ladies turnin' pink in his wake. Highest marks all through school. Plays that horn of his in church every Sunday. He's caused more women and children in this county to aspire to the heavenly choir than even Preacher Baker."

"Didn't play ball in high school." Pepp shrugged again. "His mother said this morning Skylar wasn't accepted by any of three colleges he applied to."

" 'Didn't play ball'? Is that you talkin', Pepp?"

"Handsome. Chick Hanson."

"Pepp, I figure I know you about as well as anybody. The

thing I know about you is that you're the biggest intellectual snob in this county. You barely tolerate the way us county folk talk, and think. To you, if someone hasn't read *The Decline and Fall of the Roman Empire* backwards in the original Egyptian, he's hardly worth a word."

"Haven't read that myself, Hiram. Even frontwards. But I don't think *The Decline and Fall of the Roman Empire* was originally written in Egyptian."

"There you go: correctin' an ol' duffer who belongs on a golf course. If you didn't have to run for election like the rest of us, I doubt you'd ever give anybody in this county the time of day. You'd prefer to live with your nose stuck in a book than in county affairs. And that's an actual fact. Whether a kid has ever played high school ball has never meant pie-diddle to you, Pepp. Was Mary Lou Simes murdered for sure?"

"Beaten to death."

"Couldn't an animal have done it? People are always rumorin' 'bout a bear 'round here."

"Haven't got the autopsy report yet. Looked to me like somebody beat her to death with his fists."

"Did Skylar Whitfield kill her?"

"Some evidence." The judge kept looking at Pepp expectantly. "Earlier in the evening, Mary Lou was at a party at Whitfield Farm. When Skylar showed up late at the party, apparently there was some screamin' and shoutin' between Mary Lou and Skylar."

"An argument?"

"Not described to me as such. More like play."

"That boy makes people scream and shout all over the county. Just somethin' 'bout him makes people scream and shout, what I know. He's a traveling three-ring circus."

"But apparently, at the party, Skylar and his friend Dufus embarrassed Mary Lou somehow, ruined her dress, sent her off in a huff."

"Dufus."

"Later, Skylar and Mary Lou both were at the same place at the same time, the Holler, but not together." Pepp scraped a line in the dirt with the edge of his sneaker. "I gather this county thinks Mary Lou Simes and Skylar Whitfield always are supposed to be together. They weren't together at the Holler. Maybe didn't even speak to each other."

"So you suspicion they'd had a real argument? A lovers' quarrel?"

"Skylar's pocketknife was found at the scene of the crime."

"She wasn't stabbed, was she?"

"I don't think so. Autopsy . . ."

"Then why is the knife relevant?"

"Places Skylar at the scene of the crime. Even he says he had the knife the day before. I'm sure we can find witnesses to testify to the fact he had the knife the day before. There's not a spot of rust on that knife. The murder scene is in deep woods, Judge. Not exactly a busy intersection."

The judge sighed. "I'd go for a B.H.S."

"The perpetrator may be a bushy-haired stranger. I hope so, too. If it weren't for the knife . . ."

"You know why I'm here instead of playin' golf as the good Lord means me to be doin'?"

"Bail."

"The Whitfields are polite people. They didn't telephone me. In fact, I telephoned them to tell them I'm sorry for their trouble. Just about everyone else in this county did call me. Pastor Baker. Senator Wilkins. Even the original Mary Lou, M.L. Simes. Mother of the dead girl. In tears, assuring me there's no reason to clap Skylar in jail."

Pepp said, "There's reason."

"Is there reason to keep him there?"

Pepp nodded, *Yes.* "I think so, Hiram. As you indicated, Skylar is a highly intelligent, imaginative, energetic, popular boy. No tellin' what he might do. Or what might happen to him. I suspect this is the first difficulty he's ever had in his life. If he is guilty, he needs time to think things over. The county needs time to get used to the possibility."

"You're telling me I shouldn't respond to all this until Monday morning."

Pepp smiled. "You wouldn't if it were a Republican president of the United States, Hiram."

"Is he in a cell by himself?"

"I think so." Pepp hoped Deputy Hanson hadn't done something stupid and mean regarding Skylar's jail accommodations. "We have plenty of vacancies."

"Check on that."

"Yes."

"Pepp, what do you think bail should be?"

"Not my problem, Judge."

"I know that. Just thinkin' out loud. The Whitfields aren't real wealthy folks. Dan runs that insurance business. Monica works in the library. I suppose they're maybe fifty thousand ahead, would you say? That land can't have a mortgage on it, after all these years. Guess I can find out about that. I suspect holdin' on to that land is sort of a struggle for them, seein' farmin' on that scale seldom pays for the farmland, these days."

"Sounds wealthy to me."

"Wayne's done well, up North, or so I hear. People say he's a genuine millionaire."

"His son, Wayne's son, is staying at Whitfield Farm right now."

"That so?"

"Name's Jonathan. Haven't seen him."

"So brother Wayne could be called on."

"You know, Hiram, I'm sort of in favor of keepin' that boy in jail."

"Why's that?"

"There's something about him. . . . Well, I sense he's resented . . . by some."

"You think he might be in danger, walkin' around?"

"Well, I know of one who was happy enough to hit him unnecessarily."

"One of your deputies?"

"In the police car, Chick wept openly."

"All right, Pepp." The judge swung his legs into the car.

"Guess you're right. Let's leave it till Monday. Let the boy and everyone else in this county calm down, get used to the possibility, as you say. You want a ride back to where you hide your car?"

Pepp looked at his bare arms. "Yes. I'm cooled off now."

7

When Pepp entered his house through the back door, he called
out in as friendly a voice as he could manage, "Hello!" He
believed in keeping as much as possible the forms and tones
of a workable, if not happy, marriage.

There was no answer.

He did hear the slight scrape of wood on wood from upstairs, perhaps the vanity's stool being moved on the floor.

Nor was there any activity in the kitchen at 6:45 Saturday
night to indicate food preparation was in progress or imminent. The kitchen was filthy. Dirty pots were on the stove,
dirty dishes in the sink; everything, including the table and
the floor, needed a good scrubbing.

He went through the dining room. Newspapers, magazines,
pamphlets, were piled on the dining-room table. That was
Martha Jane's work, her "search for evidence," as she called
it. The pamphlet title Pepp read was, *Man the Oppressor,
Woman the Oppressed.*

Looking at the living room, he could not figure exactly what
it was in particular that made it look so unwelcoming. Everything was askew, the pillows on the couch, the pictures on the
wall, his footstool to his chair. Every surface needed dusting.

Climbing the stairs now gave him a sense of fear, of anger,

of hopelessness. Many nights he had climbed those stairs to face scoffs, insults, rejection, in his bed. Even early in his marriage, he had seldom faced other than indifference in the marital bed, no matter what he had done. Martha Jane always had thought, had said, she expected sex to happen to her, without her contributing to the act. He never could convince her otherwise. Often he had wondered what there was in her background, in her nature, to make her think, feel, such a thing. Always she had lain as still and as indifferent as the bed itself. Her only physical response would be to clasp his wrists with her hands, to keep him from "pawing" her. If he ever succeeded in freeing his hands and touched her breasts, tears would flow. With increasing frequency, Pepp had not climbed those stairs at bedtime, preferring to spend the nights reading and sleeping sprawled in his red leather chair and footstool in the living room.

Why had he put up with such a marriage in which he, as male, was the declared enemy? Over the years, he had gone through this mental and emotional exercise thousands of times.

Pepp loved his daughter, Samantha, more than anything or anybody in the world, more than he had ever loved anyone.

Pepp, who would rather have worked toward a college education himself, have his copious reading enhanced by guidance, instruction, instead had found himself being a small-town cop, reading scattershot, eclectically, virtually concealing his reading from the town's people, buying his books out of town as some citizens bought their hard liquor, never permitting himself to be seen with a book in hand, or on the car seat next to him. When he first ran for sheriff, he lost. The second time he ran, he won. Since then he had done his job, bought a small house, supported his family.

And Samantha had won acceptance, but without much scholarship help, at Duke University, where presently she was a junior.

Just as his wrists had been held in bed, Pepp had been restrained otherwise by Martha Jane. The usual bitterness of divorce necessarily would divide the county and make the next election that much more difficult for him to win, probably cost him his job as county sheriff.

Even if he succeeded in winning the next election somehow, he knew the cost of divorce would almost certainly mean the end of Samantha's private education. And Pepp wanted Sammy to go as far in education as her interests and talents would take her.

As he entered the bedroom, Martha Jane stood up from the dressing table. She was dressed in a boxy suit.

Smiling, he said, "Didn't you hear me shout hello from the kitchen?" Of course she had.

She looked at him and at the door behind him as if he were some sort of physical obstacle to her leaving the room.

He moved out of the path between Martha Jane and the door.

"Going out?" he asked. "What about supper?"

Looking at his gray sweatsuit, her nose wrinkled. "I've eaten."

"What about me?"

Martha Jane sorted pamphlets and papers and newspaper clippings from the bureau and put them into her soft leather briefcase. "It was a male God who said I had to shop and cook and clean for you."

"Was that the same feller who said I had to take financial responsibility for a family all my adult life?"

To appear even less threatening, Pepp sat on one hip on the bed. He propped his head on one hand.

When she didn't answer, Pepp said, "I've said enough times I'd be happy to stay home, shop, cook, and clean, if you'd go to work and support the family financially. I'm not so hide-bound I see the divisions of family responsibilities necessarily defined by sex."

" 'Necessarily,' " Martha Jane quoted. "You realize how much *attitude* is behind that one word?"

"My attitude is that there are jobs to be done. We have to do them. I have a job, and you have a job. I've told you time and again we can rearrange them any way you like."

Feet widely separated on the bedroom rug, standing in her

boxy suit, her chin held high, Martha Jane said, as if swearing at him, "Maybe I will get a job. Start a business."

"God, I wish you would." Fingers clasped, Pepp stretched his arms over his head. "You've said that enough times, but you've never done a thing about it. I'd rather you do anything than sit eight, ten hours a day, watching talk shows devoted to the evils of males. 'What Daddy, Hubby, Boss Did to Me.' Dirty laundry that sells soap."

She said, "I have a meeting."

"And go to meetings." Pepp sat up on the edge of the bed, shoulders hunched, hands folded between his thighs. "Martha Jane, you know how I feel about your attending all these meetings."

"Of course I do."

"I believe I'm sympathetic to the plight of women. I understand that some women, maybe all women, need support groups." Pepp rubbed the back of his neck with his hand. "I'm still physically sick from seeing the body of a teenaged girl who was beaten to death early this morning. We assume she was beaten by a male. I expect she didn't have a chance to defend herself."

"Mary Lou Simes."

"You've heard."

Martha Jane's voice took on the volume and the cadence of someone giving a speech. "Mary Lou Simes permitted, she caused, men to think only in terms of physical beauty when regarding a woman, to think only in terms of sex. She allowed herself to be exploited by all these beauty pageants to the detriment of every other girl, woman, female, in this county, in this whole world!"

Pepp's stomach lurched. "Are you saying that little girl deserved what happened to her?"

"No woman deserves what any man does to her."

"But you are saying Mary Lou Simes put herself in the way of what happened to her. . . ."

"Is there any real difference between a girl's putting herself up on a stage in a bathing suit, allowing herself to be exploited by letting a lot of men stare at her and get sexually excited, judge her as a sexual object, a piece of meat, and her being beaten to death by a man? Is there any real difference between a man's eyes and his fists?"

The bedroom rug blurred in Pepp's eyes. "Yes." He blinked. "I think so." He tried to concentrate on a blister on his hand, pick it. "We can enjoy each other without harming one another." He took a deep breath, trying to clear his vision, calm his stomach. "At least I thought so when I got married." His hands gripped the edge of the mattress. "I didn't make this world, Martha Jane. No council of men made this world. There is the fact that there are men and there are women, and there is sex."

"And there is violence."

He nodded. "There is violence. Men didn't vote that in, either, I don't think."

"I'm late."

"Martha Jane, I'm asking you not to go to this meeting tonight."

Filled briefcase under her arm, she looked down at him. "Why?"

"I can't debate these ancient issues with you full time, all my life. At these women's meetings, you say things about me, against me. What you say gets back to me, you know. Some of the things you say are true. Sometimes maybe I can be a little insensitive, use the wrong word. Some of the things reported to me you say are not true."

"I've never said anything not true."

"Over the years, I've asked you to be interested in my work, share with me, campaign with me. . . ."

"Yes," she said. "You've tried to exploit me."

"Please realize that my paycheck is the only income we've got. If you can't work with me, please don't work against me, for your own sake. Surely, you have to see the logic in that."

Martha Jane shook her head. "This is manipulation. Man the Income Provider says, If you don't obey me, I won't shelter or feed you. Little woman, you stay barefoot and pregnant in the yard, and if you dare open your mouth to say one word against me, I'll see that no food gets put in that mouth ever again."

"Martha Jane—"

"You've gotten away with this enough centuries."

"Martha Jane, if you go to that meeting tonight, please don't come back. I mean, ever."

"You're still doing it, Pepp. Manipulating. Threatening."

Samantha is a junior at Duke, Pepp recited to himself. *Maybe the timing of divorce would work out. If not, maybe she could manage to win her college diploma by herself, with student loans or something.*

"Martha Jane, I want a divorce. If you want your independence, please take it."

"No way, mister. You don't get out of it that easy."

"Out of what?"

Martha Jane's face was pale, her eyes were hard with fury.

Pepp wondered when was the last time he had seen anything he had even thought was love for him in her eyes.

He said, "I just can't stand this anymore. I'm far from perfect, I know that, but I've done the best I can. I don't believe for a moment I deserve this constant punishment." He dropped his voice. "Martha Jane, if you don't divorce me, I will divorce you."

Oddly, Pepp found himself wondering if he ought to have used the word "shall" instead of "will" in his last sentence.

"You'd better watch yourself, boy."

Pepp looked up from the bed at Martha Jane. "How's that?"

"You're pretty vulnerable, you know."

" 'Vulnerable'?"

"You're the county sheriff. You have to be reelected. Your reputation is important to you."

"I know that. And you know that."

"You'll never divorce me." Martha Jane's eyes looked too hard ever to have held a loving look. "Don't even think of trying."

"Are you hongry?"

Tandy stood on the roof of the jail looking down into the cell. The cell was lit only by a dim corridor light.

Next to her stood Dufus in the position of a weight lifter holding one end of the metal slab hatch as high as his chest.

Skylar clambered up the jail-cell bars. He grabbed on to the edge of the roof with his hands and pulled himself up. He swung his bare right foot onto the roof.

During the day, the jail was like a broiling oven; during the night, a baking oven.

Even at that hour of the night, Skylar's body was slick with sweat.

On his smelly mattress, he had been awakened by a scratching noise on the roof. Then the scrape of a crowbar sliding between the metal slab and the edge of the roof.

Then the sound of whispers and giggling.

He had gotten off his bunk and looked up.

In the cell next to him, the bulky shadow also rose from the bunk.

In a third cell, Tony Duffy, who regularly performed every Saturday night in the town jail, sometimes Tuesday and Thursday nights as well, if he had sufficiently lubricated his vocal cords with raw alcohol, had tired of rendering "Onward Christian Soldiers" and gone to his deserved sleep two hours before.

Skylar guessed it was about four in the morning. He had had perhaps an hour's sleep. He had been disturbed by his memory of Mary Lou Simes lurching out of the Holler the night before. . . .

"Dufus, please don't drop the roof at this moment," Skylar said.

Dufus grunted.

Tandy grabbed Skylar's bicep and helped him to his feet on the jail roof.

"Right nice they gave you the corner cell," Tandy said,

"where the roof lifts up. I expect we're mighty obliged to Mr. Fleas Adam Haddam for that. He usually tries to accommodate the innocent criminals in that cell. He was similarly kind to my brother that time he kindly slapped that truck salesman upside the head." In the moonlight, she looked at Skylar's stomach. "Are you hongry?"

Her fingers patted his stomach sympathetically.

"Taters and beans."

"Mr. Fleas recognizes his cooking isn't so good that innocent criminals should suffer from it."

Dufus was still holding up one end of the metal roof slab.

Tandy leaned over the edge of the roof. She called down into the cells. "Anybody down there want anything?"

The hulking shadow in the next cell answered. "No, ma'am. I belong in here. Maybe some fried chicken?"

"All right," Tandy said.

Dufus lowered the metal hatch on the jail roof.

Leading Skylar and Dufus to the edge of the roof at the rear of the building, Tandy said, "Years county's been tryin' to raise money to fix the jail roof. Seems to me, no one wants it fixed at all!"

At the edge of the roof leaned the top of an extension ladder. The bottom of the ladder was braced in the bed of Skylar's pickup truck.

"Seems to me," Tandy said, munching a barbecue sandwich, "Mary Lou Simes has been murdered bad, and the sheriff thinks you done did it. Are those the simple facts, Skylar?"

"Sounds about right to me."

Tandy, Dufus, and Skylar were sitting cross-legged in a rocky dell east of Whitfield Farm eating the barbecue sandwiches Tandy had prepared. They passed a half-gallon plastic jug of milk among them.

Sunday was dawning.

"Skylar, why would you kill Mary Lou?"

"Jealousy," Skylar said. "I don't know. Maybe because I'm not going to college."

"I see." Tandy nodded shrewdly. "That's right. Mary Lou Simes set herself up as an expensive lady, all those beauty contests she's won. Sure, she'd have to marry a white-neck. She'd have no more interest in you, if you're not goin' on to college, would she? That's what the old 'uns would think, natural enough."

Dufus reached into the rubbish bag for another sandwich. "Skylar probably beat her to death with that tin horn of his."

"Yes, sir," Tandy said, "I can see that clear as day. Sure enough, Mary Lou was killed by someone who knew her."

"Why do you say that?" Skylar asked.

"She'd never walk a quarter-mile through the woods beyond midnight with anyone she didn't know. I'm surprised she did so at all."

"She was pretty drunk," Dufus said.

"People won't be quick to believe that," Skylar said. "Not Mary Lou Simes."

"She would have gone with you, Skylar. And if she was alone and beginnin' to walk home," Tandy said, "then she was goin' in the wrong direction!"

"She was just wanderin'," Dufus said. "Wanderin', knee-walkin' drunk. That's how come I went after her. She had no idea what she was doin', where she was goin'. I've gone into the woods from the Holler to sleep enough times." He looked around. "Hardly a patch of woods 'round here I haven't gone to sleep."

"Men have lay-out nights," Tandy said. "Ever hear of a woman havin' a lay-out night? Mary Lou Simes?"

"Booze is booze," Dufus said.

"I hear vodka has a way of catchin' up to you unexpected like," Skylar said. "First you feel little or nothin', then wham! Mary Lou was drinkin' vodka at our house, pretendin' it was white wine."

"Straight vodka?" Tandy asked.

"She was pourin' her own from the bar," Dufus said. "It wasn't no white wine."

"Time my brother, Alec, drank straight vodka," Tandy said, "he rode a horse into the river, and it drownded." She looked at the remains of her sandwich in her lap. "He was so drunk, he even tried to give the horse mouth-to-mouth resuscitation. It didn't work well enough to save the horse, but it just might have saved him."

"Just can't think why anyone would want to kill Mary Lou," Skylar said.

" 'Cept you," Tandy said. "They've got a pretty good case against you, Skylar. You have to give 'em that."

Skylar said, "Miss Tandy, I'm not appreciatin' your humor all that much."

"Sexually frustrated, that's what you are."

"Yeah."

"Just tryin' to see it as others see it," Tandy said. "You're a rejected homeboy, out on a lonely farm all by yourself with no one but Dufus and me around. No tellin' what you might do." Tandy began putting the sandwich wrappings back into the rubbish bag. "I'm tryin' to say somethin' here, Skylar."

"What's that?"

"Seems to me someone murdered Mary Lou bad, and if it wasn't you, you had better wriggle your buns findin' out precisely who done did it."

"Sure," Skylar said. "Beat the police at their own game."

"Sheriff Culpepper don't care about you, Skylar. He's a fair man. He'd just as soon hang you as Dufus."

"Tandy . . ."

"I'm sleepy now." Dufus had finished the milk. "Goin' to sleep." He wandered to one edge of the dell. He put his back against a tree, slid down, and folded his arms across his chest.

Skylar said to Tandy, "Thanks for rescuing me."

"I had to rescue Dufus this night, too."

"Dufus?"

"Yeah. I told him through the window of his shed what we were fixin' to do, come collect you from the jailhouse, and told him to hurry up and get dressed. He was sound asleep, I guess. I waited for him in the truck. Few minutes later I heard a big thump. Then he began hollerin' like a calf who couldn't find no tit. I got out of the truck and went lookin' for him.

He'd been in such a hurry he hadn't tied his sneaker strings.
Rushin' out the shed, he slammed the door on them. They
throwed him to the ground. Still half-asleep, poor Dufus
couldn't figure out how to reach around and open the door to
free himself. If I hadn't heard him fall and bawl, he'd probably
be lyin' there still."

Eyes closed, Dufus said, " 'Tis true."

Next breath he snored.

"I brung you some soap, too." Tandy stuck her head inside
the garbage bag. "And a towel." She put both in Skylar's lap.
"Guess you can bathe in the river." She left her hand on his
leg. "Guess we hadn't ought to."

"No," Skylar said.

"Not now."

"Not now."

"No way."

"No way."

"Not with Mary Lou not even buried yet."

"Right."

"Even though you probably especially need to."

"Suppose I do."

"Me, too."

"It wouldn't be right."

"That's what I'm sayin'."

"Anyway," Skylar said.

"Anyway."

"I need you to go sneak me fresh jeans, a shirt, boots."

Hand still on Skylar's leg, Tandy said, "You goin' to
church?"

"It's Sunday."

"Suppose it's all right?"

"To go to church?"

"Yeah."

"It's never wrong to go to church, is it?"

"You want your trumpet?"

"No," Skylar said. "I'm in mournin'."

8

"Sheriff Culpepper? This is Coroner Murphy."

Pepp propped pillows higher behind his head. "Mornin'."

In Greendowns County, people grew up together as close as maggots under a rock, knew each other's most intimate secrets, their weaknesses, their strengths, had at least two or three nicknames for each other, but when it came to doing formal business with each other, even by telephone early Sunday morning, were apt to refer to themselves and each other by formal titles, if they had any.

"Sorry to call you so early Sunday morning, but wanted to catch you before you went to church."

And used the formality of presumption. Sheriff Culpepper was not a churchgoer. Neither was Dr. Murphy. And each so knew about the other.

"That's all right," Pepp answered.

The other side of Pepp's bed had not been disturbed. If Martha Jane had returned home the night before, she had done so late and had not slept in her own bed.

As soon as Martha Jane had left the night before, Pepp had commenced his increasingly frequent routine of housecleaning. First he cleaned the refrigerator, removing everything, judging whatever food by sight and sniff, dumping the majority, which was rotten. Last night, as divorce had been explicitly mentioned, requested, as he had asked her not to return home if she went to her meeting, he seriously considered throwing out her vast supplies of refrigerated wheat germ, yogurt, and other such foodstuffs he didn't know by name, but he had not done so. He noted the irony that the more exclusively the refrigerator became filled with health foods, the chubbier Martha Jane got. And the meaner. Perhaps after she had left the house, she had allowed herself to think of what she was doing to him, his reputation, their income, their marriage, and just gone to spend the evening with friends. He scrubbed the refrigerator shelves.

After eating two bologna and mustard sandwiches with a can of beer, Pepp cleaned the kitchen generally. He started with the sink, cleaned the stove, loaded the dishwasher, scrubbed the counters, washed the floor. He vacuumed and straightened the front hall, the living room. He had the temptation to trash the dining room, tear up and scatter her "evidence," as she called it, all her clipped newspaper feature stories and pamphlets reporting specific cases generalized regarding man's inhumanity to woman. He would have felt as justified in doing so as he had in throwing out rotten food. It was poison to their lives together, their marriage, his career. He did not do so. Instead, he vacuumed the dining-room carpet. While polishing the furniture in the house, he left the papers on the dining-room table untouched.

He cleaned the stairs, the upstairs hall, Samantha's bedroom, their bedroom, scrubbed the bathroom, changed the sheets on their bed, loaded and started the washing machine.

It was shortly after eleven when he got into bed with a book, Shirley Hazzard's *The Bay of Noon*. Before going to sleep, he reviewed his reasons for cleaning the house alone on a Saturday night, after a week of work capped by an especially bad day, one of the worst of his professional life. Pepp simply could not stand dirt and mess. He tried not to see it as an insult to him. Nor did he intend his cleaning efforts as an insult to Martha Jane. He just couldn't stand living with everything in the house, wherever he looked, smudged, filthy, askew. To him, such mess indicated a disorderly mind and, to an extent, disordered his mind. Too, the physical work was a kind of therapy. It calmed him. If he had gone to bed without such activity, his anger would have given him a sleepless night. He had had more than enough sleepless nights.

His night had not been restful, anyway. Surging below the surface of his light sleep was the vision of Mary Lou Simes, facedown on the riverbank, little skirt tossed up, pretty legs dirty, positioned unnaturally, her head beaten into a bloody mess; her mother, M.L., trying unsuccessfully to control herself, maintain dignity at hearing the worst news of all; the expressions of incredulity, dismay, helplessness on the Whitfields' faces while Deputy Hanson was shoving their son, Skylar, handcuffed through the front door to the police car.

Yet he had not heard Martha Jane return to the house.

"I'm awake, Coroner," Pepp said into the telephone because he wasn't entirely awake and because his mind was not entirely on police business. "What have you got?"

"First, may I report something personal to you?"

"Of course."

"Chandler was at a meeting with your wife last night." Chandler was Dr. Charles Murphy's wife.

"Yes." *So Martha Jane had attended the meeting. Enough wishful thinking.*

"Martha Jane said some rather ripe things about you, Pepp. In public."

So: very nearly the end of hope.

Pepp felt prickly heat on his forehead. "What did she say?"

"Figure you'd better ask her that yourself, Pepp."

"Okay."

"I've reported this much to you for two reasons, Pepp. First, I want to assure you I don't believe a word of it. Neither does Chandler. She was shocked. She thinks Martha Jane is just embarrassing herself. I take it more seriously than that. Second, I think you had better begin defending yourself. As we used to say in the schoolyard, 'Get your dukes up.' "

"Thanks, Charley." Official conversations in Greendowns County might begin formally, but personal knowledge of each other was too intimate, concern for each other was too great, there were too many relationships cross-wired, for conversations, official or not, to remain formal, impersonal, very long. "We are having difficulties."

"Figured that. Hope you don't mind my speaking up."

"Not at all."

"I'm sure you'll hear about it from other sources."

"Yes."

"I just want to assure you there are at least two of us, Chandler and myself, who do not believe a word of what Martha Jane says, for whatever motive."

"Appreciate it."

"Now, to get to this other nasty business." Dr. Charles Murphy took a deep breath, as if changing the air in his lungs would help him change his focus. "You might consider this a preliminary report, Sheriff. Pathology, as you know, is not my specialty, thank God. But I knew you wanted a first reading as to what happened to Mary Lou Simes as quickly as you could get it. I spent most of the night with her. Everything is reasonably intact, in case you want to move her to the state pathology labs." Dr. Murphy paused. "What I mean, Pepp, is that I have done what I can do and have not screwed up, ruined evidence, inhibited anyone else's subsequent work on her."

Pepp said, "I know." He wondered, with respect, at the mind trained in science that obliged Dr. Murphy to make this preliminary statement to a preliminary report, all early on a Sunday morning. Reaching for a pad of paper and pen on his bedside table, Pepp said, "Go ahead, Charley."

"Okay." Dr. Charles Murphy sighed. "Mary Lou Simes was murdered."

"Okay." Pepp also wondered at the mind trained in science that was obliged to state the obvious.

"She was beaten to death. Ninety-plus-percent chance by a right-handed person. Two separate blows fractured her skull. One of those blows, or a third, broke her neck. She was beaten more lightly, causing bleeding, about the face and upper body, after she was brain-dead—in my opinion, Pepp.''

"To disfigure her?''

"Maybe. Maybe rage. That's all for you to discover.''

"Raped?''

"No.''

"No?''

"No.''

"Charley, was there evidence she put up a fight?''

"Not that I can see. Her hands, arms, are not bruised. Her fingernails are not broken. There is no foreign skin or blood I could discover under her fingernails. And, as I said, almost all evidence of light beating seemed to have taken place after Mary Lou was totally defenseless.''

" 'Almost all'?''

"There is a very light bruise on the back of her neck, which I also date from Friday night, but I think several hours earlier. The sort of bruise one would get bumping into something. A minor ouch. It might have stunned her, surprised her, but no way would have caused her to lose consciousness, fall down, anything like that. Mary Lou was a strong, healthy young woman.''

"How do you bump into something with the back of your neck?''

"There's a good question.''

"What time did all this happen?''

"That's harder for me to say with precision. Possibly as early as one A.M. Possibly as late as four-thirty A.M.''

"That's not very precise.''

"My supposition is that Mary Lou was brain-dead considerably before her healthy, young other organs turned themselves off. She may even have rolled herself over, onto her stomach. I say that because all the blows, including those I refer to as taking place during 'a light beating,' seemed to have been directed to her front—her face, her ribs, et cetera. Of course, the perpetrator could have rolled her over, say with his boot, after he had finished with her.''

"Charley? How did Mary Lou Simes die?''

"What do you mean?"

"Supposing there was an auto accident. Kids joyriding. Swigging beer. Car, truck, went off the road, hit a tree. Mary Lou sustained these injuries. Kids panicked. Hid her body in the woods, maybe believing she was already dead. Hid the vehicle."

"Wishful thinking, Sheriff."

"Not possible?"

"Pepp, Mary Lou Simes was beaten to death."

"What weapon?"

"Fists."

"Just fists?"

"Fists."

"There is no evidence of any use of a knife?"

"Knife? No."

"Not even a tiny cut, maybe meant to intimidate?"

"No. In fact, in my general practice, Pepp, I've seldom seen such an unblemished body. Not of anyone over the age of three or four. Mary Lou didn't have even childhood knee and elbow scars. Of course, a cut such as you describe could be hidden under other, subsequently inflicted skin breaks, but given the total surface area of the body, that would be statistically unlikely. Let me amend that. Her legs had a few scratches, very fresh. Scratches she would have gotten walking from the Holler through the woods to where Tommy found her."

"So we know she walked there. She was not carried, et cetera."

"She walked. There's a question you haven't asked, Pepp."

"Ask it for me."

"Roughly midnight Friday night. We know Mary Lou was at the beer joint, the Holler. She was found murdered a quarter-mile from the Holler."

"How much had she had to drink?"

"She was stinko."

"Stinko drunk?"

"Let me put it this way. She could not have driven a car ten feet in a desert without hitting something. If she were not as young and healthy as she was, I doubt she could have walked a quarter-mile without collapsing. I don't think she knew where she was going, or what she was doing. Incidentally, she couldn't have fought off an attack by a two-week-old kitten."

"Mary Lou Simes? Beer . . . not used to it, I guess."

"Hard liquor, Pepp. A lot of it. With beer on top."

"My, my. Any other chemical substances, Charley, drugs?"

"Not that I can detect. Some such are very hard to detect. You'll need the state pathology boys to answer that one for sure."

"Mary Lou Simes . . . Did you see evidence that drinking for her was a frequent occurrence?"

"Can't tell. Especially not at her age. In order to manifest physical deterioration by alcohol at her age, she'd have to have been a twenty-four-hour-a-day stumbling drunk, right up there with Tony Duffy. Our knowledge of Mary Lou says that's not so. For someone to drink that much at one time, one suspects she's tasted the grape before, or, in this case, the potato. But I rather think this was a single occurrence, maybe not unique, of Mary Lou Simes getting stinking drunk, as people sometimes do."

"Potato."

"Right. Vodka. So our beauty queen knew something about booze. How to conceal at least the first stages of her drinking."

"My, my. I wonder if she was upset about something."

"Probably. Realize that this county, Pepp, her school, church, family, heaped a lot of pressure on Mary Lou Simes, a long time ago. And kept it there. It's hard being put on a pedestal, Pepp, and told you must never fall off. Never had the experience myself, not really, but I, as a small-town doctor, and you, as county sheriff, have to have some sensitivity to Mary Lou's general situation."

"Upset about something specific . . ."

"You're thinking out loud again."

"Charley, I don't like what I'm seeing. How do you see what happened?"

"Some most likely right-handed person, most likely male,

definitely powerful, therefore most likely young, encountered Mary Lou in the woods and beat her to death with his fists.''

"Without sexually assaulting her.''

"No evidence of sexual anything.''

"Therefore without being sexually rejected?''

"Mary Lou was soused, Pepp. Anyone who beat her this bad easily could have overpowered her sexually.''

" 'Encountered Mary Lou in the woods' . . .'' Pepp mused. "Bushy-haired stranger. She surprised someone in the woods, some tramp asleep . . .''

"Why would such a person beat her to death?''

"Didn't want anyone to know he was there, be seen, escaped convict. Someone crazy on drugs . . .''

"More likely someone followed her from the Holler.''

"In her condition, could Mary Lou have run that far, a quarter-mile through the woods in the dark, you know, I mean, to escape somebody?''

"I suppose so, at her age, in her physical condition. Not without falling down more than once. Which she could have done. Yes, she could have been running from someone.''

"Or someone she knew could have walked with her . . .''

"Yes.''

" 'Rage,' you said.''

"I think after slugging Mary Lou, very powerfully, while she was still standing, the guy sat straddling Mary Lou's hips while she was on the ground and worked over her face and ribs with his fists. Nice, uh?''

"Would the murderer get blood on his clothes?''

"Possibly. Not necessarily.''

"Would his hands be hurt?''

"Mine would. My knuckles would be bruised. But the hands of a man who works with his hands, you know, farm work, factory work, I doubt his hands would show any notable bruising.''

Pepp heard noises from Samantha's room. Martha Jane had returned home, at some point during the night, and slept in the other room.

Damn. How can I do my work, keep my mind on it, keep this family running, pay the bills, Samantha's college expenses, while constantly having to fight a rearguard assault from my wife?

"Dr. Coroner Murphy, I think we've got someone who knew Mary Lou Simes very well."

"That's for you to say. 'Got someone,' did you say?"

Pepp put an asterisk at the bottom of his notes. "Got him."

"Did you sleep well, Jonathan?" Monica Whitfield asked kindly at breakfast.

"Not very." In fact, Jon was pretty sure he had slept better than his aunt and uncle. At breakfast in the kitchen, both his aunt and uncle looked as if they had not slept at all. Truth is, Jonathan Whitfield more than once during the night had found himself suppressing giggles. The situation was so ludicrous. Within twenty-four hours of his arriving at Whitfield Farm, partly, he was pretty sure, to reform his country cousin, that same cousin got hauled off to the local lockup and charged with murder! Of course, Jon knew it wasn't really funny; it had to be dreadful for his aunt and uncle. But to be assigned involuntarily a task at which he, Jonathan, had failed so readily, quickly, thoroughly, and dramatically, did have its humorous side. In fact, Jon had slept very well.

However, Jon was a trained and experienced houseguest. For the most part, he had always been a houseguest, even in his own home, or at least had to behave as one. Taking on the joys and griefs of whosoever's house he was guesting in was only polite.

On Sunday morning, Dan Whitfield, apron around his suit pants, was serving bacon and eggs to his wife and nephew straight from the stove to the kitchen table.

His uncle being in suit pants, shirt, and necktie on Sunday morning, Jon knew, was a hint to any polite houseguest that family churchgoing was imminent and that the houseguest was expected to accompany family to church.

Jon had come to breakfast in his bathrobe.

And had other plans.

"I'm not sure I can eat," Monica said to the fried eggs newly arrived on her plate. "I can't help wondering how Skylar passed the night."

"He's fine," Dan said, bringing a plate of toast to the table and sitting down. "Skylar's a big, strong boy."

"You hear such terrible things," Monica said, "about what goes on among the people in jails."

Yeah, Jon wanted to say. *Those guys should be locked up!*

"Skylar can take care of himself," Dan reassured his wife, not looking at all assured himself.

"I don't know. Rose Holman said something the other night about how sexy he is."

"Sexy?" Dan said. "Skylar?"

"What did she say? He has more sex than a church organ. Would you believe that?"

"How would she know?" Dan asked. "Eighty-three years old and never married."

"I'm not sure I get the joke about the church organ, either," Monica said.

"Maybe that's why Rose never married." Dan smiled. "She's other-directed. Gets turned on by church organs."

"And Skylar . . ." Monica was not eating. "Other people always seem to know one's own child so . . . differently—see him in ways his parents don't. Jonathan? Is Skylar sexy?"

"How would I know?"

"I mean, you're just a little older than he."

While Jon's eyes roamed the kitchen table, he remembered Skylar sticking his tongue into Mary Lou's ear, stepping nude from his shower into the waiting hands of another absolutely gorgeous, joyful girl. . . . "Girls take a lot from him."

"A lot of what?" Dan asked.

"May I have another piece of toast?" Jon asked.

"I trust you don't mean *abuse*, Jonathan."

"Abuse? Who said anything about abuse?"

Dan was watching Jon's face closely.

Monica wept into her hands. "Mary Lou . . ."

"Come on," Dan said. "Mary Lou is dead. There is nothing

we can do about that. We all know Skylar did not harm her, in any way, ever. I finally got ahold of Frank Murrey this morning. He was down at the river until late last night. He's going to get on to the sheriff. . . ."

Monica distracted herself by leaning over and petting the dog. "Poor Julep. Looks so confused. Was he noisy during the night, Jonathan?"

"He did whine. I took him into my room with me."

"Did you?" Monica looked at her nephew with raised eyebrows. "How very nice of you."

"Moved his bed." Jonathan finished his breakfast. "Aunt Monica? Uncle Dan?" They looked at him expectantly. "I'm sorry for your trouble. . . ."

Despite being damp and red-rimmed, Monica's eyes became hard. *"Our* trouble?"

Instantly, Jonathan was confused. "Skylar and all . . ."

"Whatever are you saying, Jonathan?" Monica asked.

Jon heard the ice crack beneath his skates. "I just think I should leave," Jonathan said. "Go home." A crack in the ice was approaching him. "The Simes girl's death . . . Skylar in jail . . . No time for you to have to put up with a houseguest. . . ."

His aunt and uncle stared at him over their unfinished breakfasts. Dan glanced quickly at his wife and then back at Jon. Monica's stare did not waver.

Jon felt the section of ice he was on beginning to sink.

Dan's nose twitched. " 'Houseguest' . . ."

"I only meant . . ."

"Are you pretending to be considerate of us, Jon?" Monica asked.

"Well, yes. I . . ."

Monica sighed. "Jonathan, Jonathan. Where do we start with you?" With her thumb, she pushed her breakfast plate forward, away from her, and rested her forearms on the table. "Jonathan, Jonathan."

"You'll be busy," Jon said lamely, feeling his feet cold. "With Skylar in jail and all."

"Family." For a moment, Monica said nothing more.

Dan cleared his throat. "The point is . . ."

Finally, Monica said, "Skylar is your cousin, Jonathan. I know you two boys don't know each other well. Maybe you two don't like each other much. Maybe you never will. Skylar is in trouble. At the moment, he is in jail, accused of murder, which is about as much trouble as one can ever have. When someone in a family is in trouble, whether you like each other or not—unless there are much bigger issues between you than there can be between you and Skylar—you rally around. You support. You defend."

"You're not a houseguest," Dan said. "You're family."

"Have you no sense of family, Jonathan?"

Jon frowned.

"Point is," Dan said, "if you, Skylar's cousin, ran out on us now, suddenly left after two days being here, went home—"

"How would that appear?" Monica asked.

"—it would do more to convict Skylar than any piece of hard evidence possibly could—even if the courts find him entirely innocent, which they will."

"It just isn't done," Monica said. "Your leaving now would signal the world that you believe Skylar guilty as charged. That you want nothing to do with the situation. You do not disassociate yourself from the innocent, Jonathan."

Dan gently put down his knife and fork. "Your leaving here would make things much more difficult for us, you see."

"Do you believe Skylar's innocent, Jonathan?"

"I, uh . . . how would I know?"

"You know he is your cousin."

Jon spoke in a monotone. "I've never been greatly concerned with appearances."

"Neither was your father," Dan said.

"What your uncle Dan means," Monica said, "is that your father is very concerned with appearances. You know it."

"Different values is all," Dan said.

"I'm a stranger here," Jon said. "Everyone's made that pretty clear."

"You're family."

"You're making that pretty clear right now. I mean, that I'm a stranger here. You're asking me to care about something—"

Monica gathered up the breakfast dishes. "You're not leaving Whitfield Farm, Jonathan. You're not running off while your cousin is in trouble, looking to all the world like a snotty kid who has made a value judgment from inside the family and decided to abandon it. Us." She brought the dishes to the kitchen sink and began rinsing them.

"We're not going to let you do this, Jonathan," Dan said softly, "for your own sake."

" 'Value judgment,' " Jon said.

"Values," Monica said from the sink. "And right now, young man, you are going to go upstairs, put on a clean shirt, suit, and tie, and accompany us to church, whether you share our values or not. Whether Skylar is in jail or not, we shall appear as a family."

Jon had already looked up the airline's telephone number.

9

"Breakfast?" Pepp asked.

Martha Jane had entered the bedroom in an oddly rough and bulky bathrobe for a beautiful late-spring morning. With a spoon, she was eating from a bowl something that made her munch, mixed nuts and dried fruit, Pepp imagined, *more squirrel food*. Munching, she nodded affirmatively. She looked at him with eyes that did not warm to him.

Naked after shaving and showering, Pepp was sitting on the edge of the bed cleaning his fingernails.

With mild surprise, he realized he was embarrassed at having his wife of twenty-two years looking at him naked.

"You attended the meeting last night," he said.

She nodded.

"What did you say about me?"

Martha Jane smiled. "You worried?"

"Of course I'm worried. A person can say anything he or she wants about another person, especially a wife about a husband. Or a husband about a wife. What did you say?"

Smiling, Martha Jane said, "I just said you have more energy than you naturally should. Man your age."

"More energy?"

"Yes. Put in a full day's work. Go running all over the

county in short pants. Read your books until all hours." Martha Jane snickered. "Come home and clean house . . ."

Pepp shook his head. "I don't get it."

The telephone rang.

Martha Jane said, "You're not foolin' me for one minute, boy."

Pepp answered the phone. "Hello?"

Martha Jane threw a towel in his lap.

Looking at her, Pepp picked the towel off him with two fingers and dropped it on the floor.

"Sheriff, this is Frank Murrey."

"Yes, Counselor."

"Sorry to call you at home on a Sunday morning, but I wanted to catch you before you and Martha Jane go to church."

"Yes, Counselor."

Frank Murrey generally was considered the best trial lawyer in Greendowns County. He and Pepp had been on opposite sides of innumerable criminal trials.

Pepp not only respected Frank Murrey but considered him a friend.

Pepp watched Martha Jane putting her breakfast bowl on the bureau, wandering around the bedroom collecting her day clothes.

Pepp said into the phone, "Frank, may I bring up a personal matter first?"

"Of course."

"I wonder if you and I might get together sometime this week to discuss divorce."

Martha Jane threw Pepp a quick glance.

Then smiled.

On the telephone line, there was a momentary pause. "I'm sorry, Pepp. I understand. Of course. Call me tomorrow morning when I'm in my office."

"I want everything frank and straight."

"Okay. Sorry for your trouble, Pepp. Maybe this isn't a good time to talk about this other matter."

Clutching her clothes to her stomach, Martha Jane went into the bathroom and closed the door.

"No. That's okay. Go ahead."

"Dan Whitfield called me this morning."

"I see."

"Asked me to represent his son, Skylar."

"We arrested Skylar Whitfield yesterday afternoon and charged him with the first-degree murder of Mary Lou Simes yesterday morning."

"You moved pretty fast on this, Pepp. Did you say 'first degree'?"

"We may not be able to make that stick. The district attorney . . ."

"This is surprising, Pepp."

"Why?"

"Good family. Skylar's an odd duck, I guess, but a good boy. Never been in trouble before, not even a speeding ticket. Straight-A student. Works the family farm. Plays his trumpet at church."

Speaking more carefully than normal, Pepp said, "Frank, I try very hard not to be prejudiced in favor of people of so-called good families. Also not to be prejudiced against people whose families have always been trouble."

"I know that, Pepp. May I ask you the hard evidence?"

"Earlier in the evening, Mary Lou was at a party at Whitfield Farm, where she drank heavily."

"Drank?"

"Can't guess where else she'd get that much vodka. Surely not at home."

"Vodka? Mary Lou? Was she drunk?"

"According to Coroner Murphy: very."

"Oh."

"Skylar arrived late at the party. Some kind of yelling went on between Skylar and Mary Lou. At first, I guess it was playful, but then it turned serious. Anyway, Mary Lou stomped off with her party dress ruined. Later they were both at the Holler at the same time, where they both had drinks, but, I guess, ignored each other. They did not speak to each other. Mary Lou arrived with other boys. She apparently left the Holler by herself, drunk, probably confused. Too drunk to drive, according to the coroner."

"That's it?"

"Tommy Barker found her body the next morning a quarter of a mile distant from the Holler in the woods. He was hunting groundhogs, or something. She had been beaten to death, Coroner Murphy says, by fists, probably by a young, right-handed male. You may be glad you didn't see the body, Frank."

"Nothing conclusive points to Skylar."

"Found his pocketknife near the scene of the crime."

"Fifteen feet away from the corpse."

"Fifteen feet isn't much in untraveled woods. What was it doing there? What doesn't make much sense to us is that Skylar says he went looking for Mary Lou in the woods around the Holler yesterday morning, without calling at her house. So why would he think she was missing?"

Frank hesitated. "I don't know the answer to that."

"We think he went looking for his knife."

"Pepp, you don't have anything absolutely conclusive."

"Plus the fact that Skylar and Mary Lou grew up together, neighbors, always an item. . . . Skylar, I guess, was the closest person to her, other than her family."

"Pepp, you mean to leave that boy in the county jail?"

"That depends on what you, the attorney general, and Judge Hall decide to do, Frank. All I know is that the judge decided not to move on this matter over the weekend."

"I mean, it seems like you've got a long way to go, Pepp, to tighten your case."

"Do I? I don't think of the evidence as ill as you do, Frank."

"I mean, you don't want to be wrong here, Pepp. I know you're distracted, upset by personal matters at this point—"

"Now don't you judge my professional performance by a personal comment I just made."

"—but have you tried to develop evidence to convict someone else in this case?"

"We've had preliminary conversations with some of the people at the party, some of the people at the Holler, her family, his family, people in the community generally about the relationship between this young man and young woman. Nothing else is showing up."

"Motive?"

"What happens between a young man and a young woman? A beautiful young woman?"

"If Mary Lou had been sexually assaulted, you would have said so by now."

"She had not been."

"Skylar's not such an ill-lookin' and actin' piece of goods himself. Isn't he the boy who always escorted Mary Lou through those beauty pageants?"

"Exactly."

"So?"

"So we don't know what their relationship really was. Maybe Skylar felt he had rights she didn't feel he had. Jealousy . . . We'll find out in time. In the meantime, the suspect is softening up in the county jail."

"Okay, Pepp. I'll appeal to the court to set bail in the morning."

"Okay."

"You going to fight me on that?"

"I'm not. Maybe the D.A. will. This was most likely a crime of passion, premeditated or not, and such things ordinarily do not repeat themselves. I don't think Skylar is a genuine threat to the community."

"You know, Pepp, you don't sound at all convinced that Skylar Whitfield is guilty."

"He hasn't been convicted yet."

"In fact, I suspect you think you've made a mistake."

"I'm a cop, Frank. I have to go with what I've got."

"Okay, Pepp. Regardless of what my client says in direct response to his rights, I do not want him further questioned, by anyone, without my being present. Understood?"

"Yes, sir."

"I have to ask you: Has Skylar said anything incriminating to this point?"

"No."

"I understand from Dan Whitfield your deputy hit Skylar a few times."

Pepp hesitated. "I'm not going to say anything incriminating, either."

"You don't want to get into trouble here, Pepp."

Pepp said, "I'll call your office for an appointment in the morning."

Pepp had his trousers on and was pulling on his boots when Martha Jane came out of the bathroom dressed for the day. Her hair had not been combed.

Pepp asked, "What do we do now?"

Quietly, she said, "I heard you, of course. As you meant me to."

"Martha Jane, I thought I was pretty clear in what I said last night."

"You clearly threatened me."

"I clearly spelled out my wishes and how important they are to me, I believe, to us, including Sammy. You completely disregarded my wishes. In fact, you seem to have escalated somehow this war you wage constantly against me. I gave you choices. You made your choice. Now I don't see that I have any choice."

Martha Jane used her arm as if batting away a fly. "Don't lecture me."

Boots on, Pepp studied the bedroom carpet again. "We can't talk. That's the point." Elbows on knees, he put his face in his hands. "There's just nothing left, Martha Jane, to our marriage . . . nothing left but bitterness, anger, recriminations, why I don't know. . . . I've done my best. . . . I didn't intend things to be this way, ever."

Martha Jane sat at her dressing table and began brushing her hair. "You don't care about me, Pepp. All you care about is your precious image as county sheriff, and how I fit into that image as sheriff's wife." She slammed the back of her brush down on the glass-topped table. "Well, I won't do it!"

"Do what?"

"Just be what you want me to be. The good little wife, with no ideas, feelings, life, of my own. Walking behind you, stars in my eyes, praising you, agreeing with everything you say like a brainless idiot. That's what you want, isn't it?"

Pepp took his gun belt off the top shelf of the closet and slung it around his waist. "I guess I thought we were, would be, a team."

" 'Team,' " Martha Jane scoffed. "You're the team. I'm just supposed to be some sort of a bubble-headed cheerleader for you. Isn't that all you want from me?"

"No. I've always tried to talk to you about my work, involve you, get your opinion, your advice."

"You've lectured me. Tried to tell me what to think, to say, to do."

"I am apt to think things out pretty well before I say them. I'm sorry if what I say sounds like I'm lecturing."

"You *tell* me, Pepp. You don't *ask* me anything."

"If you don't agree with me, do you have to disagree with me, in public?"

"Oh, go down to the corner and direct traffic."

Pepp stood in the bedroom door. "Martha Jane, what I don't understand is that if we don't work and live together as husband and wife, what is your vision of how we're supposed to live? You know, it's okay with me if you want to run against me for county sheriff. Is that what you want to do?" The telephone rang. Pepp said, "Never mind. I'll answer it downstairs."

Crossing the landing to the stairs, Pepp heard Martha Jane shout, "You see, Pepp? You just naturally presume the telephone is for you!"

The telephone call was for Pepp.

It was Adam Haddam, the County Sheriff's Department's dispatcher, jail keeper, file clerk.

"Sheriff, Skylar's stepped out."

"Fleas, what?"

"Guess he didn't expect my breakfast was worth hangin' 'round for."

"Skylar Whitfield has escaped jail?"

"Said."

"When?"

"Wasn't there when I just brought breakfast back to the cells."

"Shit, Fleas. He's charged with Murder One!" Fleas said nothing. "That boy gets into the woods around here and we'll never find him." Fleas said nothing. "Who's patrolling?"

"Deputy Aimes, this hour."

"Have you communicated with him?"

"Called you first."

"Fleas, I think you'd better roll Handsome out, too."

"Yes, sir."

"Damn, damn, damn!"

"Sheriff, you've been lookin' to get a new jail roof all these many years. This rate, you just might get yourself one."

"*R*ock of ages . . ."

In the little wooden country church, Jonathan Whitfield stood nearest the aisle and sang as loudly as he could to drown out the noises made by the ancient organ. Besides being badly played by a fourteen-year-old myopic girl, the electric organ also seemed to be suffering from frequent power surges. Half-notes changed pitch a quarter of a scale; whole notes, half a scale. First hearing the organ, Jon decided the torturing noise produced by the church organ had to be accepted as punishment for sins most heinous. It was such a spiritual punishment, clearly it would get any sensitive listener to heaven faster, or at least would make getting to heaven sooner rather than later seem damned desirable.

As they were getting out of the Whitfield Ford outside the church, other families, enjoying the morning sunlight, last cigarettes before a cleansing sermon, greeted Monica and Dan Whitfield quietly, sympathetically, said a few words regretting Skylar's incarceration for murder, met Jon or said hello to him again.

Jon recognized the Simes family, Andy-Dandy first, then Jack, the senior Simes, M.L., and John. In the shade, they, too, were surrounded by sympathizers. The Simeses and the Whitfields exchanged glances. In the shade of the stumpy church steeple, the two families slowly, wordlessly, came together. Monica and M.L. hugged each other and wept together; the males, including Jon and Andy Divan, shook each other's hands.

While the congregation stood aside, the two families entered the church together.

". . . Cleft for me . . ."

Singing loudly, Jon was thinking hard about how extraordinarily everyone was behaving: Within a day of a daughter of one family being found beaten to death, the son of another family being charged with her murder, the two families embraced outside a church door, and were embraced by the congregation, their community. Such circumstances, such an occasion, such behavior, Jon realized, previously had been inconceivable to him.

". . . Let me hide myself in Thee . . ."

Someone nudged Jon's elbow. He moved to his left, away from the aisle, to make room for the latecomer.

Without looking at the late arrival, Jon held the hymnbook more to his right, to share with his pew mate.

"Ha, Jon Than. How're ya doin'?"

Jon's neck snapped as he swiveled his head. Still drawing breath for the next verse, Jon choked. He dropped the hymnbook.

Skylar caught it.

Skylar looked toward the altar with cherubic face.

"Jon Than, as I live and breathe, you sing right pretty, I do declare, you do."

Jon sat down. His knees felt weak. His head swam.

After pulling in a few deep breaths, Jon looked around at what he could see of the still-standing, still-singing congregation.

No one else seemed ruffled. The man indicted for the murder of the daughter of a family a few pews away had entered the church and now was singing at the top of his lungs, even *lustily*, Jon thought.

In fact, if Jon's ears did not deceive him, the congregation's singing seemed generally to improve. The volume increased, the rhythm accelerated, the key became more certain. Even the organ seemed to waver less.

Yet no one openly was looking at, appeared to notice, Skylar.

Except Andy-Dandy Divan Simes.

From a few pews in front, the boy turned around, looked at Skylar, grinned, and winked.

No one, including his aunt and uncle, seemed to notice that Jon had collapsed on the bench, either.

After a while, Jon, remembering his breakfast conversation with his aunt and uncle (and beginning to feel hungry for lunch), stood up with his cousin.

At the church door, Skylar shook hands with the preacher. "Sorry to be a little late this morning, sir. I was otherwise detained."

"You didn't bring your trumpet, Skylar."

"No, sir, I didn't. Figure I have to travel light for a while."

Preacher Baker continued holding Skylar's hand. "Sorry for your trouble."

"Shoot, Preacher, I got the worst trouble in the whole world: A friend was cruelly murdered."

"Trust in the Lord, son, and things will come right for you."

"Amen," Skylar said.

"Skylar." Dan Whitfield took his son's elbow. Unhurriedly, they walked together down the church steps and into the bright sunlight. They stood among the parked cars and trucks, in plain view of the congregation milling around the front of the church. "Skylar," Dan said.

Squinting in the sunlight, facing his father, Skylar said, "Yes, sir."

"Skylar, I don't think you've been released from jail."

"Only in a manner of speaking, sir."

"You escaped."

"Yes, sir."

"That will get the jail roof fixed, for sure."

Skylar watched the Simes family come out of church. "I always do my best for the county, sir."

"I talked with Frank Murrey this morning. He means to appeal to the court to set bail for you tomorrow morning."

"I see."

Dan said, "We can't bail you out of jail, Skylar, if you're not in it."

"I do see the reasoning behind that, yes, sir, I do."

"In fact, I may be wrong about this, I'm no lawyer, as you know, but I do believe escaping jail is a crime all by itself."

"It is? I'd refer to it as a fortuitous circumstance, myself. Is it a crime to escape from jail if'n you don't belong in there?"

"I believe it is. Even if you're innocent, I believe you're supposed to wait for the Law to wend its ponderous way and release you."

"Shoot, sir. That's askin' for a passel of patience from the pure-hearted innocent."

"You see, Skylar, you were in jail because someone—the sheriff, in this case—thinks you're guilty, or might be."

Skylar said, "Sir, you have no idea how thick the air is in jail. Why, I suspect the air in that jail has been in constant use since the institution was established."

"Skylar, did you happen to think, before climbing through the jail roof, that your escaping jail just might cause some narrow-minded people to think you're as guilty as hell?"

"No one would think that."

"Some actually might, Son. Some people are actually convinced that one good reason for escaping jail is to avoid the

conviction and punishment the inmate might know he deserves. Yes, sir, Son, that is the main reason for escaping jail,
the way some people think."

"I agree, sir, that would be downright narrow-minded of
them. . . ."

"Be that as it may."

"Sir, there's another way of lookin' at this-here situation
which has developed."

"I expect there is."

"Someone escapes jail 'cause he knows he doesn't belong
there. Consider that."

Dan nodded solemnly. "And the air is thick."

"Right thick."

"Son, I'm askin' you to escape back into jail."

"So you can get me out?"

"So we can get you out legal-like."

"I think I'll let my statement stand."

"What statement is that, Skylar?"

"I escaped jail 'cause I don't belong in there."

"They'll be lookin' for you, Skylar. Huntin' you with guns.
You've escaped jail on a murder charge. You ready to be shot
for the sake of a breath of fresh air?"

Skylar raised his chin. "Sir, if I ever do anything that ought
put me into jail, I'll be the first one to escape into jail volun-
tarily, thick air or no. You won't be able to keep me out. Till
then, I'll be as free as an innocent citizen ought to be. You can
tell people that. 'Sides, all this trouble goin' on, I felt a real
strong need this mornin' for the comfort of church."

Dan Whitfield watched his son, in white shirt, jeans, and
sneakers, turn and wander through the cars and trucks, cross
the dirt road, jump the fence, and lope across a pasture toward
the trees. Up the hill the other side of that pasture, above those
trees, Dan remembered there was a seldom-used timber road.
He was pretty sure Skylar's red truck was waiting for him
somewhere on that road.

After Skylar disappeared into the trees, Dan Whitfield
smiled.

10

Tandy stood in the open door to the sheriff's office. Very quietly, very shyly, she said, "Please, sir, may I see Skylar Whitfield?"

Pepp looked toward the door. He had been sitting at an angle, studying the tips of his boots on his desk. "What?"

"Skylar," Tandy said. "May I see Skylar?"

In short shorts, sneakers, rim socks, and a T-shirt obviously without bra under it, to Pepp Tandy was not anything he expected to see in his office on this otherwise grim Sunday afternoon. Her hair gleamed in the bright sunlight from the window. Her bright eyes seemed to pulse. Her tight dark skin over the muscles of her arms and legs was luscious.

His boots fell to the floor.

The girl held up a greasy bag. "I brought him some fried chicken."

Pepp turned his chair to face his desk. "Who are you?"

He was sure he had never seen this girl before.

"Tandy McJane. I live on the Whitfield Farm." Both statements sounded like questions to Pepp. "I brought Skylar Whitfield his lunch."

"We provide lunch."

Smiling, Tandy held up the brown bag. "Fried chicken?"

From where Pepp sat at his desk, he could smell the chicken. At that moment, there was nothing in the world he wanted more than that fried chicken—that fried chicken from that girl.

Frowning at his desk, Pepp asked, "You a friend of Skylar Whitfield?"

"All my livin' days."

"Well, your friend is in considerable trouble."

"I mean to talk to you about all that." In shorts and T-shirt but with the dignity of an old lady, Tandy entered the office and sat perched on the edge of a wooden chair facing the sheriff's desk. "Skylar never killed no one."

"You mean he always killed someone?" Pepp smiled.

The girl's eyes grew large as she looked in his face.

"Never mind," he said. "I understand what you mean to say."

"He surely never killed Mary Lou."

Scratching the back of his head, trying to appear bored, Pepp said, "Murderers all have friends, I expect."

"Why would he?" Tandy asked. "You just tell me why he would kill Mary Lou Simes."

Pepp asked, "You know everything that goes on between a man and a woman?" Tandy smiled. "A boy and a girl?" The smile entered Tandy's eyes. "Skylar and his girlfriend?"

"Yes, sir, I surely do."

"What?"

Tandy tapped her index finger on the sheriff's desk. "Things between Skylar and Mary Lou Simes weren't at all as people thought."

"What did people think?"

"That things were hot and heavy between Skylar and Mary Lou."

"And they weren't?"

"No, sir, they surely weren't. Skylar didn't need much from Mary Lou, if you catch my meanin'."

"Gay?" Pepp wondered if that was what Chick Hanson had been trying to tell him, or perhaps did not even know, consciously, but perhaps had intuited. "Do you know the word 'gay'? Are you telling me Skylar Whitfield is homosexual?"

The girl's smile was as wonderful to see as sunlight on a river. "Don't you suspicion, Sheriff, there has to be a certain intensity between friends for one to kill the other?" Tandy asked reasonably.

"I suppose so."

Tandy shrugged. "What Skylar and Mary Lou were was like two sports cars parked right next to each other, if you take my meanin'."

Pepp studied the steady, patient expression on Tandy's face for some moments.

Finally, he said, "I guess you're trying to tell me something, but I'll be damned if I know what."

Standing up, her brown bag of fried chicken still in hand, Tandy said, "I sure do thank you, Sheriff, for seein' me. I do appreciate it."

As she was leaving his office, he said, "Leave the fried chicken with the man at the desk out front. Mr. Haddam."

Going through the door, without turning around, Tandy waved the bag at him.

Pepp sat at his desk a long moment before pressing the office intercommunications button.

"Fleas? Did that dazzling young woman who just left leave a bag of fried chicken with you?"

"What young woman?"

"The young woman who just left."

"No one left a bag of fried chicken with me." Untypically, Fleas added, "No one has ever left a bag of fried chicken with me."

Pepp took his finger off the button.

That young woman came here knowing Skylar Whitfield is not here, in fact, has escaped.

I'll wager she even knows where he is.

He pressed the intercom button again. "Fleas, didn't you see which way that young woman went? What kind of a vehicle she was using?"

"What young woman? Sheriff, you want fried chicken, I'll go get you some. . . ."

"I don't want fried chicken. Have you heard from the patrol cars yet? Anything on Skylar Whitfield?"

"No, sir."

Pepp released the intercom button. *I wouldn't even believe there was fried chicken in that bag, if I hadn't smelled it.*

"Hi, Sam." Because he was in his office, Sheriff Culpepper had charged his usual Sunday afternoon at four-thirty call to his daughter on his personal credit card.

"Bonjour, mon père. Ça va?"

Pepp laughed with pleasure. He drawled thickly, "Now you just quit that Yankee talk right now, you hear?"

"How goes it?"

"How goes it with you?"

"Fine and dandy. Got my history paper back with a 'B' on it."

"That's good."

" 'C' on the chem exam."

"I guess chemistry's hard."

"Biology Tuesday."

"You'll do fine. How's English?"

"Ugh. Chaucer."

"You know I got *Canterbury Tales* out of the library when you told me you were having difficulty understanding Chaucer. I didn't see how anything in English could be so difficult to understand."

"Do you see now?"

"Yeah. It's like reading through somebody else's eyeglasses."

"The professor thinks Chaucer's funny. Can you believe that? Chaucer reminds me of Pimples."

"What pimples? Your pimples? You never had any pimples."

"I certainly did. My loving dad, the sheriff, just overlooked them. I mean, Pimples, that kid in the sixth grade, Pimples Norton. He never really had pimples, either, but I guess his father had. He was the son of Pimples Norton, and so he was Pimples, Junior."

"I know. How does Pimples, Junior, relate to Chaucer, please?"

"Every time he had a captive audience, in the school bus or anywhere, Pimples would tell these long, long dirty stories that never seemed to have a point or an end. Their purpose, though, always seemed to be to laugh at people, put them down."

"If you were called Pimples long before you ever had one, wouldn't you want to put people down, too?"

"Definitely."

"Listen, Chaucer isn't so bad, I discovered, if you read him quick enough."

"Dad, in college you're not allowed to read Chaucer quick. We have to be responsible for every word. Every damned word."

"I suppose so."

"How's Mother?"

"Fine. Sam, you know your mother and I are having difficulties."

"You always have."

"Just think about it. Okay? How's that boyfriend of yours?"

"He broke his ankle. His left ankle. Playing croquet. Would you believe that?"

Pepp wasn't sure what croquet was. "How did he manage that?"

"He was swinging down hard planning to send someone else's ball into the bushes, when someone spoke to him, and he smashed his own mallet into his own ankle. Everybody laughed."

"That boy have trouble concentrating?"

"Not really. He's just always too curious about what people are saying, I guess. He's concentrating on his pain okay. Stumping around here on a crutch with a heroic expression on his face, doing the wounded athlete bit. Everyone's still laughing. How are things in Greendowns County, Sheriff?"

"Real bad."

"What do you mean?"

"Mary Lou Simes."

"What about her?"

"Beaten to death early Saturday morning not far from the Holler."

"Oh, Dad, that's terrible! Not Mary Lou! Beaten to death?"

"Yes."

"Any idea who did it?"

"We're detaining Skylar Whitfield."

"*Skylar!* Not Skylar!"

"Skylar."

"Dad, the only way Skylar Whitfield would kill anyone would be by making her die laughing."

Pepp hesitated. "We've got some real evidence."

"Well, those are about the two most adored kids in the county."

"Not everyone adores Skylar."

"Everyone must be pretty upset."

"Very. What's more, the little jerk escaped."

"Escaped what?"

"Jail."

"You've got to do something about that roof, Dad."

"I've been trying. Skylar's in the woods somewhere. Got a call a while ago mentioning that he attended church this morning."

Samantha giggled.

Then Pepp found himself laughing.

She said, "See what I mean, Dad? See what I mean about Skylar?"

Still laughing, Pepp said, "It's not funny, Sammy."

"He's a riot."

"Right now he's an escapee wanted on first-degree murder charges."

"God, no one would shoot Skylar, do you think?"

"I think someone just might shoot Skylar."

"You've got a real problem, Dad. You'll never find Skylar in the woods of Greendowns County."

"Well, he was arrested and jailed without either boots or a shirt. He showed up in church this morning wearing boots and a shirt."

"What does that mean?"

"That means he went home. I have someone watching Whitfield Farm right now. I would have put someone on it before, as soon as I knew he'd escaped, but somehow I thought Skylar would be too smart to go home."

Samantha giggled again. "Or attend church."

"Or attend church."

"Poor Mary Lou. Do you think she suffered much?"

"Not sure. She was badly beaten. She may have lived for some time after she was beaten. But she was, to use the coroner's expression, stinko."

"Drunk."

"That doesn't seem to surprise you."

"Not really. I never thought Mary Lou was as plastic as people wanted to think her."

"Sammy, is Skylar a male?"

"What do you mean?"

"Is he interested in girls?"

"Oh, yes. The boy with the electrical touch. He's a lot younger than I, but when he touches you, zowie."

"He's touched you?"

"Sure. Just playin' around. I think Skylar learned when he was knee-high to a rabbit that if he did *not* touch a girl, she'd fall ill with conniptions."

"Okay, girls like Skylar, and like him to touch them. But does Skylar like touching girls?"

"He knows just how to do it. When, how, with the right expression on his face, never gives offense, he just gives off electricity. Zap zowie, if you get what I mean."

"I don't, but that's okay."

"Why do you even ask? Are you asking if Skylar is gay? I assure you he is not."

"It's just that someone said something to me I don't understand."

"What?"

"Well, just that Skylar and Mary Lou just weren't, I don't know . . . Someone just said that Skylar didn't *need* Mary Lou."

"I see."

"Do you understand that?"

"No. Well, maybe I do. Maybe Skylar saw Mary Lou as some kind of a trap."

"What do you mean?"

"I'm not sure. They were very good friends. But I don't remember Skylar ever being that attentive to her. I mean, privately. Maybe it's like when you grow up and everyone—families, friends, the whole county—presumes you two are going to get married and make beautiful babies and uphold all of our ideals, you might pull back from all that, pull back from each other, if you see what I mean?"

"Maybe. Maybe I do."

"They were very good friends. They knew each other very well. But you know, thinking about it, it seems to me their friendship was based on a kind of mutual sympathy. Does that make any sense?"

"Maybe."

"I don't really know what I'm talking about. I've been at Duke three years. To me they're still little kids."

"Yeah. Skylar's a little kid that can make you say 'zap! zowie!' or whatever."

"Some males are like that, Dad. Sorry for all your trouble."

"Trouble is in keeping my mind where it needs to be."

"That bad?"

"More later, I guess."

"Dad?"

"Yes, Sam?"

"Whatever you and Mother decide, I'll understand. I'll try my best to be fair."

Pepp felt tears right behind his eyes. "I know, Sammy. I appreciate that. Talk to you next week."

11

"Fleas! Put me through to the sheriff right now!" Deputy Tom Aimes's voice over the police radio was excited.

At the Sheriff's Department dispatch desk, Fleas's voice wasn't. "Can't."

"Why not? Where is he?"

"Joggin', secret like."

"Shit! We've got Skylar!"

"Got him?"

"We'll get him. You listenin', too, Chick?"

"Hear ya loud and clear, Tom," Hanson answered through his patrol-car radio.

"Where are you?"

"Courthouse Square."

"Okay, Chick. Listen. Skylar just left Whitfield Farm. He's drivin' his daddy's green Ford. Drivin' toward town as if he doesn't have a damned care in the whole damned world. Fat-headed son of a bitch. I'm followin', givin' him plenty of room."

"Whyn't you grab him?" Deputy Hanson asked.

"You want to be in on this arrest, Chick, or not?"

"Sure do."

"I mean, Skylar was your original arrest and all."

"Sure was."

"Okay. You position yourself right there at the corner of Main and Wilkins. You hear me?"

"Loud and clear."

"Position yourself so he can't see you as he drives into town."

"Roger."

"I'll stay well behind him all the way into town. As he approaches Wilkins, I'll speed up. You stay on the radio."

"Roger."

"Just as he gets to Wilkins, you pull out in front of him, cut him off, and I'll cut him off from behind."

"Green Ford?"

"Two-door. Got it?"

"Roger."

"Stay on the air, Chick."

"Where you at now, Tom?"

"Just passin' Clayborn's place. You movin' yet, Chick?"

"Wait a damned minute. Got to fasten my seat belt."

"Chick? You in position yet?"

"Roger."

"Corner of Wilkins and Main?"

"Roger."

"Can anybody see you?"

"Dunno. I sure can't see nobody. Where're you at now?"

"We're on Main headed for Wilkins."

" 'Course you are."

"Skylar's ahead of me by about a quarter of a mile, but he's in sight, all right."

"That much? How far are you from me?"

"Mile and a half. I'm beginning to pull up now. Just passed the senior citizens' bus."

"Did you see my grandmother?"

"Grandmother?"

"Grandmother Abbott. She's on that bus."

"Didn't see her, Chick."

"They were carried out to that catfish farm for lunch this afternoon. You ever been to that catfish farm, Tom? Out by Sander's Creek? Hear it's real good."

"Chick? Where are you?"

"Corner of Wilkins and Main."

"Shit, Chick. I've passed you."

"Yes, sir. I saw you go by."

"You were s'posed to pull out in front of the green Ford."

"Warn't no green Ford, Tom."

"Of course there was!"

"In fact, there warn't."

"Did you see the green Ford?"

"Tom, no green Ford went by here."

"Shit! Where's Skylar?"

"Well, my best answer to that, Tom, is he must have swung off Main just before Wilkins, on Paragon."

"I didn't see him do that."

"You didn't see my grandmother, either. There goes the senior citizens' bus. Hidy, Boo-boo."

"Boo-boo?"

"Yeah. We've always called Grandma Abbott Boo-boo. It's 'cause, when we were little—"

"Listen, Chick."

"Wish I was full of catfish right now."

"Why would Skylar turn into that road? It's residential."

"S'pose we could find him and ask him?"

"Pincer, Chick."

"Pinch who?"

"Pincer maneuver. You go down Main, cut onto Paragon. I've gone left on Collins now. Makin' up time. Get out of my damned way, Dr. Murphy. Okay. Hurry up. I'll get to the fork by the V.F.W. Hall before you. You come up from behind. We'll have him both ways to Sunday. . . . Chick, you movin'?"

"On Paragon headed east."

"Say somethin'."

". . . On Paragon headed east."

"You see Skylar? You see the green Ford?"

"Lord God Awmighty!"

"Chick! What!"

"Sally Mae Crandall in a short green dress the likes of which I have never seen before in all my born days!"

"Chick! Do you see Skylar?"

"No. Wow! I mean, I knew Sally Mae has red hair and pretty legs, but that green dress! S'pose she got it here in town?"

"Chick, just tell me what you see."

"I have been."

"What do you see now?"

"I see you, waitin' at the fork."

"I see you, too. What I don't see is a damned green Ford."

"Where's Skylar?"

"Here we are, Tom, sitting in our cars at the fork lookin' at each other, talkin' to each other on the radio. S'pose we could get out and—"

"Deputies, this is Adam Haddam. Sure is educational listenin' to you all."

"Chick, either he turned left or right off Paragon."

"You two sure do beat Sunday afternoon commercial radio."

"Would have turned right toward town, I reckon, as that is where we conjectured he was headed."

"Did you see him?"

"Guess I didn't get on Paragon in time. So he must have taken one of his first rights."

"Why would he do that?"

"Might be he's evading us."

"He didn't know I was followin' him, Chick. I swear!"

"That boy's as cute as a fox with a warm rat in his mouth."

"All right. Let's move it."

"He must be in the west end of town. Chick, you three-sixty

and go back along Paragon to Main, left on Main, left on Collins again."

Fleas said, "One-eighty."

"I'll go back the way I came, along Collins. Pincer him. . . . Say something."

"Right. Roger."

"You've got to make up time, Chick."

"Phew."

"What, Chick?"

"In that green dress, Sally Mae is just as good comin' as she is goin'."

"Chick, you on Collins?"

"Yes, sir."

"Whoa! There he is!"

"I see him! Duckin' into that alley beside the hardware."

"I see him."

"Chick, you got time to get around and cut him off the other end of the alley?"

"I doubt he's goin' more than three to five miles per hour."

"Yeah, but if we pursue him down the alley—"

"He can't get out. That television-repair man, what's his name, Dan Arthur Coolidge-Samuels, always illegally parks his truck down there Sundays."

"Right. I'm in the alley right behind him, Chick. The truck is there. Skylar's backing up. Support, Chick! I want support! Come right in the alley behind me."

"I already did. I'm right behind you, Tom."

"We've got the bastard!"

Fleas said, "Now, boys. Be nice."

"Out of the car, you son of a bitch!"

There was a large man dressed in khaki with a badge pinned to his shirt leaning into the driver's-side window of the Whitfields' green Ford. There was another leaning through the passenger-side window. They were each very red-faced.

The one on the passenger side stuck a very large handgun through the car's window and pointed it at the driver's head.

"Keep his hands in sight," passenger side said.

"Keep your hands in sight!" driver's side said. "Don't move! Put your hands up!" He opened the door. "Get out! Don't move!"

"Would you please clarify your instructions?" Jonathan Whitfield asked politely.

"Son of a bitch!" On the driver's side, Deputy Tom Aimes grabbed Jon by his hair and pulled him out of the car. Jon's face scraped the top window frame of the car door.

Pulling Jon by his hair, Tom swung him around the car door and flung the top of his body facedown onto the hood of the car.

Aiming his handgun generally at his fellow officer and their prisoner, Deputy Chick Hanson scooted around the front of the car.

Kicking Jon's feet apart, grinding his bleeding face into the dirt on the hot hood of the car, together the deputies handcuffed their suspect.

"Gave us a pretty good run, didn't ya?" Tom asked. "Made us chase you all over town. Up this road, down that road. Pretty damned cute!" With the flat of his hand, he ground more dirt into Jon's face.

"I didn't know where I was," Jon said through his squashed nose.

"Oh, he was lost!" Tom laughed. "Skylar got losted in town."

"I don't know where the grocery store is," Jon said through puckered lips along the car hood.

"You caused a police pursuit," Chick said.

"I didn't know you were pursuing me."

"Wonder you didn't run over a little girl, or something."

"Why should I do that?" Jon asked.

Holding Jon's neck down on the car hood, Tom said, "Call in, Chick. Tell 'em we're bringin' the bastard in."

"I'm not a bastard, either," Jon said. "So far, the level of your accuracy is dismally low."

Tom rubbed Jon's face more in the dirt on the car's hood.

Chick sat sideways on the seat of the patrol car. Breathing heavily, he said into the car's radio microphone, "Fleas? Got the bastard. In the alley beside the hardware store. We cut him off. Trying to escape. He caused a police pursuit. Skylar Whitfield. Murder One."

Fleas said, "I'll set an extra plate."

"Tell the sheriff we're bringin' in Skylar Whitfield."

"Wrong again," Jon said. "I'm not Skylar Whitfield."

"All right, you." Tom pulled Jon erect by the neck.

Standing arms akimbo, his shaking pistol aimed at the left front tire of Tom's patrol car behind him, Chick Hanson's eyes grew wide. "Who the fuck are you?"

"What?" Tom asked.

Face streaked with blood, sweat, and dirt, Jonathan Whitfield answered, "Jonathan Whitfield. Did I do something to cause the ire of you officers?"

"Shit!" Tom said. "That's not Skylar."

"How did this happen?" Chick asked Tom.

"I swear it was Skylar I was followin' from the farm."

Chick said, "Yeah. They must have switched places on the way into town."

Tom said, "There was only one in the car when we left the farm!"

"You Skylar's cousin?" Chick asked.

"I have that dubious distinction."

"Are you or are you not, damn it!"

"I am."

"A kid drivin' Whitfield's car! Of course it was Skylar!"

Putting his face near Jon's, Tom shouted, "Where the fuck is Skylar?"

"Have you surveyed the local churches?" Jon asked.

"Shit." Now absently aiming his handgun toward a panel of Dan Arthur Coolidge-Samuels's television-repair truck, Chick leaned against the Ford's fender. "Now what do we do?"

"Bring him in anyway," Tom said.

Chick studied his fellow deputy's face.

Tom said, "Causing a police pursuit. Endangering county property. Resisting arrest. Pissin' me off."

"Conspiring with a fugitive from justice."

Tom smiled. "Hostage, is what I mean."

"Shoot," Chick said, uncertainly.

Jon said, "Hostage?"

"Yeah," Tom said. "Maybe if we keep you for a while, throw the damned book at you, just maybe your cousin would have the decency to turn himself in."

Jon said, "I sincerely doubt that. Skylar doesn't seem at all that sort of decent chap to me. Does he to you?"

Tom said, "You Whitfields stick together, isn't that right?"

"Not me," Jon said. "I don't stick together."

Chick said, "Shit! I told Fleas we were bringin' Skylar in. Told him to tell the sheriff."

"S'pose we can sneak him by Fleas? Boo-boo always used to say, 'A bird in the pie is better'n two in your neighbor's tree.' "

Chick grinned. "The ol' boy's eyes ain't what they used to be, now, are they?"

"Whyn't you mess up his face a little more for him?"

Chick stood up from the hood of the car. "Yeah."

"Officers," Jon said, "I consider your scheme highly inadvisable."

"Jeans," Chick said. "Sneakers. Hair's too dark."

Tom spit on his hands. "You still got that Huntsville Stars cap you took off that D.U.I. in your car, Chick?"

"In fact, I do."

Using the spit on his hands, Tom was slapping more dirt from the Ford's hood onto Jon's face.

"Hell, yes." Chick put the baseball cap he had fetched from his car onto Jon's head and pulled it down. "We can hustle this kid into the cells so fast, all ol' Fleas will see is a blurred fart."

"Officers," Jon said, "you are violating about every right guaranteed me by the Constitution of the United States except my right to assemble."

"Boy, we don't care too much about your right to ass-whatever. What we care about is our right to catch Skylar."

" 'Course, you could save us all a lot of trouble by tellin' us where Skylar is," Chick said.

Tom said, "That would be right nice. You could even call it aidin' and abettin' the police."

"Police," Jon groaned. "Give me liberty or give me crooks."

Y ou on shit, boy? You floatin', or crashin'?"

Having been hustled through the front of the police station, down the dingy corridor of jail cells, and hurtled so forcefully into the last cell his chin bounced off the wall, Jon sat on the edge of his bunk rubbing his wrists. At least the deputies had removed his handcuffs.

He looked to his right. In the cell next to him was a large shadow moving slowly back and forth.

The shadow had asked him a question.

"So what you done wrong this time, boy?"

"Oh, I got lost. Couldn't find the grocery store."

"Uh-uh. I know how that is. Yes, I do. Indeed I do."

"I suspect Aunt Monica simply wanted to do some cooking tonight. As therapy. You've heard of cooking as therapy?"

There was a long silence from the next cell.

Finally, the deep voice rumbled, "Well, proly your friends will come pop you through the roof again."

S heriff, you back in your car yet?"

"What, Fleas."

"Judge Hall wants you to stop at his home."

"Tonight?"

"Soon's you finish your run, he said. He said he don't care what you smell like."

"About what?"

"Didn't ask."

"Okay."

"Boys brought someone in."

"Who?"

"Pretended it was Skylar."

"Say again?"

"Ran him by me like horse traders tryin' to sell a mule. Yellin' 'Skylar' at him."

"Did they catch Skylar Whitfield or not?"

"Not."

"I don't understand you, Fleas."

"Well, the boys gave themselves some excitement, caught somebody in an alley, brought him in, and locked him up sayin' he's Skylar."

"But he isn't?"

"Skylar never had a shirt like that. No one in this town's ever had a shirt like that."

"Then who is it?"

"Doesn't even belong here. Went back in the cells to see who it is. The boy said, 'Please, sir, could you tell me precisely where the grocery store is? Next time, I'd like to know.' Talks funny. Damned Yankee, I'd say."

"Does he even look like Skylar?"

"Somewhat. Can't tell. He's marked up."

"Damn! The boys marked him up?"

"Can't tell how much, between the dirt and the blood."

Driving toward town, Pepp was trying to imagine what his deputies had done and why.

Always just below the surface of his mind, Pepp wished people thought and acted the way people do in books: cause and effect, cause and effect.

It was the illogic of real people that drove Pepp to read voraciously, to stay sane.

"Sheriff? Shall I let him go?"

"No, Fleas. Not if he's marked up. Better hold him till I get there and have a talk with . . . whoever the hell he is."

12

"Hell, Pepp. You didn't have to put your sweatpants back on to come visit me on a Sunday night."

Grinning, Judge Hiram Hall held his front door open to Pepp.

The judge was wearing shorts with a bright flowered pattern and no shoes. An aquamarine tennis shirt, loose in his shoulders, was stretched over his stomach.

Entering the house, Pepp said, "Never seen you in shorts before, Judge. Didn't know what I've been missin'."

"Don't wear them outdoors much around here. Have to maintain the decorum of the bench, you know. Can't have someone I'm about to sentence to hard labor for public indecency giggling with the thought I might be envious of whatever he's already exposed."

In the dark foyer, Pepp concealed a shiver. The air-conditioning was too much so soon after his six-mile run.

It crossed Pepp's mind to ask the judge if he could take a shower before they talked.

"I wear 'em in Florida," the judge said. "In Florida if you don't expose your baggy knees, however indecent they may be, they charge you with first-degree modesty, or something. So I hear, anyway." He turned and walked toward the back of the foyer. "Come into what's called 'round here the liberry, Pepp. It's where we watch television."

In the library, the judge faced Pepp and studied his face. "Want a drink, Pepp?"

"No, thanks."

"Some nice bourbon?"

"Could swallow some orange juice."

"Don't you drink, Pepp?"

"Sure."

"When was the last time you had a drink?"

"Last night."

"What did you have?"

"A beer."

"One beer?"

"Yes. With my supper."

"Want a beer now?"

"Just finished joggin', Judge. Rather have a orange juice."

"Okay." The judge removed his eyes from Pepp's face. "One orange juice coming up. Have to go to the kitchen to get it."

Returning to the library where Pepp was still standing, the judge said, "Some time ago I observed that only men can jog. Women joggle. Have you noticed?" Chuckling, he handed Pepp the glass of orange juice. "Sit down, Pepp."

At the mahogany bar at the side of the library, the judge mixed a bourbon and soda. "Anything new on the Simes murder?"

"Nothing I'd care to talk about."

"Seems the Whitfield boy went through the roof." The judge chuckled.

"He did."

" 'Least we can't get him for jumpin' bail. He never gave us a chance to set bail."

Pepp sipped his orange juice.

"Hear he showed up in church this morning lookin' like a shiny new silver dollar. Both Mr. District Attorney and I got calls from parishioners saying how glad they were to see Skylar free. Too late, of course." The judge sat in an easy chair. "Escaping jail makes him look guilty. Going to church with his alleged victim's family makes him look innocent. I think the message that boy is transmitting is that Skylar's goin' to continue bein' Skylar whatever comes his way." The judge looked at his drink on the arm of his chair. "Yes, sir: Skylar's a real southern boy, I'll be damned if he isn't." The judge thought a moment. "Seems to me there's a tide in life, anyway. When you're young, obstacles are not taken seriously, they're just to be gotten around. When you're older, you know you can be defeated by obstacles, and they sort of make you dig yourself deeper into whatever trouble you're already in." The judge noticed Pepp's empty glass. "Can I sell you a bourbon now, Pepp?"

"No, thanks."

"More orange juice?"

"No, thanks, Judge."

"Yes, sir. That boy has a certain style. I don't see him beatin' his girlfriend to death with his fists, Pepp. He seems more the type who would think his way around obstacles, if you know what I mean—the nonviolent type."

"I'm not sure Mary Lou was his girlfriend."

"Oh?"

"At the moment, I'm confused about all that. Tell me about the McJane family."

"McJanes? I don't think there's any family there, exactly. The Joneses have always been part of Whitfield Farm, goin' 'way back. Carrie Jones married Rob McJane. Seems he ran off before his feet got warm in the bed. I forget the timing of it all. Anyway, Mrs. McJane—that is, Carrie Jones McJane—has always lived out in a tenant house on Whitfield Farm, keeps house for the Whitfields generally. She has two children, Alec, a boy in his twenties, no better'n he should be, I expect you've run into him, I have—"

"Yes."

"I seem to remember taking his driver's license away from him once, just a week before he had a head-on collision with

Preacher Smithson's parked car." The judge chuckled. "He had the damned audacity to show up at court ridin' an ancient motorcycle that probably never did have a muffler. For which he didn't have a license, either, or registration, or insurance, of course. I asked him what he thought he was playin' at. He said, 'Well, Judge, I'll tell you what: My horse drownded, and I needed a way to go.' "

While the judge laughed, Pepp smiled wryly.

"There's a girl, too, somewhere, younger, I forget her name."

"Tangy or something?"

"I wouldn't be surprised."

Pepp was surprised to hear himself say, "As lithe as a cat."

"What?"

"She called on me this afternoon."

"The daughter?"

Pepp nodded. "Are the McJanes any sort of kin to the Whitfields?"

"God, Pepp. In the South, who knows who is kin to who, 'cept a few old women up the hollers. You know that as well as I do. The so-called 'social structure' in the South, so-called 'good families,' so-called 'trouble families,' black, white, is the South's Great Deception. Meant to fool the Yankees and other foreigners, I've always suspected. Never been a society like it anywhere in the world, I expect. A strong, self-protective illusion, is what it is. Can't tell you how many near relatives I've sent to jail. Remember two, three years ago, that old boy you brought in for hijackin' that Budweiser beer truck?"

Pepp nodded. "Pried open the back and started selling beer for a dollar a case Saturday night in County Courthouse Square."

"Not the smartest individual I've ever met. Just before sentencing him, I asked him if he had anything to say. He said, 'Well, Cousin, I'd take treatment from anybody else right hard, but seein' you're family, I trust you to do what's right for me.' 'Fine,' I said, 'That's six months in the county lockup, Cousin.' 'Yes, sir, I knew you'd be fair.' " The judge laughed. More seriously, he said, "The people have to believe in us elected officials, Pepp, us elected officials of the law."

"Could the McJane girl be any relation to Skylar Whitfield?"

The judge shook his head. "Your guess is as good as mine. I know Dan Whitfield real well, but I haven't been with him every minute of his life. Why do you ask?"

"She puzzles me." Having a new idea, Pepp asked, "Could Mary Lou Simes be any kin to Skylar Whitfield?"

Again the judge shook his head. "If so, I doubt you'd find it in the county records. I tell you, Pepp, that's what's so mysterious about the South. You find yourself laughing at Maxie with Moe, and you'll find Minnie's whole family agin ya. It's why we're all so pro-found-ly courteous." The judge sipped his drink. "John Simes wasn't always the sourpuss, the hard man, he is now, you know. He came back from that war a changed man. Distracted. Mind somewhere else. You know, his whole platoon was shot out from under him. M.L., of course, always was twittery, even as a child. I admit, it seems some kind of a miracle that those two should have three such beautiful children."

Pepp said, "People seem to be saying that the relationship between Mary Lou Simes and Skylar Whitfield was more like brother and sister than girl-boy. Yet Skylar's masculinity doesn't seem in doubt. Beautiful girl like that . . ."

"Anyway." The judge emptied his glass and rattled the ice. "Wasn't there some kind of a fracas this afternoon in the alley beside the hardware store?"

Pepp nodded affirmatively.

"Have to do with the Simes case?"

Despite the air-conditioning, Pepp now felt sweat upon his neck. In a low voice, Pepp said, "Hiram, we run separate elections."

"I know that."

"You get elected. I get elected. We run separate elections for separate offices."

"Just makin' conversation." Still, the judge waited for an answer.

After a moment of silence, in the same low voice, Pepp answered, ''The deputies seem to have jailed someone as Skylar Whitfield who Fleas says isn't Skylar Whitfield.''

''Why?''

''God knows. I haven't been back to the jail. Fleas told me you wanted to see me right away.'' After another hesitation, Pepp looked directly at the judge. ''I suspect they picked up the Whitfield cousin, the kid from the North.''

''On separate charges?''

''No. As Skylar Whitfield.''

''What sense does that make, Pepp?''

''You tell me. Judge, you know the average police officer in this country has less training than any other profession you can think of.''

The judge nodded. ''It's a profession that requires talent.''

''That's exactly right.''

''And your deputies are not overly burdened with talent.'' Pepp did not answer. ''So why haven't you told Fleas to let this boy go?''

Again in a low voice, looking directly at the judge, Pepp said, ''Because he reports to me the boy's face is bleeding.''

The judge said, ''Shit.''

''Thought the matter could wait until I have a look at him.'' More quietly, Pepp said, ''You know, find something to hold over his head, to avoid suit.''

The judge stood up. ''Can I make you a drink now, Pepp?''

Still holding his empty glass, Pepp said, ''No, sir.''

The judge went to the bar.

Pepp said, ''Hiram, you didn't call me here this afternoon just to make conversation.''

After putting fresh ice in his glass, the judge said, ''I've always thought you could be a real talented police officer, Pepp.''

Pepp said nothing.

The judge poured an ounce of bourbon in his glass and covered it with soda.

''However, now that the spurs have been put to you, you

seem to be runnin' a little awkward." The judge turned around and said, "Drugs." He took a sip. "Cocaine, ice, other stuff." He sat down again in his chair. "Last six or eight months, this county's developed a real drug problem, Pepp. Why, at this late date, I can't imagine. You'd think with all the so-called 'educating' going on . . . do you suppose the 'educating' is popularizing the stuff? The American people are used to being 'educated' about breakfast cereals and soap powders. When is education advertising? 'Yeah,' the baseball hero says. 'I pitched the whole World Series eating Bunchies for breakfast and taking crack.' Confusing world."

"Yes, it is."

"One thing I'm pretty sure of is that drugs couldn't be anywhere without police compliance. Any more than moonshine was, and is, in these areas without police compliance." The judge wrinkled his nose at the sheriff. "There's so much money in drugs, Pepp."

" 'Police control crime,' " Pepp said.

"What?"

"From a book I read. There's damned little 'shine around here, Hiram, and you know it. A few old boys keepin' up the old ways for tradition sake, makin' home brew for home consumption. Nobody's makin' money off it. I swear, not the Sheriff's Department."

"You're in great shape, Pepp. Run six miles a day. How old are you now, forty-four? Drink little or nothing. How many books a week do you read?"

Pepp said nothing.

"Trouble with me," the judge chatted on, "is that I can't tell when someone is using, or what he's using. Usually, you and I don't know if someone has got a bad case of drugs until he's in the lockup and begins climbing the walls. Isn't that true? I guess that's the point of it. Usually, one can't tell if someone is using. A grown man not drinkin' is a sign, I hear. I read people think they can control their energies with these drugs. Is that right, Pepp?"

"I'm real curious about what you're saying, Hiram."

"I've known for a while your marriage is none too happy, Pepp."

Pepp snorted. "Martha Jane's been preachin' on it."

"Do you suppose that's why you've been usin' up your energies runnin' and readin' so much?"

Quietly, Pepp said, "Might have somethin' to do with it."

The judge said, "Last night, at some women's meeting or other, Martha Jane turned it around and said you are the way you are because you are using."

Prickly heat was in every inch of Pepp's skin. "She said that?"

"I understand she allowed quite clearly for everyone to so infer."

"I was warned she said something last night, but I didn't know what."

"That's what."

Pepp said, "Before she left for that meeting last night, I told her I want a divorce. I'm calling Frank Murrey for an appointment in the morning. She knew that last night."

"Umm. I guess I've been sort of elected to talk with you about it."

"Talk *with* me?"

"Martha Jane's implied as much before. Might as well tell you, Pepp, the state boys have already checked your bank accounts. Here and in St. Albans."

"I don't have a bank account in St. Albans."

"You seem to go there a lot."

"I buy books there. I use the library there."

"They say you could have bank accounts anywhere, under any damned name you choose."

"Right at this minute," Pepp sighed, "I wish I did have a concealed bank account."

"Such habits can be mighty expensive, so I hear. You could be being paid off simply by being supplied with stuff to support your habit. Or so I hear."

"Shit, Hiram." From the air-conditioning, the sweat on Pepp's face felt cold. "Why in God's name would anybody believe such shit?"

"How long you been married, Pepp?"

"Twenty-two years."

"When the woman you've been married to for twenty-two years says something, reports your personal habits, she speaks with a certain authority. People are apt to listen."

Pepp leaned forward and put his hands in his face. "She hates me, Hiram."

"According to her testimony last night, she hates you because you're on drugs."

"She hates men. All women get, from television, newspapers, magazines, these days is anti-male shit disguised as feminism. It's destroying the American family, Judge."

"There are women," the judge said. "And there are women. Many want their independence and don't know how to go about getting it. I'll give you that. But, if statistics are correct, there are so many people in this country using drugs, most of them must be concealing it pretty successfully."

Pepp sat back. "Do you believe what Martha Jane says about me, Hiram?"

"I'd rather not."

"Do you believe that before Martha Jane went out to that meeting last night, I told her definitely I want a divorce?"

"I'm a judge, Pepp." The judge got up to refill his glass. "You said something privately to your wife in your home. No corroborating witnesses. Your wife said something publicly in a church basement. Many corroborating witnesses." Without measuring it, the judge splashed bourbon into his glass. He did not add soda. "One thing is clear: Your wife is ruining your chances for reelection, which affects your family income, her way of life. What sense does that make?"

The judge sat down. "There's been a murder. You made an arrest within hours. Apparently, your deputy beat on the accused in the process of arresting him. The alleged murderer has escaped. Your deputies apparently have arrested the alleged murderer's cousin, on no grounds whatsoever. And beat on him. Sheriff, are you in control of your department?"

Pepp looked the judge in the eye. "That's not for you to ask, Judge."

The judge shrugged. "It's important the people believe in us, Pepp. It's a very thin membrane between order and chaos. If the people don't believe in the dispensers of law and order, we all suffer. Mightily."

"Jesus," Pepp said. "Jesus Christ."

"I don't know what your personal habits are, Pepp. I don't know what your relations with your wife are. I know tonight the whole damned county is laughing at the Sheriff's Department."

Pepp stood up. "Guess I'll be going."

Remaining seated, the judge smiled. "Sure you don't want a drink?"

Fresh air entered the cell. From his smelly bunk, Jon saw stars. A heavy figure held up one side of a section of the roof. A smaller, lighter figure, hands on knees, leaned over the roof edge.

"Hey, mister! You hongry?"

Jon jumped up.

From the next cell, a heavy voice grumbled, "That my fried chicken?"

"Speedy delivery," the girl said. "A whole bucket!"

Chuckling, the big shadow in the cell next to Jon was also standing, looking up. "I just knew you wouldn't forget me."

"Can you climb up a little?" the girl asked. "Don't want it to spill on that floor. Why, I'll bet that floor hasn't been scoured since it had the honor of hostin' the dirty socks of Yankee soldiers."

The shadow stood on the bottom horizontal bar. As he reached up, the girl on the roof handed him down a bucket.

Jon smelled the fried chicken.

"Don't know how you're gonna get rid of the bucket," the girl said, "so Mr. Haddam won't find it."

"That's all right." The deep voice chuckled. "I'll prolly eat the bucket, too."

Standing erect, the girl on the roof said, "Okay, Dufus."

"Hey!" Jon said. The roof section was lowering. "Hey!"

"Stop a minute," the girl said.

Hands on knees again, she peered down into the jail cell.

"That you, Jon Than?"

"Yes."

"What're you doin' down there?"

"Got lost on the way to the grocery store. Apparently, it's a crime around here to demonstrate ignorance of local geography."

"Miz Whitfield's been wonderin' where her pork chops got to. Thought you made off with the grocery money, I think."

Carefully, Jon said, "I did not abscond. I was kidnapped by the police."

"You committed any real serious crimes, boy?"

"You mean anything more serious than murder?"

The deep voice from the next cell, sounding more rubbery, said, "Good chicken."

"They've got me here instead of Skylar. I was drivin' Uncle Dan's car. At first they thought I was Skylar. Then they decided to dump me here. Probably because they cut my face."

"Your face is cut?"

"Not badly."

The big boy holding up the roof said, "Ughhh."

"Just a New York minute, Dufus." The girl stood, arms akimbo, against the starry sky. "Reckon you want out of there. . . ."

Jon said, "Yes, please."

"I mean, you wouldn't mind escaping jail, is that it?"

"They have me in here for nothing," Jon said.

"And you don't like it much down there?"

"Not much."

"Jon Than, I notice in this conversation you haven't used my name, not once."

"No," Jon said. "I haven't."

"You know my name, Jon Than?"

"I can't recall it."

"We've met."

"I saw you yesterday morning, in the bathroom."

"You saw me at breakfast, too. You could have seen me at the Holler Friday night, if you hadn't been lookin' around like a rooster at barnyard shit."

"Ughhh," Dufus said.

"I'm sorry I don't know your name," Jon said. "Is that Dufus?"

"What's left of him. He's fadin' fast."

"Ha, Dufus," Jon said, carefully. "How're ya doin'?"

"Ughhh."

"You almost got that right," the girl said. "My name is Tandy McJane."

"Okay."

"You goin' to forget that?"

"Never!" Jon said.

"Okay." Tandy McJane leaned over and stretched a hand down to Jon. "Hurry up on out of there. Skylar's waitin' on us."

Jon put up his arm.

Her hand was out of reach.

"Climb the bars, boy!" Tandy McJane said. "Hain't you never 'scaped jail afore?"

13

"Jon Than? You ride with me." Across the road from the sheriff's office, Skylar reached across the seat of the pickup truck and held the door open for his cousin.

On the sidewalk, Jon leaned over and looked into the truck. "No way."

"What do you mean, 'no way'?"

"I'll ride with Dufus and Tandy McJane."

"I told them to go straight home. They've already done gone."

"Oh, no."

"Oh, yes."

Saying he wanted nothing to do with it, Jon had lurked in the shadows of downtown Greendowns, while Dufus, Tandy, and Skylar had proceeded to remove Dan Whitfield's green two-door Ford from the police parking lot.

"Come on, Jon Than. You escaped from the same jail I did. I'll drop you off nearby the farm."

"Skylar, you might have murdered somebody."

"Might've. Didn't."

"The Law is looking for you."

"That's one good reason, Jon Than, for not loitering all that long in front of the county jail. Hell, if the counties happen to investigate out their window and notice us, and catch up to us, I'll just throw them you again. They've already shown they have no discrimination at all, at all.''

''I know you just stole a car from the police compound.''

''Stole a car? How can anybody steal his own daddy's car? He needs it to go to work in the morning.''

''Well, you removed a car from the police compound.''

''What right do the police have to keep it? Why, Jon Than, that car is as blameless as alphabet soup. It hasn't even spelled anything embarrassing.''

''Well . . .''

''Jon Than, you want to walk home? It's fourteen miles, and more'n likely the wharupadangs will get you on the way.''

Jon got into the truck and slammed the door.

''Yes, sir,'' Skylar said, accelerating. ''The Law's the Law, but never catch yourself foolin' around with the wharupadangs.''

Jon said, ''You told Tandy and Dufus to go straight home?''

''I did.''

''Does that mean we're not going straight home?''

''Damn, Jon Than, you're smart!'' Skylar turned off the town square onto the road toward the highway. ''You smart like a sunburn! No wonder they let you out of school without obligin' you to take final examinations.''

''You know about that?''

''Mama mentioned it to me while I was burnin' the midnight oil.''

''Burnin' the midnight oil screwing who? Or what?''

''You're a hard one to figure, Jon Than. As good-lookin' as a fresh coat of paint, as rich as pecan pie, and as smart as a bee sting! How can one boy have so much?''

''I don't figure you, either, Skylar.''

''Why, I'm just a lopsided, dung-walkin', flea-bitten, sore-assed hayseed.''

''Principally what I can't figure is why women like you so much.''

''Women?''

"That Tandy McJane adores you. Damn it, Skylar, she helped you escape jail on a first-degree murder charge."

"She's a friend." Skylar speeded down a steep hill. "Helped you escape, too."

"I wasn't a prisoner. I was a hostage."

"I'll say one thing for the counties, Jon Than: They sure improved the appearance of your face considerably. Is the real Jon Than beginnin' to emerge?"

Jon wiped his cheek with his fingertips and looked at the grime and dried blood on his fingers in the dim light from the dashboard. "No girl ever towel-dried me after a shower."

"You without friends, Jon Than, or a towel?"

"At the party, Mary Lou Simes may have been swearing at you, but her eyes were penetrating yours, diving straight down and rolling around inside your pants."

"It's nice and warm down there. Cozy. Expect she knew that."

"You stroked the bare leg of the waitress at the Holler and, damn it, Skylar, she shivered with the delight of a drunk taking his first drink of the day."

"You ever hear tell of sexual pleasure, Jon Than?"

"I've heard tell of it."

" 'Course you have. For a minute there, I forgot you're sufferin' a social disease."

"What about sexual pleasure?"

"Well, early on I discovered there isn't all that much of it in this world, despite reports to the contrary. Wouldn't you say, Jon Than, that mostly what's practiced is sexual relief, rather than sexual pleasure, you know slam-bam, thank you, ma'am, here's a brat for your side yard?"

"And that's not what you do?"

"Hell, no. Not when there's so much more pleasure to be had when you're both havin' fun."

"So where'd you learn better, hayseed?"

"Mrs. Duffy."

"Mrs. Duffy?"

"She used to be thinner."

"When? How old were you?"

"Goin' on nine."

"That's criminal."

"Some folks I know think it's criminal to take violin lessons. For some, it just might be."

"Mrs. Duffy teach Dufus, too?"

" 'Course not."

"Dufus didn't attract her in the same way, uh? Skylar, how do you rectify all your fucking around with your Bible-thumpin', singing at the top of your lungs, praise-the-Lord churchgoin'?"

"Ah, Jon Than. For someone as smart as a stubbed toe, you don't understand the difference between a snowflake and a moonbeam."

"Cut the damned metaphors, Skylar! How can you be such a churchgoin' fuckhead?"

"Guilt, Jon Than."

"Guilt?"

"Yes, sir. Guilt is the X in ecstasy."

Jon choked.

"You ought to try it, Cousin. Yes, sir, as the first step toward bringin' you along, I'm real interested in makin' a regular churchgoer out of you."

"Jesus," Jon said. "Churchgoin' as an aphrodisiac."

"Laugh and you live; cry and you die," Skylar said. "Shucks, Jon Than, I'll bet you caught that social disease without even crackin' a smile."

Jon pushed the wing window into position so the air blew more in his face. "Tell me about Tandy McJane. How come she's willing to risk jail for you?"

"Why, Jon Than, wouldn't you do the same? She just did the same for you, and you're not even likable."

"Tell me about Tandy."

"Well, sir, I will, as long as you ask. Week, ten days ago, she was driving this very same truck along Stillwater Creek Road all by herself. And there was this big, beautiful rainbow."

"So?"

"So she told me she seriously considered stepping into it."

"Into the rainbow?"

"Yes, sir. She regretted she didn't have time to stop. The rainbow was *that* close, she said."

Jon stared across the dark truck cab at Skylar.

"She came home and asked me if I had ever stepped inside a rainbow, and, if I had, what it had felt like."

Jon watched his cousin a moment, expecting a punch line, a laugh. Skylar remained silent.

Jon said, "Somehow, Skylar, that isn't what I expected you to say."

"Sayin' and doin' what is expected of you is downright bordering-on-the-rude boring, wouldn't you say, Jon Than?"

They rode over hill and across dale in silence.

Finally, Jon took a deep breath. "Okay, I give in. Where are we going, Skylar?"

"Las Vegas Motel."

"Las Vegas Motel. Okay. The Las Vegas Motel wouldn't be a thousand or more miles away in Las Vegas, Nevada, would it?"

"No, sir. The Las Vegas Motel is right here in Greendowns County. Out on the highway."

"Is that where fugitives from the law stay?"

"I have no idea."

"Is that where you're staying?"

"Me? I've never stayed in a motel in my life. Never needed one."

"Skylar, why are we going to the Las Vegas Motel?"

"Well, sir. There was a man at the Holler the other night. I expect you noticed him. An older man with longish hair and a scraggly beard."

"There were lots of them."

"This one looked as wore-out as a nightshirt in March."

"They all did."

"He wasn't from around here."

"Oh."

"You might remember I went up to the bar to get you all drinks so you wouldn't be embarrassed by my hearing Mrs. Duffy call you an ill-mannered, pompous, presumptuous mother-fuckin' son of a bitch?"

"I'm glad you missed all that."

"Well, sir. This man spoke to me. He offered to buy me a drink. He asked me if that girl down the bar was Mary Lou Simes."

"Was she?"

"Yes."

"So?"

"Why was this stranger interested in Mary Lou Simes? How did he know of her? In fact, he did recognize her. He was just asking me for confirmation."

"What did you say?"

"I didn't tell him yes or no."

"Why not?"

"Jon Than, I didn't know him!"

"You don't speak to anyone you don't know?"

"I might speak to 'em. But I don't tell 'em anything."

Jon said, "Mary Lou has put herself up for all these beauty contests. Isn't the purpose of such so-called pageants to publicize oneself?"

Skylar Whitfield thought a moment without saying anything.

Jon said, "There must have been pictures of Mary Lou in the newspapers."

"The pageants Mary Lou and I were in were as local as the town's one taxi. That man at the Holler wasn't from within a thousand miles of here. Furthermore, he didn't look like any sort of pageant promoter or talent scout to me."

Jon said, "Cousin, you are such a mixture of innocence and craftiness."

Skylar looked at his cousin. "Is that an insult? If you're goin' to insult me, Jon Than, use words I can understand. Can you say 'sombitch'?"

"You think this creep is at the motel?"

"If he's still around. The Las Vegas Motel is the only place to stay 'round here, unless you've got either friends or a ground sheet."

"What are you going to do?"

"Sit outside the motel and wait to see if he goes either in or out."

"Oh, boy. Now Cousin Skylar's playing detective."

"That old boy was tryin' to confirm the identity of Mary Lou Simes in a bar shortly before and nearby where she was killed. Doesn't that make you curious, Jon Than?"

"Leave it to the cops!"

"A man has the right to defend himself, Jon Than." Bright lights appeared in the rearview mirror. "If I left it to the cops, I'd be hot, hungry, being prune-shriveled in a jail cell right now. Who's that?"

Jon turned his head to look directly through the pickup truck's rear window. "Someone's driving about eighteen inches from your rear bumper, Skylar, with his high beams on. Why don't you let him pass?"

"I believe he's gonna ram us." Skylar stepped on the accelerator.

As soon as he did so, the truck shuddered.

"What's happening?" Jon yelled.

"He rammed us."

"I told you to let him pass!"

"You don't get the point, Jon Than. Not at all, at all."

The truck shuddered again as its rear bumper was hit from behind.

"What is the point?" Jon asked.

"That's the question of the ages," Skylar said. "Don't philosophers call that question the jumpin'-off point?" As Skylar continued to accelerate the truck, it was hit from behind a third time. "In this instance," Skylar continued, "the point is obvious: Somebody means to kill us."

"Kill us? Just because you wouldn't let him pass?"

"The road to the quarry's right down here. We'll lose the sucker. Hold on to your shorts, Jon Than."

Just as Skylar was skidding into a turn, his truck was hit from behind again, putting it nicely onto the dirt road to the quarry.

"Wowee!" said Skylar. "Didn't even tip over. Praise the Lord!"

" 'Wowee,' " Jon muttered. " 'Praise the Lord.' We're going to get killed."

The other truck, bigger, more powerful than Skylar's pickup, had skidded to a stop on the main road. It reversed and turned onto the dirt road.

"We'll lose ourselves in here," Skylar said. "Go to ground and be as quiet as a church mouse while the preacher is preachin'."

"Skylar!" The pickup was bouncing and swaying over a dark, narrow dirt road. "Let me out of this truck!"

"Can't stop now, Jon Than."

"Let me out, damn it!"

"Can't you see someone's pursuin' us?"

"They're pursuing you, damn it! Not me!"

"In fact, they're catchin' up faster'n a horny 'gator with poor eyesight who's spotted a fresh oak log."

"Will you stop that shit!"

"What shit's that, Cousin?"

"The way you talk!"

"Just mean to be entertainin'."

The pickup was rammed hard.

"You're entertaining enough! I can't stand any more entertainment! Let me out of here!"

"You can always jump, Cousin."

"Slow down!"

"Like hell."

Skidding around a corner, the pickup was hit again. It nearly tipped over.

Jon said, "Jesus Christ!"

"Now, Cousin," Skylar admonished. "I don't like hearin' you take the Lord's name in vain. Not at all, at all."

"In vain? I'm praying!"

"I just knew it would work out that I'd be a right good

influence on you, Jon Than, sooner or later, somehow or other.''

''Jesus, Skylar! Stop! That rock!''

''I mean to slew around it.''

'' 'Slew'?''

Skylar threw the pickup's wheel at a last moment. The truck skittered to the left around an enormous rock.

The pursuing truck skidded to the right around the rock.

''Now we just slide down here,'' Skylar said.

Bouncing and banging, the pickup fell down a steep decline. Jon could see nothing to their left but air.

Braking hard in the dust, Skylar advised, ''Bit of a curve down here.''

In the headlights approached a solid wall of rock.

The pickup came to a full stop a few inches from it.

Proceeding slowly, then, Skylar made a hairpin turn to the left. They jounced down another leg of declining road.

At the bottom, Skylar turned off the headlights and accelerated.

''Skylar, you can't see . . . the light. . . .''

''Shoot, Jon Than. That's what someone said to the snake that got into the preacher's drawers.''

Skylar turned the truck around.

The heavier truck, well lit, was above them, on a higher cliff level.

''Well, I'll be a bear's left titty,'' Skylar said. ''That's ol' Jack up there.''

''Jack who?''

''Jack Simes.''

''Mary Lou's brother? The football player? The halfback?''

''Shoot. He knows this place as well as I do.''

Without turning his head, Skylar reversed speedily.

''Let me out of here!'' Jon yelled.

''Now I just can't do that, Jon Than.'' Skylar wheeled around and went forward rapidly without headlights. ''This here ol' quarry's a big place. You'd just get yourself lost in here.''

''I want to get lost. I need to get lost.''

"What would your daddy say if he found you lost?"

"Skylar, you know where all the boulders in this place are?" Mammoth rocks, higher than the truck's cab, were going by Jon's window faster than he could focus on them.

"No, sir, I surely don't."

"Then how do you dare drive this way? What the hell do you know?"

"I know where they ain't."

"Skylar, you're as witty as . . ."

"How about a kitty in her first snow?" The pickup truck began limping, jouncing rhythmically on its front right wheel. "Hot damn!" Skylar said. "I've got a stob in my casin'."

" 'Stob'? 'Casin'?' " Jon recognized the truck's problem. "Damn. We have a flat tire!"

"That's exactly right." Skylar limped the pickup between two boulders and stopped. "Correct even to your use of the proper pronoun."

"What's a 'stob'?"

"This is as good a place to stop as any, I reckon."

"There is no such word as 'stob.' "

"There isn't?"

"There is not."

"All this time I thought there was."

Directly in front of them, truck headlights and roof lights turned on.

Skylar's door was pulled open.

Skylar said to his cousin, "You wanted to get out. Now's the time."

Skylar was yanked out of the truck by his neck.

He landed on his feet. "Ha, Jack. How're ya' doin'?"

There were three large young men besides Skylar visible in the other truck's headlights.

Jon leaned across the seat of the pickup truck and slammed Skylar's door shut. And locked it. And rolled up the window.

He had already locked his own door and rolled up the window.

Jon sat in the locked truck watching through the dusty windows.

"For once, Skylar," Jack Simes said, "I suggest you keep your mouth shut."

Skylar said, "Haven't much to say anyway."

Jack smashed his fist against Skylar's mouth.

Skylar did his best to wrap his only two arms around his only head.

In the dark at the side of the truck, taking quick glimpses through his arms, Skylar could not tell where all the blows were coming from. Mostly they were coming from Jack Simes, but the two other men got a blow or a kick in as they could.

When he felt his ribs had taken enough, Skylar knelt on the ground. Arms still around his head, he lowered his head near the ground.

After a solid kick in the ribs, Skylar quickly extended his body like a snake and slithered under the truck.

The blows stopped.

After a moment, Jack Simes said, "Ah, leave him."

After a decent interval, Skylar slowly slid out from under the pickup.

There was no sign, lights or sound, of the other truck.

There were no bulky shadows of people.

Kneeling, reaching up, he grabbed the pickup's door handle. He pulled himself up.

Jon sat in the truck with all the dignity of a judge with a new robe.

Skylar knocked on the window.

"Open the damned door." His lips and teeth hurt.

Jon turned his head to look at Skylar. "What?"

"Unlock the damned door!"

Jon unlocked Skylar's door.

Skylar pulled the door open and sat sideways on the driver's seat, his feet on the ground.

He heard Jon rolling down the window on his side of the truck.

Frogs were croaking in the damp spots of the quarry.

Skylar lisped through sore teeth and cut lips, "Has it occurred to you yet, Jon Than, that two against three could have had a better chance than one against three?"

"It occurred to me immediately," Jon said, "that I have no reason in the world for being beat up for you."

Skylar said, "We could have fought back."

"We both would have gotten beat up. Why in hell should I get beat up for you by people I don't even know or care about?"

With his thumb, Skylar wriggled a loose tooth. "It would have been companionable."

"Skylar, I don't even like you!"

Skylar sighed. "Now you tell me."

"Now will you take me home?"

"Uh-uh." Skylar wrapped his ribs with his arms. "Got to change the wheel, first."

14

"Never known you to be here this hour Sunday night," Fairer said.

"Don't think I ever have been," Pepp answered.

"Never seen you order pie and coffee before, this late."

"Missed supper."

"Never seen you in a sweat suit this time of night, either."

"No." Pepp made an exaggerated sniff. "I haven't even showered after my run this afternoon."

"You're usually home this time Sunday nights, I reckon."

"Usually."

They were alone in the coffee shop.

Fairer said, "You don't want to go home, do you, Pepp?"

"Big troubles," Pepp said. "Taxpayers never would agree to put a new roof on the jail." He sneezed into a paper napkin. "Place leaks like an old boot."

"Yeah. I've heard about all that."

"Guess everyone in the county has." Pepp's sniff was genuine this time. "Right now I have an armed-and-dangerous all-points bulletin out for a boy in this county who is more popular than the town pump after the senior prom." He looked through the coffee-shop window out into the dark.

"Hopeless. That kid knows the woods around here better than a hawk. He's smarter than a fox. And probably over ninety percent of the people in the county don't believe he's capable of killing the Simes girl. They would aid him as a fugitive from the law without a second thought." Pepp hesitated. "A small percentage would be quick to believe anything against him, and might just shoot him down out of sheer, irrelevant resentment."

Fairer smiled. "Holding his cousin as hostage didn't work, uh?"

"Is that what the deputies thought they were doing?"

"That's what they were whisperin' to each other when they were in here havin' supper. Figured it wasn't any idea of yours."

"Surely wasn't. I tongue-lashed them so loud and fast, I never gave them a chance to say a word." Pepp shook his head. "Stupid. Far as I know, police work has little to learn from Mideast politics."

Fairer put her elbows on the counter. "I've heard what-all Martha Jane's sayin' about you, Pepp."

Below the short white sleeves of her uniform, Fairer's bare arms were slim, firm, with healthy color, a little light blond down on them.

Pepp said, "You probably heard before I did."

"Probably."

"Anything you don't hear in here, Fairer?"

"Not much, I reckon."

"Sheriff's office ought to hire you. We need an intelligence wing."

"Food's like liquor, Pepp. Eatin' or drinkin' loosens people's lips."

"Hard to keep my mind on my work." Pepp studied the bottom of his empty coffee cup. "I try to think where Skylar is, what's the next thing to do on this case, and my mind swings back to twenty-two years with Martha Jane . . . Sammy at college . . ."

Fairer popped her lips and ran her eyes up the wall behind Pepp's head. "Impossible for you to go home, I reckon."

Wryly, Pepp smiled. "We've got at least one empty jail cell I know of."

"Have you slept there before, Pepp? In a jail cell?"

"Yes."

"Some marriage."

"It's been difficult for a long while."

Fairer stood straight. "I've got to close up. Why don't you go upstairs to my apartment, Pepp, and take a shower? I'll be up after I finish cleaning up."

Pepp stared at Fairer. "I can't do that."

Fairer shrugged. "Why not?"

"I'm getting a divorce. I can't go to your apartment tonight. Not even for a few minutes."

Fairer looked down at her ice-cream coolers. "I meant I was hopin' to spend the night with you."

"It wouldn't be fair to you. If we did that, it would be all over the county faster than an alligator bites."

Fairer looked at Pepp out of the corners of her eyes. "No one's ever had any gossip about me, Pepp. Not lately, anyway. I live and work twenty-four hours a day in plain view on the town square. No one except Martha Jane has ever passed any gossip about you, that I know of."

"I remember Fairer Kelly from grammar school. What you looked like then. Yellow pigtails and scraped knees."

"Shoot, Pepp. I've always been sweet on you. Didn't you ever suspicion that?"

Pepp laughed. "If you've thought so much of me, how come you've given me a little container of cream for coffee I drink black nearly every day for twelve years?"

"Just tryin' to get you to notice me."

"You're a quiet one."

"You're just slow."

For a moment, they smiled into each other's eyes across the counter.

Pepp felt internally warm. "I've been noticing." His throat was tight. "I just remember your saying, when you took over this place, the coffee shop, once everything was all right again, you were finished with men."

"I was," Fairer said. "I meant it. I have been." Fairer wore no makeup. She needed none, except for the shadows of tiredness under her eyes. Her fourteen-hours-a-day, seven-days-a-week work in the coffee shop had kept her slim. She wore her blond hair braided at the back of her head. "Go sit in the bathtub, Pepp. I'll come up and remind you of something."

Slowly, he stood up and put money on the counter.

Fairer put the money in the cash register and put his change on the counter.

"That's all right," he said.

"Thanks." Fairer slid the change into her hand and dropped it into a jar on the shelf behind the counter.

"You serious?" he asked.

Again she shrugged. "I'm sure serious about your needin' a bath."

Confused, Pepp stood in the middle of the coffee shop. He looked toward the back. "You know, I don't know how to get up to your apartment."

"Some detective. That door marked Fire Exit. The stairs are at the back of the hall."

Pepp turned, took a few steps in his running shoes, turned back.

Fairer had been watching him walk.

Pepp said, "You know . . ." She cocked her chin at him. "You know, I haven't had much of a sex life lately."

"Better'n mine, I expect."

"I mean . . ." Pepp swallowed. "I don't know if I'm up to it. What I'm up to."

"Go take a bath." Fairer picked up a sponge to wipe the counter. "Let's just see what happens."

Julep was licking Skylar's face.

Waking up, Skylar pushed the dog aside with his forearm. "What're you doing here?"

Sitting up in his sleeping bag, Skylar saw the beam of a flashlight.

In the moonlight filtered through the trees, he saw Tandy climbing over the truck's tailgate. In one hand, she held the flashlight, in the other a paper bag.

She said, "Someone straightened out your rear bumper for you, Skylar."

"What time is it? What are you doing here?"

"I heard you were hurtin'." Tandy sat cross-legged on the bed of the pickup truck next to Skylar. She shined the flashlight at him. "Your face hurtin' you? It's just killin' me!"

He averted his eyes. "I've got a headache."

"Brung you some aspirin."

"I was asleep."

Tandy peered into the paper bag. "Also some ointment and bandages."

"Mostly my ribs."

"Any broke, you think?"

"Hurt too much."

"That's good."

With a great sigh of relief, Julep flopped on the floor of the truck bed.

"Hello, Julep." Skylar petted the dog. "How are you, boy?" Lying still, the dog beat his tail faster than a hummingbird's wings.

"He's missed you," Tandy said. "He moans and groans. He was out on the balcony outside your room. Reckon Jon Than threw him out there."

"How'd you know I'm hurtin'? Jon Than tell you?"

"Jack Simes."

"Jack?"

"Heard the cattle disturbed. Looked out the window. Saw the shadow of his big pickup. Went out. He was nowhere in sight. He came up behind me."

"You see a truck in the yard this time of night, you ought to stay in your bed, Tandy. Yell for Dufus."

"I knew it was Jack's. Skylar, how come Jack Simes has

such a new, fancy truck and his daddy drives that beat-up old Plymouth?''

"Personal choice, I guess."

"What does his daddy do, anyway, I mean, for work?"

"He travels a lot."

"Is that work?"

"I think he's in some kind of real estate business."

"Mr. Howell's in the real estate business, and I doubt he ever leaves the county. Besides, he drives a shiny new Buick."

"Maybe he sets up shopping malls, something like that. Housing developments."

"Hardly any of those around here."

"That's why he travels, I guess."

"I mean, if there aren't any shopping malls or real housing developments around here, how'd he ever get into that business anyway, bein' from here?"

"Anyway, all I know is he goes and comes a lot."

"Wonder why he doesn't wear his gold wristwatch anymore."

"What?"

"Remember, he used to wear a gold wristwatch?"

"No."

"Haven't seen it lately. Anyway, Jack Simes came by, past midnight."

"Jack Simes's the one who whupped me. He and two friends."

"I know. He came to apologize."

"That's what he said?"

"He said, 'I know you know where Skylar is. Tandy, please tell him I'm real sorry what happened tonight, what I did. I know Skylar never killed my sister. Tell Skylar tonight I just had to whup someone.' "

Skylar said, "Uh," and lay back down.

"Want a kiss?"

Skylar said, "No," and then he said, "Ow" as something stung his lips. "What's that?"

"Ointment. It sting a little?"

"It stings a lot."

"Then it's doin' its work. You got any other cuts?"

"No. I don't think so. Just sore all over."

"Where'd all this take place?" Tandy asked.

"Quarry."

"Jon Than was with you."

"Sort of. He stayed in the truck."

"While they were beatin' on you?"

"Locked himself in."

"Whyn't you think of that?"

"What?"

"Sounds sensible to me. Three guys want to beat you up, you might just lock yourself in."

"Didn't have a chance."

"While they were beatin' on you, Jon Than locked himself in the truck?"

"He had the time to do it."

"You were already grabbed out of the truck, and he didn't get out to help you?" Tandy was taking off her sneakers.

"No. He didn't. He didn't even get out after they'd left. If they'd killed me, he just might have sat there forever."

"My, my," Tandy said. "I got cousins better'n that." She pulled off her T-shirt. "I might just as well have left that boy in jail."

"You're tellin me Jon Than went back to the farm and didn't mention I'd gotten beat up?"

"Never saw him. Lights out in his window." Standing up, Tandy took off her jeans and placed them on the side of the truck bed. "Guess that sickness he's got makes him sleep well."

"Sombitch. He didn't help much while I was changin' the wheel, either."

"Got a flat?"

"Casin' took a stob. They wouldn't've cotched us, otherwise."

Tandy held out two aspirins to him. "Dry-swaller these."

Skylar opened his eyes and saw Tandy standing over him

in the truck bed in the moonlight dressed only in her underpants and socks. "What're you doin'?"

He swallowed the aspirin.

"I'm fixin' to get in that there bedroll with you and hold
your ribs tight."

"I thought we said—"

"Move over."

He rolled on his side. Her body was cool and smooth sliding
down his hot, naked body. She wrapped her arms around his
ribs and placed her face against his chest.

She said, "Go to sleep."

Then she said, "Jimmy Bob got that job, drivin' that
eighteen-wheeler."

"Your hair's wet." Fairer stood in the bathroom doorway.

Reclining in the warm tub of water, Pepp had not heard her
enter the apartment.

He brought his knees together.

She left the doorway.

He sat up in the tub. He pulled the plug.

Then he replaced the plug.

And sat there.

Let's just see what happens.

He caught her sounds and her shadows as she moved
around in the bedroom.

Fairer's apartment was large, well furnished, and as clean
and neat as the coffee shop downstairs.

He had finished running warm water into the tub before he
undressed. Carefully, he folded his sweat suit over a chair in
the bedroom.

Although alone in the apartment, he wrapped a towel
around his waist, walking the few feet from the bedroom to
the bath.

In the tub, he experienced a strange combination of relax-
ation and anticipation.

Barefooted, wearing a long dressing gown, Fairer came into

the bathroom. "I threw your sweat suit into the washing machine."

From the tub, he grinned up at her. "Then I guess I can't go anywhere very soon."

Standing near the tub, she opened her robe. She let it slide down her body to the floor.

Pepp was greatly surprised. Her body was splendid, for a woman of any age. She had the tight breasts and reasonably flat stomach, slim, strong legs of an athletic woman much younger than she.

With a tight throat, Pepp said, "What a waste."

Fairer cut her eyes at the bathroom mirror. "What's wrong with my waist?"

"That's not what I meant."

"Oh." Fairer held her foot over the water. "Move your legs. I'm coming in."

Pepp spread his legs to make room for her.

As she stepped gingerly into the tub, Fairer's eyes sparkled over his body. "And you were afraid you couldn't get it up."

Pepp looked down at himself.

Crouching, her back to the faucets, Fairer said, "Why, Sheriff, I do declare you could hang a flag off that, and people would stand tall, and, salute."

"Of what were you going to remind me?" Pepp asked.

"Oh, nothin'."

In the bed, they had made love slowly and simply and gently.

"What?"

"Thought I might need to remind you of something to encourage you. Seduce you. Get you some confidence back." Fairer nuzzled his shoulder. "No need."

"What?"

"When my little girl died. When Stella died."

"Oh." Pepp tried to remember the details. Sitting in the warm bathtub, he had recollected that he had been in Fairer's previous home, the circumstances that had brought him there. The home of Fairer Spinner. Mrs. Tucker Spinner. He knew he still had the file somewhere. "I had little to do with that."

"You saved my mind." She brought her whole body closer to his, entirely against him, as if seeking refuge in him. "You could have landed me in jail."

Pepp tried to remember. "Have you ever heard anything at all from him?"

"No."

"Truly?"

"Never a word."

"I've never asked, have I?"

"I appreciate it."

I should have asked. Pepp thought.

In the dark, he knew her hand was wiping tears from her cheeks.

Pepp said, "I always figured Tucker thought Stella was too much of a burden on you, on both of you. You were killing yourself trying to take care of her."

"I didn't mind."

"Maybe he thought she was in too much pain, inexplicable to a three-year-old. Leukemia, wasn't it?"

"I never thought that, Pepp."

"No?"

"If he did it for me, for us, how come he disappeared, and I've never heard word one from him all these years?"

"He was facing jail time."

"That's what I mean. If he'd killed Stella deliberately, intentionally, after thinking about it, he would have calculated the jail time, faced it. He wouldn't have just done it and run."

Pepp remembered climbing the stairs of the Spinner house. Fairer was below him, in the front hall, crying into her hands. He entered the bright yellow-and-blue nursery. There was medical equipment in the room. Neatly on her crib, uncovered, lay the three-year-old girl. Her forehead had been struck once, hard, broken with a hammer. The hammer lay beside her shoulder, like an ignored toy.

Also in the crib was a handwritten note that read, *I killed Stella.* It was signed, *Tucker Spinner.* Her father. Fairer's husband.

The only fingerprints on the hammer were Tucker Spinner's.

Fairer said, "I don't think there was any love in what he did. Not for Stella. Not for me."

"Domestic violence is still the biggest problem we have around here," Pepp said.

Fairer said, "I left Stella with him as little as possible. He almost liked to pretend she didn't exist. I mean, he'd never make a special trip upstairs to see her, when he came in. He never went in to see her before we went to bed, or when we got up in the morning. When I did leave him with her, and he had to tend to her for an hour or so, when I came back he'd look more exhausted than he'd look after a week of work."

"He must have realized how much caring for her was taking out of you."

"I think that day I left him with her, the day he killed her, I think he just went plumb out of his mind. He couldn't stand the sick child. Poor whining, demanding sick child."

Pepp remembered Tucker Spinner worked for the telephone company.

Pepp said, "He took his fishing gear. His shotgun. His clothes. That doesn't sound like a man out of his mind."

"I think he killed her, then couldn't face what he had done. I'd say he did it entirely for himself, surprised himself, then ran."

"Maybe." *At least, I should have been combing the telephone companies around the country these past years, looking for Tucker. Why haven't I?*

"I went crazy."

"You went into a bottle. And corked it."

"I thought I was numbing the pain. I guess I was, a little. I was purging self-pity."

"You had three car accidents in a month. Something like that."

"Every time on the way to the liquor store, or on the way home. I didn't go anywhere else." Fairer giggled, just a little. "Last accident, I beat up the cop."

"You really hurt him."

"I broke his nose for him. I was real tired of his arresting me for drunk driving, at that point."

"Jim Blackwell."

"Where's he at now?"

"Drivin' a bulldozer."

"You could have had me in jail."

"Drinkin' and drivin' wasn't your problem. You needed help with the pain. You needed rest. Therapy."

"Then you talked me into takin' on the coffee shop." Fairer kissed Pepp's warm forehead. "How come you understood, Pepp? How could you so understand a hurtin' woman?"

"Fairer Kelly." He put his leg over her hip. "Yellow hair in pigtails. Scraped knees."

"You could have been the macho sheriff out lookin' to gun down Tucker Spinner. 'Stead, you took care of his hurtin' wife."

"Got to sneeze." Pepp rolled away from her and sneezed into his hands.

When he came back from the bathroom, he said, "I guess you've got my confidence up again."

"I see that," she said.

She had turned on the lamp over the bed.

Pepp pulled the sheet away from her slowly, looking at her body as it was revealed.

Then he got onto the bed at an odd angle. Upside down from her, he put his legs between hers and slid himself to her so that their crotches were pressed against each other.

They lay like two scissors open on each other at the crotches.

She looked puzzled at him.

He said, "After you insert me, hold my hands, and pull."

As she was inserting him in her, she said, "How you know about this?"

Pepp said, "I read books."

Later, the light was out again.

Fairer had gotten Pepp a box of tissues for his runny nose. The box was on the floor on his side of the bed.

"Fairer?"

"Um?"

"I noticed twice we didn't do anything to prevent child-birth. Et cetera."

"I wouldn't mind," Fairer mumbled. "I wouldn't mind another child now. As long as she is yours."

He kissed her forehead, then stroked her cheek with his thumb.

"Will you stop giving me those little containers of cream now, every time I order coffee?"

"Sure. No need to, now."

"I thought you were indifferent to me."

"No obligation," she mumbled. "I never thought I'd be this happy."

15

"How'd you get in here if it's locked?" Adam Haddam stepped through the door of the coffee shop Sheriff Culpepper had opened for him. "Where's Fairer?" He looked at the sweat suit Pepp was wearing and recognized it as the same Pepp had been wearing the night before. "Oh, I see."

After closing and relocking the door, Pepp went back behind the counter. "You see nothing."

Without disturbing Fairer's sleep, Pepp had gotten out of bed, used the bathroom with the door closed, showered but did not shave. He had dressed in his clothes he found in the dryer off the kitchen and come down the stairs to the coffee shop. He lit the burner under yesterday's pot of coffee.

During the night, Fairer had reacted to him and reacted to him and reacted to him. And he to her.

There had been nothing phony or one-sided about what had happened between them.

In the morning, Pepp cursed himself.

For years he had been living with a woman, faithful to a woman who sexually had been reacting to him with indifference relieved only by abuse.

Evidence that there was nothing sexually wrong with Pepp increased his rage at Martha Jane. And at himself.

After he had turned on the coffee burner, he searched behind the counter for a packet of seltzer tablets.

Fleas had knocked on the glass door of the coffee shop.

While Pepp was covering two seltzer tablets with water in a paper cup, Fleas said, "I've been looking for you over an hour."

With a tight jaw, Pepp said, "It is not yet seven A.M. Monday morning."

"You weren't at home."

"No. I wasn't."

"Martha Jane told me you hadn't been home all night."

"I'm sure she did."

"Jack Simes is dead."

Pepp dropped the cup in the sink. His head snapped up to examine Fleas's face.

"His daddy found him," Fleas said. "Sunrise. Apparently beaten to death. In his driveway."

Pepp said, "Shit."

Hands in his back pockets, wordlessly Fleas watched the sheriff behind the counter of the coffee shop.

"Jack Simes . . ." Pepp said. "Beaten to death . . ." He scooped the seltzer tablets off the bottom of the sink back into the paper cup. "Jack Simes. First-string college halfback. Not possible. Nobody I ever saw around here could beat that boy to death."

Fleas said, "I'd hate to try it."

Pepp poured more water into the paper cup.

"You don't look well, Sheriff."

"Got a cold." Pepp swallowed the seltzer and water.

Fleas said, "Coffee to go."

"Come get it yourself."

Going behind the counter, Fleas asked, "Where's Fairer?"

"Guess she isn't up yet."

Pouring yesterday's coffee warmed into a Styrofoam cup, Fleas said, "Fairer's always here by this time."

"Have you been in touch with the deputies? Have you called the coroner?"

Fleas sighed. "I'm afraid you'll find them all out at the scene of the crime, Sheriff, waitin' on you."

"Shit. They'll mess the place up worse than a herd of worker ants."

"Had to do something."

Coffee cup in hand, Fleas stopped at the door of the coffee shop. "Where'll I say you've been, Sheriff?"

With red, runny eyes, Pepp looked at his dispatcher. "Shut up."

It was four minutes before eight Monday morning when Sheriff Culpepper drove into the Simeses' driveway. At the jail, he had shaved quickly and changed into uniform.

A forest-green bedspread covered a lump on the ground just outside the shed the Simeses used as a garage. In the open shed, facing away, were Jack's fancy truck, John senior's old Plymouth, the old Plymouth wagon used by M.L., once used by Mary Lou Simes as well.

The two police cars and the coroner's car were parked off the driveway.

Near the cars stood Deputies Aimes and Hanson. Aimes held the Sheriff's Department's camera in his hand at his side.

Dr. Murphy was nearest the body, walking slowly back and forth, examining the ground.

John Simes stood like a statue on the grass between the house and the driveway. His hands were at his side. He was staring across a pasture at the hillside woods.

Pepp went to John Simes. Without speaking or really looking at each other, they shook hands.

As Pepp approached the lump on the driveway, he noticed a baseball bat about two meters from the body.

"That the murder weapon?" he asked Dr. Murphy.

"I'd say so. It's got enough blood on it."

"Has anyone touched it?"

"I hope to God not."

Pepp called to the deputies. "Either of you touch this bat?"

"No, sir."

Pepp glanced at John Simes, who said nothing.

"Guess you need to see." Blocking John Simes's view with his own body, Dr. Murphy lifted the bedspread off the dead young man on the dirt of the driveway.

Jack Simes, one of the main hopes of the state university's football team, was on his stomach. Dr. Murphy lifted him by a shoulder to reveal his face. The young man's head and shoulders were so beaten there were loose strips of skin and bone fragments. Yet the rest of his body still looked powerful, neat, vital. He looked as if the top of his body had been inserted momentarily into a meat grinder.

"I'd say he was hit from behind, hard, back of his head, with the bat. Then, once he was down, or going down, set to with the bat with a vengeance." Dr. Murphy lowered the young man's shoulder. He placed the bedspread over the body again. "He did not defend himself."

"Didn't have a chance?"

"Probably not. He might have. Powerful young man, used to being hit, even from behind, on the football field. Given the worst blow, people don't go unconscious immediately, you know. Not like the movies."

"Yeah." Except for seltzer, coffee, and the apple pie the night before, Pepp had had nothing to eat. Just then he was glad his stomach was empty. Near the pasture fence someone had thrown up recently. Probably Deputy Hanson. Handsome had always just had something to eat.

Pepp sneezed twice. "Time of death?"

"Between two and four A.M., I'd say."

"Same as his sister."

"Saturday morning. Monday morning."

Pepp sneezed again. "Would he have had a chance to cry out?"

"I would think so. Crying out under such circumstances is an almost involuntary reaction."

Pepp looked at the big farmhouse. "I wonder why his parents wouldn't have heard him."

"Again, Jack was a football player. Used to being physically surprised, attacked. Maybe after seven or eight years playing football, your instincts change. You don't cry out at the surprise of pain."

"John Simes found him?"

"Opened the shade of his bedroom window when he got up at dawn, and there was his son lying on the driveway. Called your office." Dr. Murphy looked closely at Pepp. "Got a cold?"

"Yeah."

"Stop by the office later. I'll give you something for it."

"I don't think so."

"Why not?"

"I may have to ask you for a blood test. I may need proof I use no drugs whatsoever."

In the sunlight of the beautiful morning, the doctor's eyes were sad. "I see." He looked down at the covered corpse on the driveway. "What we human beings do to each other, one way or another . . ."

Pepp returned to John Simes.

"What time did you get up this morning?" Pepp asked.

"I always get up just before sunrise, year 'round, no matter where I am."

"Okay. Did you raise your bedroom shade immediately?"

"First thing I do."

"What was your first thought when you saw your son in the driveway?"

"I thought he was dead."

"Not drunk?"

"I knew he was dead."

"Could you see his head from that distance?"

"I've seen a lot of dead bodies, Pepp. Bodies that are dead look completely different from bodies that are asleep or unconscious, drunk. Even at a distance, there is something heavy, permanent . . ." Simes continued to stare forward, into the fairly distant wood.

"Whose baseball bat is that?"

"Ours, I guess."

"Do you know where it was kept?"

"In the shed, I suppose. In the garage."

"Show me, please?"

Pepp followed Simes into the car shed. Simes made no effort to skirt his son's body in the driveway.

There was an open storage area in the shed, on the side nearer Jack's truck. In it, on a shelf with loose tools, an unplugged power saw, an unplugged sander, drill, hammer, assortment of screwdrivers, pruning shears, cans of paint, clean brushes, there was an assortment of footballs, including a few deflated and decayed, baseballs, a mesh bag of tennis balls, an old and a new basketball. There was a basketball hoop affixed to poles outside the shed. Also in the shed was a volleyball net on its poles in good shape. Next to the poles were two baseball bats.

There was a charcoal grill on wheels.

The shed still smelled vaguely of its days as a carriage house.

Indicating the baseball bats, Pepp asked, "Are you sure there were three bats here?"

Simes shrugged. "There could have been three. There could have been five."

"Could there have been only two?" Simes didn't answer. "Who knows they were here?"

Slowly, a pickup truck turned off the road and came into the driveway. It stopped behind the sheriff's car.

"Everybody."

"Everybody?"

"Every young person in Greendowns County, I expect. Some adults. Over the years, just about everybody's been here, playing one game or other. I'd say everyone knows this is where this stuff is kept. Like the tools." Simes looked around the storage area. "Things get taken out and used. Put back. Borrowed. Sometimes put back." He did not attempt a smile.

Outside, two young men had gotten out of the truck. They went to the covered lump, looked down at it but did not disturb the bedspread.

They walked to where the deputies were standing on the lawn.

Pepp studied the dirt floor of the shed, looking for anything unusual, a telltale cigarette butt, odd scuff mark, footprint. In fact, one area of the dirt was patted down, depressed, smoothed, as if someone had stood there a long time. With his naked eye, Pepp could not discern anything as distinctive as a footprint.

He placed a paint can from the shelf beside the area to prevent anyone from walking on it.

Untermyer's hearse came into the driveway. At a crawl, tipping slightly, two wheels on the lawn, it passed the pickup truck and the sheriff's car.

Pepp realized he had summoned none of these people, not the deputies, the coroner, the undertaker. *Damn. Right now even I'm questioning my competence.*

Simes said, "All right if I go in the house now?"

"Of course."

"Andy-Dandy's about hysterical."

"Maybe you should ask Dr. Murphy in."

"Yes."

"I'll ask him for you."

Simes walked in a straight line to the back door of the house and entered it.

Coming out of the shed, Sheriff Culpepper said, "Doc? Saw you examining the ground. Find anything?"

"No, sir, I did not. Thought I'd spend the time policing the area before you showed up—just in case."

"There appears to be a place in the shed where someone might have stood waiting."

"I see."

"We'll hold that for the state lab. The bat. Once Mr. Untermyer leaves, we'll give this place the full photographic treatment before going over it on our hands and knees."

Pepp wondered why he said all that. *Am I trying to express my professional competence to Dr. Murphy?*

Untermyer and his assistant carried the gurney to the body. They lifted the body onto the gurney without removing the bedspread. They had to wheel the heavy body of the young man back to the hearse.

Pepp said, "Shit."

Slowly, the coroner said, "Yeah."

"Told John I'd ask you to stop in the house. M.L. The little boy, Andy . . ."

"They must be out of their minds. Mary Lou's funeral was planned for today."

"Today? Not tomorrow?"

"Can't guess what they'll do now. Well, I'm not their doctor, but I'll go in. Any idea who their doctor might be?"

"No."

"Least I can do is make a phone call for them. Get the Reverend Baker out here again. He might as well take up residence here."

Pepp started across the yard to speak to Untermyer.

Deputy Chick Hanson intercepted him.

" 'Morning, Handsome," Pepp said. "How do you feel?"

"Where were you?"

"When?"

"This morning."

"I'm here, Handsome."

"These two boys here have something to tell you."

"Is that Reg Fields?"

"Yes, sir."

"Who's the other one?"

"Frank McNally. Friends of Jack's."

Pepp knew Reg as a graduated member of the high school football team. He hadn't been good enough at either football or his studies to go on to college. He worked collecting scrap metal.

Frank McNally sat on a fender of a police car. Reg, arms folded across his chest, leaned against the same fender.

" 'Morning," Pepp said, approaching them. "You boys got something to tell me?"

The young men glanced at each other, volunteering the other to speak.

Pepp asked, "Well . . . ?"

"We were with Jack last night," Reg said. "We came across Skylar on Highway Forty-two."

"Why didn't you report it?"

The young men did not answer.

Finally, Pepp said, "So . . . ?"

"We chased him into the quarry."

"Who was driving?"

Frank said, "Jack."

"Then what happened?"

Reg said, "We grabbed him out of his truck and beat on him."

"Who did? All three of you?"

"Yes," Reg answered.

Frank said, "Mostly Jack."

In the morning sunlight, Pepp's eyes were running and stinging him. His sinuses felt ready to burst. Still, his face, inside and outside, felt just wet. His head ached, and his legs felt tired.

He asked, "Then you just left him there?"

Frank nodded, *yes.* "There was someone with him."

"Who?"

"Some other kid. We didn't recognize him. He never got out of the truck." Frank snorted. "The other kid locked himself in the truck."

Skylar's cousin, Pepp thought. *No love lost there, I'd say.*

Pepp said, "You boys know Skylar Whitfield had escaped from jail on a first-degree murder charge?"

Reg said, "Yes, sir."

"Then why didn't you report finding him?"

Frank said, "Didn't believe he was guilty."

Reg said, "We didn't really believe he was guilty of anything . . . last night. Except for bein' a general, all-'round wise guy."

"Did Jack believe Skylar guilty?"

"Not really," Reg said. "He felt a little bad about it, later."

"Then why the hell did he beat him up?"

Reg said, "That was what he needed to do, last night. Jack,
I mean."

"Why did you help him?"

Reg watched the hearse leaving the driveway of the Simes
home. "We were his friends."

"Beer?" Pepp asked.

"Yes, sir."

Frank said, "A little."

Reg said, "We were trying to be with Jack, you know? I
mean, with him."

"Jeez." Pepp shook his head. "You guys beat each other up
in the dark of the night, just to be companionable, and in the
light of the next day you're all drinkin' beer together, including whoever was beat up, tryin' to see who can give the wit-
tiest version of what happened, laughin' your fool heads off
at your own damned, raw violence. Some ways, the South
hasn't changed much, has it?"

Reg said, "We're not laughin' this mornin'."

"I hope you know I could throw you both in jail. Bring
damned serious charges against you."

Reg said, "Yes, sir."

"You may have beat Skylar up, but you kept him from
justice."

After a moment, Frank said, "We were just being with
Jack."

"How do you feel about it now?" Pepp asked.

"Do you think . . . ?" Frank slid off the car fender. He was
looking at where Jack Simes's body had lain. He looked as
though he might vomit.

"What do you think?" Pepp asked. "What time did all this
happen at the quarry last night?"

"About midnight," Reg said. "Little before."

"How badly was Skylar beaten?"

"Not all that badly," Reg answered.

"We just sort of roughed him up."

Pepp turned away. "How did you know to come here this
morning?"

Frank said, "It's on the radio."

Shit, Pepp thought. *Maybe the sheriff should take to listening to the radio.*

The Reverend Baker was turning into the Simeses' driveway.

Pepp said, "Deputy Aimes?"

"Yes, sir?"

"Get these two boys out of my sight."

"Yes, sir."

Pepp turned to them. "And don't you boys even think of drinking a beer, or beating anyone else up, or hunting Skylar, or anything else. You hear me?"

"Yes, sir."

"Get out of here."

"Yes, sir."

Julep growled, then barked.

"Shut up, dog," Skylar said.

Julep shut up.

Shortly, head down, Tandy appeared from the woods. She carried a brown paper sack.

"How're ya doin'?" Skylar, in the truck bed, his back leaning against his bedroll against the cab's rear wall, had been reading a book in the shade of the trees.

Tandy handed the paper sack up to Skylar.

Julep was wagging around the truck bed, frustrated in his greeting of Tandy.

"What's the matter?" Skylar asked Tandy. "Did you go to Mary Lou's funeral?"

"No funeral," Tandy said.

"No funeral? How can that be?"

Standing on the ground beside the truck, Tandy put her face in her hands and sobbed. "Oh, Skylar. Jack Simes is dead. Found by his daddy beaten to death in their driveway this morning."

Through Tandy's chokes and sobs, her tears and her hands, it took Skylar a moment to understand her.

It took him another moment to assimilate what she was saying.

By then, Tandy had climbed onto the truck bed. She knelt, then curled up, putting her shoulders and head on Skylar's crossed legs. "I didn't hear till an hour ago. Dufus and I were out mendin' that fence."

Skylar had put the bag of food Tandy brought him on the floor of the truck bed beside him. He had been hungry.

Skylar said, "Someone is killin' the Simes kids."

"Why?"

"Wouldn't you say two out of three is pretty indicative?"

"Skylar, the way the radio tells it, you for sure are the murderer. They know Jack Simes gave you a whuppin' last night in the quarry. They're reportin' it. Few hours later, Jack Simes was beaten to death."

"Fields and McNally must have told them." More quietly, he said: "Or Jon Than."

"The radio keeps sayin' you were already wanted for the murder of his sister, Mary Lou, that you escaped jail. . . ." Tandy cried hard into Skylar's lap.

Skylar said, "Things are beginnin' to look downright serious for me, ain't they just?"

She put her arms around Skylar's waist. "Don't you think you ought to give yourself up?"

"What chance would I have then?"

"They'll be huntin' you."

"I'd better move. After dark."

"They know you're somewhere 'round here, Skylar."

"I leave this county, I'm lost."

She sat up and looked at him through teary eyes. "Skylar, why don't you go to the sheriff?"

"Got somethin' to do."

"Like what? Get yourself shot?"

"No. Not like that. Leastways, I don't think so."

"Can I do what you have to do?"

"No. Don't think so." He pulled her back into his lap, higher, so her wet cheeks were against his chest. "Jack Simes beat to death? Lordy, Lordy."

She said, "Your heart's goin' faster than a bluebird's."

Skylar took a deep breath.

"Skylar, ain't you scared?"

"Scared shitless."

Tandy said, "Well, so am I."

"Listen, Tandy. Will you give Dufus a message for me? Will you both do something for me?"

"Sure."

"Try not to let Andy-Dandy out of sight."

"How can we do that?"

"Damn. I don't know."

"You think someone's fixin' to kill Andy-Dandy, too?"

"I don't know. Two out of three."

"Well . . . Don't know how we can. 'Spect he'll be kept close to home, anyway. Don't you reckon?"

"I guess."

"Jon Than asked me to give you a message. Saw him for a minute this morning."

Absently, Skylar said, "What?"

"He said he means to apologize to you."

"For sittin' in the damned truck while I was gettin' whupped?"

"No. He said there is such a word as 'stob.' He looked it up in the dictionary, he said."

Skylar said, "That's good."

16

"You stayed in the truck?" Pepp asked.

"Yes."

In the Whitfields' living room, Monica and Dan Whitfield seemed more curious about what Jonathan was saying than even the sheriff.

At some point earlier in the interview, Monica had said to Pepp, "We knew that Jonathan had been picked up by your deputies when we sent him to the store yesterday, and then released . . . Needless to say, we were very worried all evening. Apparently, he wasn't given the opportunity to telephone us. . . . But we knew nothing of this quarry business. . . . Jonathan must have felt that to tell us might somehow have compromised Skylar. . . ."

Released? Telephone? Pepp wondered if Monica was being diplomatic in her description of events. He guessed not. He guessed this description of events was as the Yankee boy had presented it to his aunt and uncle. Pepp thought he had not encountered a mind like Jonathan Whitfield's before, except in books. Instead of describing unpleasantness in detail and excusing it tolerantly, with humor, charm, as a Southerner might, Jonathan seemed to feel it of a higher diplomatic order to deny unpleasantness had ever happened. Pepp also doubted the young man's failure to report Skylar's being beaten up in the quarry was because of any unwillingness to compromise his cousin.

Pepp's mind was nibbling at the edges of a concept of Albert Camus he had read and thought about but had never expected to see implemented. The concept regarded commitment and involvement.

Looking around the Whitfields' living room Monday midday, looking at the stolid deputy Tom Aimes taking notes with big handwriting in a small book, Pepp felt some amazement at the discovery that minds actually are disciplined to such concepts.

Yes.

Jonathan Whitfield's monosyllabic answer landed on them all in a nearly judicial tone. It seemed to Pepp almost as if Jonathan Whitfield were conducting the interview rather than himself.

By the time the sheriff had reached the Whitfields' home, Monica, Dan, and Jonathan Whitfield knew of the murder of Jack Simes by the radio, by phone calls. Dan Whitfield had returned home from his office.

Both the senior Whitfields were pale and drawn.

"How many boys were there?" The sheriff asked.

"Three young men," Jon corrected.

"Did you know them?"

"How could I? I was informed one was Jack Simes. I don't know the man well enough to swear to it myself. It was a dark and confusing scene."

"Informed by Skylar?"

"Yes."

"How badly was Skylar beaten?"

"Bloody lips, nose. He complained of sore ribs. He was well enough to change the truck's tire, after he had taken a few minutes to recover." Jon smiled. "The tire had a stob in it."

Pepp was puzzled by the boy's smile. What was funny about a flat tire?

"Did you help him change the tire?"

"Not much. It was dark. I don't know that truck."

"But you did help him a little?"

"I wanted to get home. I mean, here. Back at the farm. I wanted to go to bed."

Monica said to Pepp, "Jonathan has mononucleosis. He's here for a rest."

Pepp said to himself, *He's here because his parents want to get him away from some girl.*

He asked, "Was Skylar upset?"

"What do you mean?"

"I mean, was he angry? How angry was he? At Jack Simes. Would you describe him as furious? Enraged?"

"Not at all," Jon answered.

"How would you describe him?" the sheriff asked patiently.

"I'd describe him as philosophical. I gather giving and taking beatings is as common around here as lovemaking." Jon glanced at his aunt. "I gather that praising the Lord, screwing around, and beating each other violently are all equal ingredients in the social and moral stew of Greendowns County."

Pepp dried his nose with his handkerchief.

Again Pepp found himself wondering, *To what extent are all theological and philosophical concepts spiritual or intellectual exercises; to what extent are they purely emotional armor?*

Surprisingly, perhaps out of some embarrassment at his frankness, Jon volunteered, "I would have been enraged. 'Vengeful' is the word for which I think you're looking, Sheriff."

"Skylar was not 'vengeful'?"

"Not to my perception."

"Where did Skylar drop you off?"

Jon waved his hand toward town. "Down the road. Within sight of the lights of the farm."

"At what time?"

"About twelve-fifteen. When I took off my watch in my room, it was just past twelve-thirty."

"Did he say where he was going?"

"No."

No.

"Jonathan, do you know where Skylar is now?"

"No."

"Do you know of anyone who does know where Skylar is now?"

It seemed to take Jon a little effort to keep his eyes on the sheriff's face. "No."

For a moment, Pepp sat silently, staring at Jonathan Whitfield, attempting to stare him down. Jon looked slightly red, slightly hot. But Pepp did not succeed in staring him down.

Finally, Pepp said, "All right."

"Another murder." Attorney Frank Murrey had looked up from his desk at Sheriff Culpepper in the doorway.

"Yes."

Frank took off his glasses. "Any word on Skylar Whitfield?"

"No."

Frank sorted some folders on his desk. "Let's not talk about that now."

"Obviously, I haven't had a chance to call you, Frank. Do you have any time for me now?"

"Sure. Come in. Take a load off."

Pepp closed the office door behind him.

Frank said, "You look tired."

Sitting down, Pepp answered, "A bit."

"Unfortunately, divorces don't happen in a vacuum. When there's a death, daily life is allowed to stop for a few days. There's a period of mourning. Although divorce has become almost as frequent as death in our society, and frequently causes much more pain, for some reason people are expected to work straight through it. There are no real mechanics for mourning."

Pepp asked, "Do you say that to all your divorce clients?"

"In fact, I do. I do make a few introductory generalizations."

"From compassion?"

"Not really. I find it helps bring a little objectivity to perhaps the most subjective of all human events. Makes it easier for me." Frank opened an empty folder and placed a blank piece of paper on its back flap. "You sure you want to initiate this litigation, Pepp, while you've got so much going on professionally?"

Pepp shrugged. "I have to. I have to defend myself. Martha Jane is making a deliberate attempt to ruin my reputation. As sheriff. I don't see that I have any choices, Frank. Right now, I've got about as much credibility in this county as I've got gold in my boots."

Still looking at the blank piece of paper, Frank said, "Your jail with the convertible top hasn't helped your reputation any."

"That's it," Pepp answered. "Even Fleas isn't taking me seriously. The deputies are doing things. . . ."

"Fleas didn't let those boys escape on purpose, did he?"

"There's only one cell in that jail from which anyone can escape." Pepp smiled. "Mostly, it's used for Tony Duffy."

"His home away from home. I mean, his home away from the trash can, or wherever he lives."

"Yesterday, Skylar Whitfield attended church. No one apprehended him. Last night, he drove his little red truck right through town and along Route Forty-two, and not one soul reported seeing him."

"I expect things are different today," Frank said.

"I don't know."

Still looking at his blank paper, Frank said, "Of course, I've heard what Martha Jane is saying about you. Accusations by the party being divorced of drug or alcohol abuse by the party threatening or initiating divorce is routine these days."

"Really? Well, maybe attorneys who handle divorces know that. . . ."

"Routine," Frank said. "Tiresome. Also essentially irrelevant. People continue to try to turn divorce cases into criminal cases." Finally, Frank looked up at Pepp. "By the way, you are not addicted, are you?"

"No."

"Have you ever used cocaine, or any of this other stuff?"

"No." In Pepp's ear echoed Jonathan Whitfield's flat answers: *No.*

"Too bad."

"Why 'too bad'?"

"If you were addicted, we could make out to the court that you are the dependent party of this divorce." Frank smiled. "Maybe get alimony out of Martha Jane."

Evenly, Pepp said, "I've never been the dependent party of this marriage."

Still looking at him, Frank said, "Pepp, I've got to observe this afternoon that your nose is red and your eyes are runny."

"Goddamnit, I've got a cold." Pepp blew his nose.

Frank grinned. "Okay." He put on his glasses. "Let's list your assets, boy. So I'll know how much to nick you." He picked up a pen. "And don't forget your secret bank accounts stuffed with drug profits."

In the laundry room off the kitchen of the Simeses' farmhouse, M.L. turned away from the washing machine. Wet sheets and pillowcases were draped on the floor from the washer to the dryer.

Taking only a few steps, she put her arms around Dan Whitfield.

Dan put his hand between her shoulders and pressed her against his chest.

While he kissed the top of her head, she wept against his shirt.

"Skylar . . ." Naked, Tandy sat up in bed in Skylar's dark bedroom. She threw the sheet off them both. She put her hand on his higher shoulder and pushed him onto his back. Then she gripped the hip farther from her with her opened hand and pressed her thumb hard into his stomach muscle. His legs drew up. "Skylar . . ." With relaxed fingers, she brushed her hand rapidly, lightly, up and down his face. "It's almost dark. Near time you got goin'."

"What are you doing?" he mumbled.

"Figured out where you were. Home in your own bed. Figured it was a good place for me, too. People are out beatin' the bushes lookin' for us both."

Skylar rolled back onto his side, facing her. "Have you slept?"

"A little bit. Remember, you want to get to the motel."

"Yeah."

Tandy lay down on her side, too, facing him. She put her knees against his stomach, her lower legs against his thighs.

"Skylar?"

"What?"

"Good bodies."

"Who?"

"Us."

"Lucky us."

"Other people. Mary Lou. Jack. Interesting. I mean, most people are pretty interesting. Each of us an energy wrapped up in skin."

"What're you talking about?"

"I'm trying to get you to wake up. It's dark out."

"I'm awake. Just sleepy."

"What I've been tryin' to figure out is how can anyone bring hisself to destroy someone else. Kill someone else." When Skylar didn't answer, Tandy said, "What in God's name can happen to a person to make him murder another person?"

"Happens a lot, doesn't it?"

"How?"

Skylar said, "Books I read say sex and money."

"Drugs."

"That's money, isn't it?"

"I don't see sex and money being a cause for murder. Sex is nice. Money don't count for all that much."

Skylar rolled onto his back and stretched every part of his body. "Not everybody is Tandy McJane."

"I ought to be able to understand some little part of murder, there's so much of it around."

"Pressure."

"Pressure is . . ." Sitting cross-legged on the bed, Tandy waited for Skylar to continue.

Rubbing his eyes, Skylar said, "I don't know. No sex. No money. I've heard it said people can only stand so much pressure. I guess people can have enough weight on them for so long they flip out. Think differently. Murder becomes possible for them. Anyway." Skylar yawned. "I expect before we're done with all this, we'll understand more."

"Have you ever felt that way, Skylar? That you could murder someone?"

"No."

"Skylar, you know there's nothing in the world sayin' you didn't kill Mary Lou and Jack." Skylar slid himself up the bed and rested his head and shoulders against the headboard. "Even I can't say it. I didn't get to the truck this morning until three-thirty, quarter to four."

"I know."

"Your knife. I didn't see you drop it that morning in the woods. If I had, I would have picked it up." Skylar said nothing. "I've just been thinkin'."

Still Skylar said nothing.

"I've been tryin' to think of how we can develop evidence you didn't kill nobody."

"So have I. That's why I'm goin' to the motel."

"Skylar, I don't mind tellin' you, I'm scared."

"So am I."

"A lot more people in Greendowns County are thinkin' of you as a murderer today than there were yesterday."

"I expect so."

The dark bedroom was silent a moment.

"Skylar, someone's knittin' a rope to hang you on as we speak."

Skylar sat up.

Tandy said, "I've always thought you're about tall enough as you are."

"They have to prove I did murder Mary Lou and Jack."

"Chick Hanson with a gun comin' across you in the woods right now doesn't have to prove much at all at all. You're an escaped fugitive from justice, thanks to little ol' me."

"Tandy, all your talk of hangin' and shootin' me is makin' me feel just a mite blue."

She put her forearms on his shoulders. "Just tryin' to get you to think, Skylar." She cupped her hands around his neck. " 'Spect you could do enough neck exercises to withstand a hangin'?"

"Somebody must have tried that."

Folding her legs around Skylar's back, Tandy slid onto his crossed legs. She pulled his face to her and kissed him.

"Tandy, I thought we weren't going to . . . Mary Lou . . . Now Jack . . ."

"You need it, Skylar." Her right hand fondled his penis, erect against her stomach. "I've got to make sure you can think straight."

While Skylar was shaving, the light went on in the guest room.

While Jon stood in the bathroom doorway looking curiously at Skylar, the balcony door to Skylar's bedroom closed softly.

"Has something happened?" Jon asked.

Skylar tightened his left cheek to shave it. "More than enough, wouldn't you say?"

"I mean, has something happened to have you declared innocent, so you can come home?"

"No, sir. Not as far as I know."

"Then how can you be here?"

"Needed a nap in my own bed. A shave. A shower. Fresh clothes. Don't you find all that reasonable, Jon Than?"

"Was that Tandy McJane who just left?"

"Yup."

Skylar saw Jon's eyes crinkle in the bathroom mirror.

"Everyone is running around Greendowns County looking for you, and you're at home in your own bed. Last place they'd look for you."

"That's what I figured."

"And now you mean to make that trip to the motel."

"You've got it."

"How are you going to get there?"

"Tandy's just gone to borrow Mrs. Duffy's car."

"Tandy can't drive you."

"She's not going to."

"People suspect Tandy and Dufus of being loyal to you, helping you, knowing where you are."

"Right."

"You can't drive yourself."

"I mean to."

"Skylar, as I remember, the route to the Las Vegas Motel takes you straight through the county, straight through town."

"There are side roads."

"I expect they'll be looking for you on the side roads."

Skylar rinsed his razor. "What's your point, Jon Than?"

"Do I owe you an apology for not getting out of the truck last night and getting beat up, too?"

"No, sir. Tandy wondered why I wasn't as smart as you are, and lock myself in the truck, too." Skylar washed the soap off his face. "Apologizin' to me about the word 'stob' was more'n I ever expected from you, Jon Than. But I still don't get your point."

"I'll drive you."

Skylar turned and looked his cousin full in the face.

"It will be perfectly safe." Jon smiled. "Everyone knows I don't give a damn about you."

17

Hunkered down on the floor of the backseat of Mrs. Duffy's car, Skylar asked Jon, "Who dat?"

The interior of the car had been flashed by bright lights from a closely following vehicle.

"Someone who wants to pass us, I presume," said Jon, driving. "Please observe, Skylar, my use of traditional road manners. Notice how I slow the car and pull to the right."

The right side of the car began jouncing.

"No need to put us in the ditch, Jon Than. Good manners don't require it."

The other vehicle pulled up alongside of them, hesitated, and then passed them.

After the lights had left the interior of Mrs. Duffy's car, Jon said, "A police car."

"Police?"

"It was marked 'Sheriff's Department' and had the appropriate symbols of authority, extra antennae, lights, probably concealed somewhere under its hood a steam whistle or whatever siren technology has reached Greendowns County. . . ."

"Did he look at you?"

"Glowered."

"Did you ignore him?"

"I waved. Forgivingly. Understandingly. In a manner I might describe as noblesse oblige. As I assured you, the local constabulary indubitably has given up arresting me." Jon shifted down to climb a tall hill. "Although why I am driving Mrs. Duffy's car through the scenery, especially at this hour on a Monday night, might be occurring to the officer as a question worth contemplating right about now."

Skylar said, "At the top of the hill, ease down a little road to your left, Jon Than, stop, and turn off the lights for a while. I need an airin'."

"Right."

"No," Skylar said. "Left."

Special Deputy Marian Wilkinson's voice crackled through the old intercom on the sheriff's desk. "Long distance for you, Pepp. Person to person."

"Okay." Pepp picked up his office phone. He had just returned from patrolling. He did not believe patrolling the roads of Greendowns County for Skylar Whitfield would result in the capture of Skylar Whitfield, but decidedly he wanted as much presence of the Sheriff's Department on the roads at this point as he could muster. He had not yet removed his gun belt to sit at his desk. "Culpepper."

"Hey, Dad."

"Sammy?" His daughter never called on a weeknight, especially at his office. "What's happenin', babe?"

"Just studying."

"Big biology exam tomorrow, uh?"

"Dad, I'd like to fly home tomorrow, after the exam."

"Anything wrong, Sammy?"

"I just want to see you. Can you come to the airport?"

"Tomorrow really isn't a good time for me, Sammy. There's a lot going on here. Have you heard Jack Simes has been murdered?"

"Yes." To Pepp's ears, his daughter's voice appeared peculiarly strained.

If Sammy had heard from Greendowns that Jack Simes had been murdered, she probably also had heard the gossip that her father was filing for divorce from her mother.

"I see." The nearest airport Sammy could fly into was almost a hundred miles away. Driving there and back would take more than four hours out of his day. "Could your mother pick you up instead?"

"Dad, I want to see you." Pepp realized that Sammy probably felt he needed reassurance of her love and support, because of the divorce. More to the point, she probably needed his reassurance.

Suddenly, the current history of Greendowns County faded in importance, meant little to him.

Pepp wanted to see his daughter.

"Good ol' Sammy," he said into the phone. "What time?"

"Three-oh-seven. Isn't it ridiculous the way airlines give their departure and arrival times to the odd minute?"

"I expect the airlines want to build confidence in us by appearing scientifically precise." The button for the sheriff's other phone line was flashing. "Induce us to think they've tightened all the bolts before takeoff."

"They don't hit their own numbers, either goin' or comin'," Sammy said. "If airlines did things to the precise minute they state, that might build confidence."

"Got another call," Pepp said. "Good luck on the exam. See you at three-oh-seven."

Pepp pushed the flashing button. "Culpepper."

"Pepp, there are a couple of real weird creeps in town."

"Only a couple?"

Over the phone, Fairer said, "I'm working in my new capacity as the Sheriff Department's Intelligence Branch."

Fairer had seen many strangers in her coffee shop. Including the Yankee who once called her "Madam," she hit with a one-egg skillet.

Pepp said, "Tell me."

"Very expensive suits," Fairer said, "like I've never laid eyes on before. I'd say, special built."

"What do you mean, business suits?"

"Fit them perfectly, even when they sat down, if you know what I mean, at the counter, without unbuttonin' their jackets, not ordinary Sunday-go-to-meetin' suits. The left sides of their jackets were bigger than their right sides, had more cloth in 'em, right about where their hearts are."

"You think they're carryin'?"

"Yes."

"Are they still there? I mean, in your coffee shop?"

"No. They left."

"Why didn't you call me? Carrying a concealed weapon for the sake of going armed is against the law around here."

"Their eyes were everywhere. Their ears, too. All the time they were here havin' sandwiches and coffee, they said nothing to each other. I was pretty sure they'd notice me picking up the phone and talking quietly into it."

"You were actually afraid of them."

"You didn't see these guys."

"Did you notice their vehicle?"

"Airport rental. I made a point of watching what they got into before calling you. Pepp, point is, they asked directions to the Simeses' place."

"Did you tell them?"

"I'd never heard of the Simeses. The Henry brothers were sittin' at the counter, and they testified they'd never heard of anyone 'round here named Simes, either."

"License plate?"

"ZED 152. A heavy new Oldsmobile. Red."

Pepp made a note. "Thanks, Fairer."

"You notice I opened late this morning?"

Pepp appreciated Fairer's phrasing. She knew the call went through the department's switchboard. "Fleas did."

"Slept better than I have in years. I have no idea why." Pepp felt he could hear her voice smiling. "Coming by for pie and coffee tonight? Saved a piece for you. You really seemed to like the piece you had Sunday night."

"Sure did." Pepp was smiling. "Better not, though. The people in the county might notice if I gain weight. I'd hate to give them a reason for not reelecting me."

"Well, okay. I'll keep it in the refrigerator for you."

Pepp said, " 'Appreciate it."

Pepp punched the button for his other telephone line and called what had once been his home.

After five rings, Martha Jane answered. "Hello?"

"Need the car tomorrow. I'll pick it up about noon. Okay?"

"Okay," Martha Jane answered. "But I'll need it by six-thirty. I have a meeting."

Pepp hesitated. It seemed unnatural not telling Martha Jane that Sammy was coming home. Yet he felt the needle in her saying she had another meeting, the next night, and he was supposed to have the family car home in time for her to attend. Another meeting at which she would smear him.

He hung up.

Jon had parked Mrs. Duffy's car under some trees at the back of the Las Vegas Motel parking lot. They could see along the row of motel rooms. Each had a little porch light outside its door under the roof.

Skylar and Jon sat silently. They watched the doors a long time.

There were only three cars nuzzling the motel rooms' doors, one a red Oldsmobile with an in-state license, one a trash compact car with Indiana license plates, one Skylar knew belonged to a local, married lawyer who could have only one reason for renting a room at the Las Vegas Motel.

Skylar memorized both the license plates he did not know.

After a long time, a tractor trailer pulled in and parked. It obscured their view of the motel rooms' doors. Jon left the car and went around the truck and watched. After the driver went into the motel office with his grip, returned to the exterior corridor, and entered his room, Jon moved the car around the truck, closer to the motel but still in the dark of the back of the parking lot. They were viewing the motel rooms' doors at less of an angle.

After another long while, Jon said to Skylar, "I thought you were conversational."

"Not if there's nothin' to say."

"It appears to me," Jon said, "you're intelligent enough to have done well enough in school to be admitted to one college or another, even if only Cow Flap U. Looks to me like your parents could afford to help you financially. . . ."

"You goading me, Jon Than?"

"Isn't that my purpose in my being here, according to you?"

Skylar said, "I've got everything I want right here. Why would I ever want to leave the farm, Greendowns County? Just tell me that, Jon Than."

Jon chuckled. "Sure. You're the perfectly happy man, all right, the perfectly contented individual. You've got everything you want, no more, no less. You've got a pretty place to live, good basic food, healthful outdoor work, and women who adore you and apparently will do anything you want."

"That's about right."

"Do you consider yourself adequately intellectually challenged, for your age?"

"Jon Than, perhaps you haven't had a chance to notice yet, but there are people around here who may not know all that you know about some things but whose minds move faster than yours, I swear."

"You sure of that?"

"Pretty sure."

"Yes, indeed," Jon said. "You have everything a man could want right here in Greendowns County: an all-points bulletin out for your arrest on two counts of first-degree murder and one of being a fugitive from justice, and, I expect, half the county of these intellectual giants are out combing the woods contesting to see who will be the first to shoot you, enjoying the hunt, as it were, not really caring very much whether you are guilty. Why would you ever want to leave Greendowns County? Why, indeed?"

"Temporary misunderstanding I'm about to set right," Skylar said.

"Sure." Jon again readjusted the window wing, trying to attract some breeze. "Though I will admit, Skylar. I'm not half as bored here as I expected to be."

"Sure," Skylar said. "You're getting the point. The tradition of chivalry is right interestin'."

"Chivalry?"

"Panache."

Jon said, "Oh, my God."

Skylar said, "Sure wish you wouldn't swear, Jon Than."

They sat in the car another long time, silently.

A motel door opened. In the light from the room, Skylar and Jon saw a slim, middle-aged man with long, unkempt hair and beard in the doorway. The light behind him went out.

"I'll be tied to a rattlesnake's tail!" Skylar opened the door of the car. "There he is! The man I saw at the Holler. Still here."

"Wait," Jon said. "What are you going to do?"

Skylar spoke through the window of the car door he had closed softly. "Why, Jon Than, I'm just goin' to speak nicely to him."

Jon watched through the windshield as Skylar approached the man.

"Ha," Skylar said. "How're ya doin'?"

The man had just opened the driver's-seat door of the car registered in Indiana. With steady reddish-brown eyes, he studied Skylar standing at ease on the sidewalk in front of the car. Skylar's hands were in the back pockets of his jeans.

Skylar said, "I saw you the other night at the Holler. You offered to buy me a beer. Doncha remember?"

Not moving a muscle of his taut, wiry body, the man said nothing.

"You were considerably more friendly then," Skylar said.

"You asked me to confirm the identity of Miss Mary Lou Simes."

Still the man said nothing.

"Now I'm downright curious why you wanted to know."

For a while, unmoving, they stared at each other.

Finally, Skylar said, "Being a stranger here and all, maybe you haven't heard it on the local radio that that very same night that very same Miss Mary Lou Simes was beaten to death in the woods not far from the Holler."

The sinewy man seemed dangerous to Skylar, a snake full of poison poised to strike.

Skylar maintained his easy stance, but his nerves were preparing for flight or fight.

"I wonder how a stranger like you, from Indiana, is it?"—Skylar made a point of looking at the license plate on the old car—"knew of Mary Lou Simes?"

After a long moment staring at Skylar, the man snorted. He got into the car and slammed the door. Starting the car, he stared at Skylar through his dirty windshield. Then, looking around, he reversed the car, stopped, turned on the headlights, and drove out of the motel's parking lot.

Through the windshield of Mrs. Duffy's car, Jon watched Skylar standing casually talking to the man beside the old compact car. Jon could not hear what was being said; he could not tell if the man was answering Skylar.

He watched the man get into the car and leave the parking lot.

On the roofed, porch-lit sidewalk, Skylar watched the car disappear in the dark. Then he sucked in a big breath, did a funny little dance, ran a few steps in place, shook his arms and his fingers, revolved his head on his neck. With straight legs, he touched his toes.

Turning around, taking something out of the pocket of his jeans, Skylar went to the door of the man's motel room. He appeared simply to shake the doorknob. He opened the door, turned on the room's light, entered the room, and closed the door behind him.

"Oh, no!" Jon groaned. "Breaking and entering. Oh, no!" Jon hit the steering wheel with the flat of his hand. "And I'm driving the damned getaway car, probably, damn it, stolen from that damned old whore!"

Minutes passed while Jon's heart thumped loudly in his chest, in his ears. What would he do if the man returned while Skylar was still in his room?

Before Jon had made a decision, the motel room's light snapped out. The door opened.

While Skylar sauntered across the parking lot with something white in his hand, Jon started Mrs. Duffy's car. He put it in gear.

Skylar started to get in the front seat, remembered, got in the back.

As soon as the door was closed, Jon jerked the car forward.

Skylar's head was nowhere in the rearview mirror.

From the floor behind Jon's seat, Skylar's voice said, "Slow and easy, Jon Than. Don't want to raise suspicion on Mrs. Duffy's car."

"'Raise suspicion'! Damn it, Skylar, you just broke into a man's room, and, I suspect, committed burglary!"

"That I did, Jon Than. You got that exactly right."

Back on the road, Jon asked, "Well? Did you discover anything?"

"The man was right taciturn. Strong-lookin' sombitch. Right-handed. That man has ridden hard and long, in this life, on a poor horse over rocky ground."

"Skylar . . ." Jon sighed. "One of these days, most likely, if all goes well, if you're lucky, you are going to find yourself making an appearance in court. I don't think your poetic descriptions of your various crimes will incline judge or jury toward leniency."

"Judge and jury?" Skylar inquired. "Shoot, Jon Than. You sure do think early and late."

Not bothering to figure out what Skylar meant, Jon asked, "What did you take from the man's room?"

"A photograph. And, to be completely honest, a motel envelope to carry it in."

"I don't care too much about the envelope, Skylar. . . . Tell me about the photograph."

"Needs interpretation," Skylar said. "Jon Than? I wonder if you'd be good enough to drive me to the house of Mr. Tommy Barker. An honored veteran and a great American."

"Who is he really, Skylar?"

"The man who found Mary Lou's body, for one. You'll be pleased to meet him, I'm sure. His cabin is on the way home. Sort of."

In the dimly lit corridor, Pepp opened the jail cell's door. In the next cell, he could distinguish the large bulk of his only prisoner in captivity awaiting trial on serious charges lying flat on his back on his bunk. The prisoner's naked torso gleamed with sweat.

Pepp swung the cell's door closed but unlatched behind him.

Sitting on the edge of the bunk, Pepp took off his boots and unbuttoned his shirt. He pulled his shirttail from his trousers.

He lay on the bunk.

The cell smelled. More of antiseptic than of other things, Pepp was glad to notice. The thin mattress on the metal bunk shelf smelled, and not of antiseptic. The county could not afford to supply a new mattress for Tony Duffy every Tuesday and Saturday night. The cell was hot and airless.

Pepp ran his eyes along the edge of the metal slab on the roof through which various prisoners had escaped over the years. They had all been local people not guilty of more than drunken misjudgment or plain high spirits. Sooner or later, they had each paid their little fines, taken their punishment with good grace, having been able to save face in their community, express their manliness by having escaped the county jail. For the rest of their lives, they had a tale to tell, with no bitterness toward the sheriff, his department, police in general, law and order, justice. Frequently, such escapees had become the staunchest friends of the Sheriff's Department.

Without doubt Fleas had thought Skylar Whitfield fit into such a category when he put him in this cell: a local good kid inadvertently tangled with the law, whose friends would rescue him soon enough, hide him until matters got straightened out. Was Fleas wrong? That jackknife. That damned jackknife.

Without doubt deputies Hanson and Aimes had put Skylar's cousin, that snotty Yankee kid, into this cell, because they knew he didn't belong in jail, so they could say, *Well, you know we didn't really mean to keep him, you know which cell we put him in.*

There had never been murders like the murders of Mary Lou Simes and Jack Simes in Greendowns County before that Yankee kid, Wayne Whitfield's son, showed up. Series murders. Senseless, apparently unmotivated murders. That snotty, physically strong, right-handed Yankee kid. Friday night, early Saturday morning, was he really asleep in Skylar Whitfield's truck outside the Holler? Did anyone see him asleep in the truck? He was present at the fight in the quarry between Skylar and Jack Simes and his two buddies. Who but he says he went to his room after Skylar dropped him off near the farm that night, and took off his watch just a little after twelve-thirty? He easily could have walked to the Simeses' house. Baseball bat; he wouldn't have known the baseball bat was in the shed. No, but he would have known there was something in that shed with which to strike a person from behind, a baseball bat, a hammer, a tire iron. With the baseball bat in his hand, he could have waited in the dark of the shed for the county's football hero to arrive home in his fancy truck, turn off the truck lights, climb down, start toward the house, sick and confused over his sister's murder. . . .

The boy's mind had been disciplined in a way foreign to Sheriff Culpepper, foreign to Greendowns County. He had a different value system, aloof, protected. He thought on a plane from which he could choose to be objective, subjective, involved or not. He had had so much in life he was probably bored, especially in Greendowns County. In the dim, smelly, airless cell, Pepp shook his head. Tomorrow, when he picked up his personal car to go to the airport to pick up Sammy, he would find his copy of *Crime and Punishment.*

Right now, Pepp was tired, too tired, too worn out from his nose cold, too depressed and distracted by personal matters, his divorcing Martha Jane, his ability to see Sammy through college threatened by divorce, loss of career, to think seriously about a kid coming into an area and committing a series of murders out of boredom, for the thrill, the experience, the statement, and, because he was sure no one would suspect him because he really didn't know the people he killed.

The fact was, that of all the people in Greendowns County, Mary Lou and Jack Simes were two the Yankee kid had met, or at least seen, knew of, probably had realized were greatly admired. . . .

The heavy, deep voice rumbled from the next cell. "You floatin', or you crashin'?"

It took Pepp a moment to realize he was being addressed. "What?"

"You floatin', or you crashin'?"

Pepp said, "Summerhouse, this is Sheriff Culpepper. If you don't shut up and let me get some sleep, I'm gonna rip off your face and stuff it in your ear."

"You in here, Sheriff?"

Pepp sneezed.

There was a deep chuckle. "I allus heard you is a user."

"Summerhouse . . ."

"A supplier, too. I heard your very own wife says so. My, my. So here you is, ain't you?"

"Summerhouse, I'm here to get a night's sleep."

"Lordy, won't it be somethin' to see the sheriff, his very own self, rise up and disappear through the roof? I just think I'll stay awake, this night."

"Shut up."

"That's all right, Sheriff. I haven't got nothin' particular much to do tomorrow."

Pepp smiled and shook his head.

His sweating seemed to be helping drain his sinuses.

When Pepp was almost asleep, he heard Summerhouse rumble, "Sheriff? I sure am glad you cotched me, anyway."

18

"You gonna shoot me?" Skylar asked.

He stood under the porch light of the log cabin.

He had waited a long time after knocking on the door. Immediately after he knocked, a light went on in the cabin. Skylar did not knock again. He heard sounds from inside. Something dropped on the floor. There was a scraping noise.

The porch light finally went on. The door opened slowly.

In red bikini underpants, Tommy Barker stood on the other side of the screen door. There was a crutch under his left armpit. There was a shotgun in his right hand, aimed through the screen at Skylar's feet.

"No. I'm not going to shoot you." Tommy pushed the screen door open with the shotgun's barrel. "Come in, Skylar."

Skylar stepped into the cabin. Jon had remained in Mrs. Duffy's car down the dark lane.

Skylar had known the veteran's left hand had only two fingers, no thumb, and that he was stiff-legged, but he had not known Tommy had no left leg at all. Standing inside the door, Skylar watched Tommy lean the shotgun against the wall and work his way on one leg and the crutch across the one room of the cabin to a Morris chair by the stone fireplace and drop himself into it. In the corner of the cabin, on the floor next to a single bed, was an artificial leg.

"How come you're not out hunting me?" Skylar asked. Despite his handicaps, Tommy was known as one of the best woodsmen, hunters, fishermen, in the county.

"I don't hunt humans anymore." Although Tommy Barker's hair was graying, it was still full and curly. His eyes were a clear, brilliant blue. His face was free of wrinkles, except near his eyes. His body had no fat on it. As he looked up at Skylar from the chair, Tommy's lips and eyes smiled. "Though I don't know how I can help you, Skylar."

Tommy, with the aid of a few friends, had built the cabin. It was authentic caulked logs. The fieldstones of the fireplace had been placed by hand. Yet between the beams sparkled a rough white plaster. The floor was polished hardwood.

Everywhere in the room were bright colors. Red, white, and blue curtains draped the windows. A large, circular blue, green, red, brown braided rug covered the floor of the sitting area in front of the fireplace. The two Morris chairs and the wood-frame couch they faced across the cobbler-bench coffee table were cushioned in forest green and canary yellow.

Against the wall across from the kitchen eating area was an entertainment center with a large-screen television and a stereo system with two massive speakers in the corners of the cabin.

Skylar said, "This place is neat."

Tommy looked around. "I try to keep it clean."

"Of course it's clean. I mean, it's neat!"

Tommy laughed. "Thanks."

Looking at the handsome, seven-fingered, one-legged man in the Morris chair, Skylar had a great temptation to blurt: *Why isn't there a woman here, with you, loving you?* Of course, he did not. Since returning from the war, from the hospital, Tommy Barker had used his government pension to work for anyone in the county, the old, the poor, the more seriously handicapped, for free. He would just show up at some needy person's home in his pickup truck, and, with little conversation, fix the plumbing, the wiring, the roof, chop wood, paint, and prune. He always paid for the materials out of his own pension checks.

Now he was not complaining that Skylar had gotten him out of bed in the middle of the night.

"Why don't you sit down?" Tommy asked.

"I'd like for you to interpret something for me." Taking the motel's envelope out of the back pocket of his jeans, Skylar approached Tommy's chair. "This photograph."

Skylar handed it to him.

Tommy leaned forward with the photograph in his hand to get the best light.

He said, "It's a lieutenant and his platoon standing around a half-track. From their dress, equipment, and the picture's background, I'd say they're about to go on patrol."

Skylar asked, "What do the inked-in black crosses on the men's chests mean?"

"It means they're dead now," Tommy answered. "Killed in action, more'n likely."

"One has a red X on his chest."

"Yes."

"What does that mean?"

"I don't know."

"Is a man missing from this picture?"

"What do you mean?"

"Someone took the picture."

Tommy looked closely at the picture. "It's not a full platoon. But platoons that saw a lot of action were seldom consistently full."

Tommy handed the picture back to Skylar. "You do recognize the lieutenant, don't you, Skylar?"

Skylar squinted at the picture. "Somehow looks familiar to me. How can that be?"

"You're too young to recognize him. The lieutenant in that picture is John Simes."

Suddenly, the facial features of John Simes popped out of the photograph at Skylar. "Of course it is." John Simes as a young lieutenant was wearing a slight smile. Skylar had never seen John Simes smile. "Mr. Barker, what do you know about John Simes, anyway?"

"Know about him?"

"Yeah. What was he like, younger?"

Tommy shrugged. "Not much. Used to be pretty handy with a pack of cards, but I haven't heard much about that in years."

"I don't even know what he does for a living," Skylar said.

"Travels. Sells heavy equipment or something."

"Heavy equipment?"

"Construction equipment or something. I don't really know for sure, Skylar. His mind always seems to be somewhere else. Doesn't exactly invite conversation."

"Do you recognize anyone else in this photo?" Skylar handed the photo back to Tommy, who leaned forward again and studied it.

"No," Tommy said.

"I do." Skylar took the photograph from Tommy Barker and slid it into the envelope. "I was talkin' to one of these men less than an hour ago."

"Good morning, Miss Holman."

Before eight on a bright Tuesday morning, Skylar had knocked on the kitchen door of the eighty-three-year-old spinster.

She answered the door in a light bathrobe over pure white cotton pajamas. Her eyes were as bright as the morning sun.

"Why, Skylar! I'm real glad to see you!"

Skylar looked around at her sunlit backyard. "Hot already," he said.

"Going to be a broiler." She pushed the screen door toward him. "Come in."

In the kitchen, she looked him up and down. "Except for the sweat already on you, boy, you look as clean and fresh and rested as a bull on his way to stud." She felt the sweat on the back of his head with her hand, then brushed his sweaty hair off his forehead. "Bein' wanted for murder doesn't seem to be affectin' your health or good nature any, Skylar."

"No, ma'am." Skylar frowned. "But I do admit I find it a bit worrisome."

"I expect it is. Are you hungry?"

"Sure."

"How about I fix you a nice breakfast?"

Skylar grinned. "I wouldn't leave none to waste."

"You like scrambled eggs?" Skylar nodded. "Country ham?" Skylar nodded. "Bacon?" Skylar nodded. "Sausage?" Skylar nodded. "Toast?" Skylar nodded. "Skylar, you drink coffee, your age?"

"Yes, ma'am."

"That's good," Rose Holman said. "This country was built on black coffee, strong whiskey, and raw tobaccy. It's goin' to hell since men began seriously reformin'."

"Yes, ma'am."

"I've got some peach preserve, too, I expect you wouldn't stick your nose up at."

"No, ma'am, I sure wouldn't."

Having a good breakfast while Jon was parked off the road in the bushes made Skylar even hungrier.

"You ever hear tell of the old maxim that the way to a man's heart is through his stomach?"

Skylar laughed. "You already got my heart, Miss Holman, you know that."

She flipped up the front of his T-shirt, making him back off, laughing. "Well, your heart better be bigger'n your stomach, Skylar, or I won't want any part of it."

As she opened the refrigerator, Skylar asked, "Can I help?"

"No, you just sit down and tell me all about how it feels havin' the law after you. That's an experience I don't expect to have, here on in."

"I wonder if I could use your phone," Skylar said.

"Sure."

"I want to call my father and the sheriff."

"Right there on the wall. If you want privacy, there's another one in by my bed, in case the sickness ever visits me in the night."

Skylar picked up the wall phone and began dialing. "I don't need privacy."

Cracking eggs into a bowl, Rose Holman shook her head.

"I don't know about you, Skylar. You gotta be quicker about acceptin' an invitation into a lady's bedroom than that."

Grinning at her, Skylar said into the phone, "Dad?"

At the other end of the line, Dan Whitfield said, "Guess I shouldn't ask where you are."

"I'm all right."

"Guess this phone isn't being tapped."

"Don't care if it is," Skylar said. "You and Mom doin' all right?"

"You know it. Mrs. McJane tells us your bed was slept in yesterday. She knows it was you from the way you left your shavin' gear on the sink." Dan said, "I don't suppose it would do me any good to ask you to present yourself to the sheriff."

"In fact, I'm about to call him."

"That's good. You could come home. We could have Frank Murrey here. . . ."

"Pretty soon, won't be no need for all that. Dad, what does Mr. Simes do? I mean, for a living?"

"He speaks loosely of being in the real estate development business. Construction. Something."

" 'Loosely'?"

"He never seems very specific. John always used to play his cards pretty close to his chest."

"That's a pretty good business, isn't it?"

"It has been."

"Developin' real estate, he must need a lot of insurance. Hasn't he ever come to you for any?"

"Not for anything except his property here, his vehicles."

"No life insurance?"

"No."

"Why not? Haven't you ever tried to sell him some?"

"Sure I have. He's always said, when I've tried to sell him life insurance, for M.L.'s sake, that he has some of that term insurance the banks sell. Not much, I gather."

"How come no business insurance?"

"The real estate he develops is out of state."

"Why? Why doesn't he develop real estate around here?"

"Well," Dan answered dryly. "I heard someone was cogitatin' on buildin' a new house over on Muckle Creek a few years ago. . . ."

"So where does he develop real estate?"

"Where?"

"I know he's always travelin'."

"Listening to him tell airlines horror stories, seems he's always either comin' from or goin' to Puerto Rico."

"I would think there would be enough people in Puerto Rico who would want to develop Puerto Rico real estate."

"And Nevada."

"Pretty far apart. Different climates. That doesn't sound too efficient to me."

"I know little of that particular business."

"Dad, would you say that Mr. Simes has not exactly been rakin' in the folding green stuff in recent years?"

"Yes," Dan said, slowly. "I would say that."

"He and Mrs. Simes drive old trash cars. Their house needs painting."

"John Simes doesn't need to do well. His family is well taken care of."

"Has Mr. Simes ever asked you to invest in his business?"

"Yes. More than once."

"Have you? I mean, invested?"

"No."

"Why not?"

"I just haven't. Your mother and I don't have that kind of money, Skylar. What little we do have, we don't risk. For one thing, we thought you might want to go to college, you know?"

"Even when he's asked you to invest, he hasn't told you much about his business?"

"I never let any such conversation get that far. I will say . . . what will I say? . . . he's always approached me sort of wrong."

"What do you mean?"

"I don't know. His attitude has always sort of been, 'I need this money now; I'll explain later,' not that he's ever said exactly that. He's always asked for bridging loans, cash money to get him over a weekend, that sort of thing."

"Isn't that the sort of thing banks do?"

"Yes. I would say John's business accounts have been stretched pretty thin, now and again. But that happens even to people who are personally well off."

"I wish I understood more."

"Why are you asking about all this, Skylar?"

"I guess I'm wonderin' why he's always such a sourpuss."

"He hasn't always been. I gather he had a rather 'bad war,' as we used to call it. He spent a lot of time in the thick of things."

"Do you know of any specific incident, anything in particular that might have happened to him during that war?"

"No. He's never talked about it."

"Ever wounded?"

"I don't believe so. Never seriously, anyway."

"Oh."

"Answer my question, Skylar: Are you going to start doing the sensible thing, and clear up this police matter?"

"Yes, sir, I am," Skylar answered. "Bye."

While Skylar was looking up the general business number of the police station, Rose Holman, at the stove, said, "Don't worry about the Simes family money, Skylar. There's plenty and more there. When Aggie Church died—M.L.'s mother?—she left enough to run the county. John and M.L. just don't like spendin' it, I figure."

"Mr. Haddam?" Skylar said into the phone. "Good mornin'. This is Skylar Whitfield. How're ya doin'?"

Fleas called out, "Sheriff?" Then he said, "I'm puttin' you through, Skylar. Soon as he gets to his desk."

"Thank you kindly for your attention, Mr. Haddam," Skylar said.

"Hello?"

"Sheriff Culpepper, this is Skylar Whitfield. How're ya doin' this fine mornin'?"

"Skylar . . ."

"You got a nose cold?"

"Mind tellin' me where you are?"

"Sounds like you got a nose cold to me. Summer colds are wicked. They keep you out of the crick. You drinkin' enough water?"

"Skylar, all we got on you is the jackknife and escaping justice. Everything else is circumstantial. Where can we pick you up?"

"Shoot, Sheriff, my kidney still hurts from the kickin' your handsome deputy gave me last time you-all picked me up."

"Nothing like that will ever happen again."

"Plus, your accommodations are not suitable for an honest citizen."

Pepp said, "Skylar, doin' what you're doin', you're just convincin' a lot of gun-happy good-old boys around here you're as guilty as someone smilin' at four in the mornin'. If you come in, we set bail, it would change things considerably."

"I do thank you for your advice, Sheriff, but may I change the topic of conversation for a moment?"

"Go ahead."

"Sheriff, I have discovered the murderer of Mary Lou and Jack Simes as sure as God taught hens to lay eggs."

"Go on."

"There was a man at the Holler Friday night, a middle-aged, tough-lookin' hombre, who offered to buy me a drink. And asked if that was Mary Lou Simes down at the end of the bar. It was."

"So?"

"So Mary Lou Simes was killed shortly later."

"Who was he?"

"A stranger to this county."

"Was he wearin' a suit?"

"Doubt this old boy owns a suit. Long hair, beard."

"Christ," Pepp said. "You've come up with a bushy-haired stranger. No one ever said you're stupid, Skylar."

"Sheriff, I'd admire you more if you don't take the Lord's name in vain."

"What? You little shit!"

"It's all right if you alienate me, I suppose."

"You're making this up."

"No, sir, I'm not. I hunted him down last night. He's stayin' at the Las Vegas Motel. He's drivin' a trash compact car with Indiana license-plate-number 691947EJ."

"Go on."

"Well, sir, a Veterans Administration envelope in his motel room gives his name as Henry Kelly and his address as 13059 Circe Road, Bloomington, Indiana. Want me to spell any of that for you?"

"I've got it."

"You ready for the hot news?"

"Anything you can dish out, Skylar."

"He's a member of Lieutenant John Simes's old platoon."

"John Simes was a captain."

"Must have been a lieutenant sometime."

"What's all this supposed to prove? Except that you are an artful dodger?"

"I'm just notifyin' you that a member of Mr. Simes's old platoon showed up in town just before the Simes kids got murdered, and I can testify this very same man was looking for these very same kids, at least one of them, and, that he was at the Holler the night Mary Lou was murdered, and, that he knew who she was. Now I'm not a po-lice man, but all that seems pretty conclusive to me."

"A 'po-lice man' would say you are trying to lead us on a wild-goat chase."

"I'm not sure you're hearing me, Sheriff. It must be the cold blockin' your ears."

"Skylar, are you tryin' to tell me you broke into a room at the Las Vegas Motel last night?"

"Did I say that?"

"Neither the Las Vegas Motel nor anyone staying there reported any sort of a break-in or disturbance."

"I was as fast and dirty as a suckling pig."

"I'll tell you one more thing, Skylar: We know about where

you are. I sincerely doubt you could have gotten across this county last night without being spotted and reported. In a word, Skylar Whitfield, you're clever, but you're full of bullshit. In fact, you're so alarmed that we're honing in on you that you call me up with this cock-and-bull story to try to throw us off."

"You don't believe me?"

"Not one damned word out of your mouth. Now tell me precisely where you are."

"I cannot tell a lie."

"Skylar, you realize how predictable your calling me up with some tale about a bushy-haired stranger is?"

"Aren't you goin' to check it out, Sheriff?"

"Hell, no. I'm tellin' you, Skylar, you've got totally unauthorized people with guns out lookin' for you right now, just for the fun of huntin' and shootin' you down. Skylar, you're only making things worse for yourself. Tell me where you are, and I'll come get you personally."

"No, thanks," Skylar said. "I don't want to catch your cold."

He hung up.

"Good boy." On the kitchen table, Rose Holman had set a tall glass of orange juice and a steaming plate of eggs, ham, bacon, sausage, toast. There was also a cup of coffee and a jar of peach preserve. "Even the sheriff of this county ought be talked to, if he took the Lord's name in vain. Now sit down, Skylar." Rose Holman sat herself at the kitchen table. "Tell me all about how it is to be wanted by the law."

"I tell you," Skylar said, forking a fried egg into his mouth, "I'm seriously beginnin' to question Sheriff Culpepper's professional competence."

"Well, Skylar." Rose Holman sat at the kitchen table to watch him eat. "Right now the sheriff has some personal problems that must be just about drivin' him crazy."

"Mighty worrisome." Skylar drained the orange juice from his glass. "Yes, ma'am. It's almost enough to make you lose your appetite. . . ."

After sitting quietly at his desk for a while, cursing the lack of equipment, even the ability to trace a phone call, Pepp blew his nose for what seemed like the nine-thousandth time in less than two days. His throat felt scratchy.

He found himself thinking about meeting Sammy at the airport that afternoon. How did Sammy really feel about the divorce of her parents? Pepp had read divorce was hard on the children of any marriage, at any age.

Talking to her, listening to her on the ride home, might be a help to them both.

Fleas stood in the doorway. "Not going anywhere?"

For a moment, Pepp wondered what Fleas meant. *Damn! That kid doesn't need to try to create a diversion for me. Martha Jane has already done so.* "Oh. No. Skylar Whitfield did not have the courtesy to leave his current address."

"Where could he have been calling from?"

Pepp shrugged. "Anywhere. The Las Vegas Motel did not report any disturbance last night, did it?"

"No, sir."

"Ol' Skylar would rather have us out pursuin' a bushy-haired stranger than himself. He must be gettin' hungry and tired. We'll come across him soon. Or, more likely, he'll turn himself in. You know, Fleas, I just had an inspiration. Have the boys check out the quarry."

"Yes, sir."

"The kids around here believe that's their own Sherwood Forest." Pepp smiled. "About the third generation to do so, I know of."

Fleas said, "While you were on the phone, Coroner Murphy and the state forensic lab called."

"Okay. I'll call 'em back. And, Fleas, I'll be leaving at noon. I won't be back until about five o'clock, I hope not later."

Fleas's eyebrows rose. "You will?"

"I will," Pepp said firmly.

"Well, if you're really needed, should I call Fairer's apartment?"

"No." Pepp glowered through red, runny eyes at his dispatcher. "Goddamnit. I will not be at Fairer's apartment!"

19

"Sammy!" Outside the airline's security gate, Pepp put his head on his daughter's shoulder and gave her a big hug. She was carrying a sack purse and a book. She hugged him back.

"Come on." Arm around her shoulder, he began walking them toward the sign that said BAGGAGE. "As soon as we get your gear, we'll be on our way home."

In the middle of the corridor, Sammy stopped. "I don't have any gear."

"No luggage?"

"I didn't bring any luggage, Dad. I'm going back to school in an hour or so." She looked at her wristwatch. "Well, my flight leaves in an hour and twenty minutes."

"What?"

Frowning, Sammy looked up into her father's face. "I just wanted to talk to you, Dad."

"The telephone was invented some time ago, Samantha. Seems to me you know how to use it. . . ."

"Don't worry. I'm spending money I earned working extra hours in the bookstore."

"Then there's the United States Mail. . . ." Pepp shrugged. "Well, what do we do?" He looked around the airport terminal. "Want a sandwich?"

"Sure. Just let me check my flight."

Feeling conspicuous being dressed in a sheriff's uniform somewhere he wasn't sheriff, Pepp stood in the middle of the airport terminal watching his daughter at the ticket counter confirm her flight back to the university. In honesty, Pepp had to admit to himself that Samantha was not the most beautiful girl in the world, nor was she the most intelligent or the most accomplished, but she was his daughter, the person he loved, had ever loved, probably ever would love, most in his life.

Having taken cold tablets, Pepp had worked through the morning feeling dry-mouthed and groggy.

He had returned Coroner Murphy's call and learned nothing new. Jack Simes had been beaten to death, probably by the baseball bat discovered at the scene of the crime, probably first struck hard on the back of his head from behind, probably by a full-sized, powerful, right-handed person. Once down, Jack's head had been beaten unmercifully. The young man had eaten cheeseburgers and french-fried potatoes, ketchup, three to five hours before death, and, nearer the time of death had drunk less than five ounces of beer. There was no other alcohol or drugs in his system. Otherwise, his body showed no injuries other than old and known football injuries.

The state forensics lab, which was now giving top priority to the Simes murders, added little information. Jack Simes had been killed by that baseball bat, but after the event the bat had been wiped clean of fingerprints with an oil-stained rag. The rag was not discovered. The patch of earth in the shed most likely compressed by someone standing, hiding in the dark, awaiting the victim, offered no real evidence of shoe size, make of boot, size of person, personal habits, duration of wait. Offered only as an opinion was that the murderer probably was a good-sized male.

That morning Pepp also had received a short, closed-door visit from attorney Frank Murrey, who, smiling beguilingly, reported the rumor he had just heard that Pepp and Fairer Spinner were having an affair, and that such, if a fact, or even if generally accepted as fact, would damage Pepp's suit for divorce. Frank questioned if Martha Jane was the source of this allegation as well.

Pepp did not respond. He sighed and looked at the walls of his office, which seemed to be getting closer to him. To himself, he wondered why he, the sheriff, could not discover the whereabouts of a teen-aged boy, while apparently the whole county knew where he himself privately had spent a few hours late Sunday night and early Monday morning. Sardonically, he realized it was because he had never done such a thing before, in his married life, that made his having done so once of such great interest.

Frank said that if there was any truth to the rumor, Pepp would be well advised to cease, desist, or postpone the relationship, or even the appearance of such a relationship until after the divorce had been settled.

A little later than he had expected, Pepp went to his house. Martha Jane was working with her "evidence" at the dining-room table. Without speaking, he found his copy of *Crime and Punishment* and carried it out with him.

As he was leaving, Martha Jane said, "Be back before six."

Instead of answering, Pepp noted to himself that Martha Jane did not ask him where he was going, or why he needed the family car. Pepp always had been scrupulous about not using the sheriff's official car for personal business.

Starting the old Chevrolet, Pepp chuckled. Maybe Martha Jane would tell people he was dashing out of the county to deposit more drug profits into his concealed bank accounts.

Before climbing the ramp onto the highway, Pepp noticed the signs for the Las Vegas Motel. He hadn't time then, but on his way home, with Samantha, he thought, he really ought to stop at the motel, question the clerk regarding one—what was the name Skylar had given him?—Henry Kelly, question briefly this Henry Kelly, if he was there, if he existed; ask to look through the man's room if he was not there. The room clerk would oblige him.

Fairer Kelly Spinner . . .

And people knew Pepp and Fairer had spent Sunday night together.

That boy, Skylar Whitfield, was trying on some elaborate joke. . . .

"Sorry it took so long," Sammy said, returning to her father in the airport terminal.

"You haven't given us much time."

"I know."

"Sandwich?"

"Sure."

"There's a food bay over here."

"I think it's called a snack bar," Sammy said, following him.

"If there was a pit and lift in the floor, I'd guess they could change your oil and give you a grease job while you eat."

"Oh, Dad."

Sammy ordered a bacon, lettuce, and tomato sandwich; he, a roast beef on rye. They each ordered iced tea.

Their table was very small. Samantha put her book and purse on it.

Not many were eating at that hour.

She took his hand in hers. "Oh, Dad."

"I guess it wouldn't do much good to ask you to try not to be too distressed, Sammy. You know your mother and I haven't been happy with each other for many years, now. If you can just tell yourself that we're doing each other more harm than good now, and that at least I don't see any way of improving the situation . . ." These were the remarks Pepp had prepared on the drive to the airport.

His daughter's face showed more pain than he had ever seen. Shocked, he stopped talking.

"Dad, can't you get help?"

"You mean marriage counseling? I suppose—"

"That's not what I mean."

"What do you mean, Sammy?"

"For drugs."

"*Drugs?*" Having shouted, Pepp looked around the snack

bar to see how much attention he had caused. "What in God's name are you saying, Sammy?"

Her hands caressing his were hot and sticky. "I know, I mean, I've read, I mean, I've read and heard how hard it is to get off cocaine—are you using crack?" There was complete sincerity in her question. "You need help."

Pepp had never fainted in his life. Now his loss of breath, his loss of focus, the feeling of weakness that slammed his body like a hurricane, made him wonder if he was about to faint. He straightened his back and sucked in as big a breath as his muscles allowed. "Sammy! . . ."

"I know." She wiped her eyes with her paper napkin. "I expect I'm the last person you'd ever want to know, ever want to have talk to you about it."

"Where did you ever hear of such a thing?" Pepp realized his mouth was working without much thought.

"I've had courses in it all through school, Dad. Even you came to the school once a year to lecture on drug abuse. At college—"

"Sammy, where did you hear I use drugs?"

"Oh, Dad . . ."

"Has your mother called you within the last day or two and told you I use drugs? Answer yes or no."

"Yes."

Fuming, Pepp breathed deeply. Because of physical distance, Sammy's being away at college, the closeness of Pepp's relationship with Sammy, he had thought her invulnerable to Martha Jane's slander.

Sammy said, "Kids have always said there couldn't be any drugs in Greendowns County without your—"

"Kids always want to believe things like that! There are damned few drugs in Greendowns County!"

"There are drugs in Greendowns County."

"There are drugs everywhere! We've made how many drug busts? . . ." Pepp was so astounded, he couldn't remember figures dear to his heart.

"Yeah." Sammy looked aside. "Getting rid of the competition, eh, Dad? Every time you've made a bust, that's what they say. . . ."

Their sandwiches and drinks were plopped onto their little table beside Samantha's book and purse.

Neither Pepp nor his daughter even looked at their lunch.

Pepp took another big breath through his mouth. His sinuses were throbbing. "Sammy, do you really think, believe, I use drugs?"

"Oh, Dad, look at you! When you greeted me out there"— she waved toward the arrival gates—"you immediately put your head down on my shoulder so I couldn't see your face up close. Your eyes are glassy. Your nose is red. Your mouth is dry."

"Jesus. I've got a cold. I don't want you to catch it."

"Sure. You've gotten so used to concealing it, you've got all the tricks. You've got a cold. Is that why you're so pale and you're having trouble breathing? Where are the sunglasses you usually wear?"

They were in his shirt pocket. "You know they're prescription."

"Do I?"

"Sammy," Pepp said carefully. "I am more shocked at this moment than I have ever been in my life."

"You have big mood swings," Sammy said as if reporting the obvious. "You're with me, other people, fine. With me you've always acted like a kid. With people you've known all your life, you act like a stranger. As soon as Mother shows up, you get as tense as an I-don't-know-what."

"I've got feelings. I react."

"You go out and run a hundred miles, and then you're up all night pretending you're reading. Who the hell do you think you've been kidding, Dad?"

"Sammy, just tell me one thing: Did your mother ever tell you I am using, abusing, addicted to, out-of-control with drugs before I told her I am divorcing her?"

"You can't just use drugs, Dad, without abusing them, without abusing yourself. And no drug user thinks he's addicted.

Sure, I'm certain my big, macho daddy thinks he's strong enough to handle the use of drugs, but no one is, you know."

"Thanks for the lesson. Answer my question."

"She told me something I always knew."

"Like hell."

Sammy took a bunch of napkins from the table dispenser and cried into the wad. "You tried to shoot Ted Callister."

"I never did."

"You did. That time he came to the house."

"Sammy, if I tried to shoot Ted Callister, I would have shot him."

"You almost did."

"That boy was no good! He's now serving time in a Texas prison for rape! I know this as a fact, Sammy."

"You shot out the window at him."

"I shot in the air! It was the third night in a row that boy had come around the house at two, three o'clock in the morning. I had tried talking with him. Did you want to be a victim of his?"

"You said he was trying to steal our hens."

"I was trying to scare him off for good and all. And I did. You can thank me for it."

"We didn't have any hens," Sammy sobbed. Again she reached for her father's hand. "Dad, you were hallucinating!"

"I was like hell!" Pepp's tone was that of a shout, but his voice was low. "I had to scare him off. I shot in the air out my bedroom window. I made a joke of it. Everybody knew we didn't have any hens. What else could I do? The boy wasn't really guilty of anything, at that point, other than being a nuisance. And of being a car thief, come to think of it."

"Sure. You can rationalize, explain away anything."

Pepp regained some objectivity. Here he was, an older man, in a sheriff's uniform, at an airport snack-bar table, with a weeping young woman trying to hold his hand.

"Sammy?" he said. "You and I have got big trouble. How about canceling your flight, coming home a few days . . ."

"I have two papers to write and a lab report to finish."

"I don't think those are the most important things in the world, right now."

"I haven't heard you deny it."

"Deny that I use drugs? I do not use or abuse drugs, and I never have."

" 'Abuse'!" she scoffed.

"I said, 'use or abuse.' "

"Oh, Dad. Denial is a part of the sickness. I'll bet you have some of that shit on you right this minute. Who'd stop a man in a sheriff's uniform carrying a six-shooter even in an airport? I notice you didn't go through the security checks to meet me. You could have."

Pepp sighed. For a moment, he was speechless.

Sammy said, "Which came first? I mean, I know how much you wanted me to go to a great, private university."

"What are you talking about now?"

"Money."

"You mean, money from drugs."

Sammy glanced at her watch. "I've got to get to my gate."

"You haven't eaten your sandwich."

"I'm not hungry." She reached for her book and her purse on the table. "Oh, Dad, I don't care about you and Mother. Well, I do care. I just want you to get help."

Pepp took his daughter's hand. "Sammy, is this really what you think of me? With your knowledge of me, do you really think such a thing is possible? From your perspective, do you honestly believe I am controlled, motivated, by a drug addiction? Is this the sum total of our relationship from your point of view?"

Sammy shook off his hand as if resettling her bracelets and stood up. "Just get help, Dad." That was the knife in his heart. She then twisted the knife by saying, "And remember: I love you."

He watched her cross the snack bar to the terminal corridor and turn left toward the departure gates. To return to the university.

Pepp had no idea how long he sat at the little table staring into the airport corridor.

Finally, a waitress stopped at his table. "Shall I clear off?"

"Sure."

"You want anything else?"

"Just to sit here a minute."

She was bending over the table, clearing away the ignored sandwiches and glasses of iced tea. "Want a drink, Sheriff?"

"A drink of what?"

"Vodka?"

Pepp remembered that he had taken cold tablets that would compound their effect with alcohol. "Sure. Bring me a double vodka."

"A double-vodka what? A double-vodka martini?"

"Sure," Pepp said. "A double-vodka martini. Why the hell not?"

"Tandy?" Skylar asked. Her sweaty face was against the sweaty skin of his chest. Even under the shade of a black-walnut tree, the late afternoon was hot.

"I'm asleep," she said.

"What do Puerto Rico and the state of Nevada have in common?"

Tandy answered, "Neither one is in Greendowns County."

"Is that all you care about?"

"That's all."

"Seriously. Answer me."

Her eyes opened wide in thought. "I've seen pictures of them both. You know, askin' me to visit there, not knowin' who they were askin'. One is a luxurious, tropical, jungly is-land; the other a luxurious, hot, deserty place."

"Tourists," Skylar said. "They have tourists in common."

"How come I never see pictures in magazines asking me to visit Greendowns County?"

"Not luxurious, I guess."

"We have a public swimming pool now."

"No umbrellas. I think it must be the umbrellas that make a swimming pool luxurious."

"Why would anybody want to be a tourist?" Tandy asked. "Why would anybody want to be someplace she's not at home?"

"Do you hear something?" They both listened. "Someone?"

"Yes." She sprang up. "Let's you go, Skylar."

He remained as he was, on the tarpaulin from the truck, his back against the tree. "I'm not going anyplace."

"That's Julep's bark."

"Yes."

"Julep is leadin' someone to us."

They remained quiet and still until Julep scooted through the underbrush. He danced in circles in front of Tandy and Skylar, greeting them.

Petting the wriggling dog, Skylar said, "What have you done to me, Julep?"

A slim, shirtless figure in blue jeans came through the woods, stopped, looked at them, then came forward.

Tandy said, "Jon Than." She put on her T-shirt.

" 'Afternoon," Jon said.

"Ha," Skylar said. "Hot enough for you?"

"I wasn't looking for you two," Jon said. "I didn't mean to find you. I was just taking the dog on a walk, following the dog."

Skylar said, "You're getting some color, Jon Than. You look almost useful with a red nose, red cheeks, and red shoulders. You could almost be put up as a Stop sign."

Jon was not standing straight. "It's so hot here, I have to force myself to move."

"Better'n bein' cold," Tandy muttered, "with your bones all brickly."

" 'Brickly,' " Jon said. "Guess I won't question that word."

"Sit down." Skylar smoothed the tarpaulin. "You're sweatin' like a hog at first sight of a skillet."

"I thought it might be cooler, walking in the woods." Jon sat on the rough ground with his arms around his knees. He looked at Tandy, then at Skylar. "Honest, I wasn't looking for you."

"I believe that," Skylar said.

"If I wasn't looking for you, and I found you, how come all the people who are looking for you can't find you?"

"Because they're lookin'." Skylar grinned. "They're operatin' on the principle we're hidin'."

"We're not hidin'," Tandy said.

"Feel the little breeze?" Skylar asked.

"Oftentimes we come here," Tandy said. "Julep knows that."

"Jon Than," Skylar said, "we were just discussin' on somethin' maybe you're smart enough and educated enough to help us figure out."

Tandy sat down cross-legged on the tarpaulin. "Has to do with umbrellas around swimming pools, near as I can figure."

"Jon Than? What do Puerto Rico and the state of Nevada have in common?"

Jon stretched his arms. "Gambling."

"Shoot," Tandy said, "gamblin's pretty common everywhere, I reckon. I mean, that's real common. Don't have to go to none of those places for to gamble. Gamblin' happens plenty 'round here. One Friday night my brother, Alec?—you haven't met up with him yet, I reckon, Jon Than, he keeps hisself pretty scarce when there are people around he thinks might belittle him, like yourself. Anyway, one Friday night he was gamblin' over at Boss Sly's big old barn, you hear tell of Boss Sly yet, Jon Than, who used to run the moonshine? Well, he still does, of course, but we say 'used to' just to be polite because they don't bother cotchin' him no more, now they got drug dealers to whistle after. Anyway, Alec is a gamblin' away, sippin' the moonshine, which, from what little I've tasted of it, is gamble enough, I mean, sippin' at it is, playin' at cards, that game where everything's supposed to add up to twenty-one or you're busted, and at first poor Alec couldn't get the cards to make twenty-one no matter what he did, how he added 'em up, so he lost his boots. And there he was, I 'spect, wearing his Sunday socks, the holey ones, bein' the only kind Alec ever had. Give him a pair of socks on Tuesday, and by Sunday, be damned if they're not ready to go to church and stomp snakes. Next hand they played, now don't axe me what Alec was playin' on, 'cept that boy was always recognized for his beguilin' grin and willingness to pay anythin' to anybody as long as it's next week, damn all if he doesn't win not one but two little pigs that Abernathy man had thrown in the pot. Did I tell you all this was happenin' on a cold night? The ground was right crunchy. Well, ol' Boss Sly, he laughs and says, 'Well, Alec, I see you lost your boots. Think you can wear them little pigs home?' "

Skylar said, "Gamblin'."

"I've been thinking about 'hisself,' " Jon said. "Either 'hisself' makes more grammatical sense than 'himself,' or I've been here too long."

"You've been here too long," Skylar said.

"Now, Skylar, you be nice. Didn't Jon Than ride you halfway around the state last night with the counties peerin' in on him every time he slowed down enough to let them pass?"

"Anybody ridden Runaway lately?" Skylar asked.

"Not at all," Tandy answered. "Nobody has since Friday."

"How about Dufus?" Skylar asked. "He might have Runaway with him now."

"I told you about Dufus," Tandy said. "He hurt hisself. He hurt his neck."

"How did Dufus hurt his neck?" Jon asked.

Tandy said, "Well, for some reason Dufus put this ladder up against this wooden rail fence down between the sheds? And he begun climbin' the ladder, only Dufus didn't stop climbin' the ladder when he got to the top of the fence, and o' course the ladder swung over the fence like a seesaw, and suddenly Dufus found hisself on the other side of the fence climbin' down it, headfirst. That wouldn't have been so bad, all in all, 'cept he was so surprised he lost his grip and started fallin' down the ladder headfirst, good thing he kept his head up and didn't let it get stuck between rungs, he was goin' so fast he might have hurt hisself considerable worse if he'd 'a' done that, but he gived hisself a pretty good wrench in the neck as it was, when his head finally hit the ground, that is, and his body fell over him."

Jon wiped laughter tears from his sweat-slick cheeks.

Tandy gave Jon her widest-eyed stare. Then she looked at Skylar. "Is that boy laughin' 'cause Dufus done gone and wrenched his neck?"

Skylar looked at his wristwatch. "I'm wonderin' if one of you might do me the considerable favor of goin' and gettin' Runaway."

Tandy asked, "Bring him here?"

"Yeah."

"What're you thinkin', Skylar?"

"That I want to go see Mr. Tommy Barker again. He ought to be gettin' home pretty soon from wherever he's been, if he's been anywhere, that is, and if he's goin' home."

Jon roared with laughter. "You two!"

Tandy was on her feet. "Jon Than can drive you in Mrs. Duffy's car again." She glared down at the laughing Yankee. "If he ever recovers from Dufus's hurtin' his neck, that is."

"Reckon I shouldn't try to get away with the same thing twice," Skylar said. "Anyway, I can get to Mr. Barker's house quicker cross-country on Runaway."

"Fences," Tandy said.

"You ever seen the inside of Mr. Barker's cabin, Tandy?" Skylar asked.

"Never had the privilege."

"Neat."

Tandy started through the woods down the hill. "I'll be back quicker'n an in-law can steal your tools."

Petting Julep, Skylar watched and listened to his cousin laugh.

Jon quoted, " 'He ought to be gettin' home pretty soon from wherever he's been, if he's been anywhere, that is, and if he's goin' home.' "

"You just wait. Watch and see," Skylar said. "It all works out."

"Yes," Jon said. "Like climbing a short fence with a tall ladder."

"Well, I do declare, Jon Than," Skylar said. "I believe you

just committed a metaphor. Time you get home, you might be speakin' halfway purty."

Jon looked into the woods down the hill. "She'll be back 'quicker'n an in-law can steal your tools.' "

"Thing is, Jon Than, in this patch of sufferin', we all still have instinct for each other. And one thing for another."

"What's Dufus's real name?"

"Duffy."

"Any relation to Mrs. Duffy, at the Holler?"

"Her son."

"I see. Mrs. Duffy was pretty strong on the point she's to be called 'Mrs. Duffy.' Are you going to swing at me if I ask if there is, or ever has been, a Mr. Duffy?"

Skylar nodded. "Tony Duffy. He fills the function in Greendowns of bein' the town drunk."

"That's a function?"

"A damned important function," Skylar said. "Warns the li'l chillen off the booze and other self-indulgences, includin' rock candy and goin' bathless long enough to bother other people. Why, if a town doesn't have a town drunk, it doesn't qualify as an upstanding, morally instructive town, wouldn't you agree?"

"Sure," Jon said. "I agree with everything you say, Cousin."

" 'Course, it's a voluntary position. We all appreciate Tony Duffy, the way he keeps himself in the gutter for us all."

"Where is Dufus now? In his shed wondering how he got *hisself* upside down on a ladder?"

"At this very moment," Skylar said, "Dufus is lurking outside the home of the Simes family."

"Why?"

"He's keepin' an eye on Andy-Dandy. Or, at least he's tryin' to. You see, the way I figure it, Jon Than, someone is murderin' the children of M.L. and John Simes. And Andy-Dandy is the only one left. Is that about the way you figure it?"

"Who?" Jon asked. "Why?"

"I'm workin' hard on the answers to both those questions, Jon Than. Yes, sir, I surely am."

20

"You were there." After watching Tommy Barker approach and sit down on the barstool next to him, the man said it as a flat statement.

"I was there," Tommy confirmed.

"Ha, Tommy! How're ya doin'?" Father Jones shook hands with Tommy across the bar. "A cold one?"

"Cold and wet," Tommy said.

What the man did not know was that Tommy Barker had followed him there from the parking lot of the Las Vegas Motel.

"When and where don't matter," the man said. "It was all the same shit."

"All the same," Tommy said agreeably, although he remembered that during that faraway war, even deep in-country, some had had it considerably better than others.

Putting a cold beer on the bar, Father Jones said, "On the house, Tommy."

"Thanks," Tommy said to Father Jones.

The bartender at the Holler said, "There's few around this county who wouldn't say 'Thank you,' to you, Tommy."

"Sure," Tommy said softly. "I'm an inspiration to you all."

"What's that?" Father Jones asked.

"I'm just thankin' Mrs. Duffy, and you-all."

The man on the next barstool had heard what Tommy had said.

"You're no more over it than I am," the man said.

Tommy said to the man seated next to him, "And all the stories are the same."

"Shit." The man resettled his shoulders.

Tommy shook his head. "You're never over it. When you're there, you use up courage and bravery and bravado you haven't got, no decent person could possibly have, you borrow it from your future, and you spend the rest of your life shakin', payin' it back, trying to make up for it, trying to rebuild a shot nervous system. Am I wrong about that?"

"Look at us," the man said, looking closely at Tommy. "Our hair's graying, those of us who still have hair, it was so long ago, and part of us is still over there."

"Yes, sir." Tommy played with a paper match folder on the counter with the four fingers and thumb of his right hand. "We came back deeply indebted to our nervous systems. And I hear tell from the experts that at first when we returned, our bravado was still with us, had its own momentum. It was only when we realized we weren't there anymore, that we didn't need to keep borrowing from our nervous systems, that we discovered our courage wells were dry, and that's when things really began to get bad for us."

"Real bad."

"Is that the way it's been with you?"

The man nodded. "It gets worse with the years instead of better."

"Divorced?" Tommy asked.

"Twice." The man smiled. "I kept marryin' women who expected me to work every day and sleep every night. You?"

"Never married," Tommy said.

The man put out his hand. "I'm Harry Kelly."

Tommy shook hands with him. "Tommy Barker."

Harry reached down to the floor near his feet and picked up a bottle in a paper sack. "Put some of this in your beer."

"Whiskey?"

"Bourbon." Harry poured a good slug into Tommy's beer.

From Harry's eyes, from the slightly slurry way he talked, from the slow, unsteady way he had driven from the Las Vegas Motel across the county to the Holler, Tommy knew that Harry had been drinking earlier in the evening, in the day, and not just beer.

"Thanks," Tommy said. He swigged the concoction in his beer glass.

"See you left a couple of fingers over there." Harry put the sacked bottle back on the floor near his feet.

"A thumb, two fingers, and a left leg."

"Really? I didn't notice about the leg."

"Like hell you didn't."

"I didn't. When you walked in and sat down."

"One thing we cannot do is lie. Not to ourselves. Not to each other."

"Just to other people."

"It's no good sayin' anythin' to other people—people who weren't there."

Harry said, "I did notice about the leg. Sorry. I did notice your leg was among the missing."

Tommy smiled at him. "That's better."

"I didn't lose any parts. Just friends."

"We all lost friends."

"Sure." The man drained his glass and put it forward on the bar for a refill.

"I'll buy this one." Tommy drained his glass quickly and put it on the bar next to Harry's.

Harry said, "I mean, I lost friends. Buddies."

Father Jones refilled their glasses from the tap and said, "You and your friend are drinkin' for free tonight, Tommy. I've been lookin' forward to buyin' you drinks for years now."

"Thanks."

Harry snorted. "Treat you like a respected veteran around here."

"I don't come here often."

"They'd make a drunk out of you. You're from around here." Again, a flat statement.

"Yes. Where you from?"

"Indiana," Harry said. "Bloomington."

Henry Kelly, 13059 Circe Road, according to Skylar Whitfield, Tommy said to himself. *What would Harry Kelly think, say, do, if I recited his full address to him right now? The trick is to stay upwind of him, come down slowly, quietly.* "That where you're from originally?"

"Yeah. Sure. I don't know. Nearby there. Who cares?"

As Harry poured bourbon from his sacked bottle into both their beer glasses, Tommy did not ask, *What are you doin' here?*

"Guess no one will mind our doin' this," Harry said, "seein' you're such a respected veteran around here."

I'm not respected just because I'm a veteran, Tommy wanted to say.

"So what do you do?" Harry asked.

"A little carpentry. Plumbing. Some basic electrical work. Yard work. I get a pretty good pension."

"I'll bet you do. You look like you spend a lot of time outdoors."

"Huntin'," Tommy said. "I do some fishin'."

"On that freakin' phony leg?" Harry asked. Then he smoothed his whiskers around his mouth. "Sorry."

Tommy laughed. "I told you not to lie."

"Just popped out." Harry looked into his glass. "I been drinkin'."

"You? What do you do?"

"Factory work, when I can get it, nonskilled, nonunion, until I can get unemployment insurance again. Then I drive around for a while. Drink. Like this. You know? I can't get ahead, anyway. A couple of courts attach anything much I make for child support, you know? As soon as they catch up to me with their liens, I'm gone like a cool breeze on a hot night."

"Don't care much about your kids?"

Harry straightened his back and put his fingers on the edge of the bar. "Not if I don't get to see 'em. Semen isn't all a daddy gets to put into the making of a kid, you know, to make him his own. Shit, these days a woman can get semen from a test tube. You ever hear of one of those artificial-insemination laboratories having to pay child support?"

Again Tommy smiled agreeably. "Don't like kids?"

Harry's back relaxed. "I guess I don't, much." He smiled at Tommy. "They don't know anything. You never had any of your own, I guess."

"No. So what are you doin' for yourself? I mean, you said things get worse rather than better. You doin' anything about that?"

"Yeah," Harry said. "I'm doin' somethin' right now."

"Drinkin'?" Tommy smiled.

"That. Somethin' else."

Father Jones filled their beer glasses again and again looked away as Harry topped their glasses with whiskey.

"What you said," Harry said, "about all stories bein' the same. That's not exactly true."

"Sure it is." Tommy felt the mess in his stomach escaping to his brain, his eyes, his tongue. He was not used to drinking. He knew he had to move against his prey quickly now. "You're sent into an accident. You get damaged. If you're lucky, or unlucky, however you call it, you get to come home again. All the same story. Just the amount of damage suffered is different."

"War is an accident?" Harry asked.

"Sure," Tommy said. "All wars are accidents. Once they're over, everybody says, 'Whoops,' explains why that particular war should never have happened. They explain all that while settin' up another accident to happen."

"Ever hear of troops fraggin' an officer?"

"Sure." Tommy knew of it to happen specifically. A green second lieutenant leading his platoon into what his troops knew was not only a useless maneuver but most likely a trap received a bullet through the back of his skull from close range. The incident was reported as sniper fire with a captured weapon. "Heard of it."

"Ever hear of an officer fraggin' his troops?"

"No," Tommy said. "Never heard of that. I've heard of officers makin' mistakes, sure enough."

"This officer made no mistake."

"Why would an officer do that?"

"He owed nearly every man in his platoon thousands of dollars he didn't have."

"How?"

"Gamblin'."

"Poker?"

"Sure, poker . . . Also what time it would rain . . . How many would return from patrol . . ."

"Why? Why would a platoon put up with that?"

"Let me put it this way," Harry said. "He'd also gamble with who'd get assigned point on patrol . . . Who'd be the first to find a route through a minefield . . . Who'd get to explore a tunnel . . . We were all just kids, then."

"Bastard."

"We gambled with him, all right. 'cept this officer was a crazy, bad gambler, a compulsive, I guess, who had to lose."

"Fraternizing . . ."

"Right," Harry said. "Exactly right. The platoon was writing up a document, names, dates, figures. We were goin' to turn the report in to a friendly colonel."

"He knew it? I mean, the lieutenant knew you-all were going to report him?"

"Guess so," Harry said. "He led us right into a trap so obvious, at first the enemy weren't even prepared to fire on us. I heard them scramblin'. Our position was so hopeless. . . . We'd been walked in to be executed just like cattle in a slaughterhouse. They could take all the time in the world exterminatin' us. And this was no green lieutenant. He knew what he was doing."

" 'Us'?" Tommy asked.

"I am the sole survivor," Harry Kelly said slowly. "I took blood off somebody else, globbed it on my shirt, played dead upside down on a stream bank with my head in the water. The enemy was still so surprised, curious, probably about why this happened, they didn't mutilate. They left me my parts."

"Where was the officer?"

"Nowhere. Nowhere at all. He knew what he was doin'. By the time I got back to base camp, he was all cleaned up like a duck's ass and pullin' a long face for his brother officers to see. He didn't look too happy to see me, though." Harry emptied his glass. "The document the platoon had been working on was gone. It had been disappeared. Missing in action, you might say. Like your leg." He looked at Tommy. "Is that enough to convince you that that particular war incident was no accident?"

"You've been livin' with this. . . ."

"Yeah. I shut up. I was still workin' on gettin' home alive. It had become a habit. The lieutenant made captain. I got a cherry lieutenant. Yeah." Harry sighed. "I shut up all this time." His eyes were red and wet. "All this time I figured I owe something to those guys."

"To yourself," Tommy said. "And now you're doin' somethin' about it, right?"

"Yeah."

Tommy's glass was empty. He held it out to Harry. "Just give me a slug of that whiskey, will you?"

"Sure." Harry poured from the bottle into both glasses.

Tommy held his glass while Harry drank fully from his.

"And now," Tommy said, carefully, his leg braced at an angle on the floor, "you have come to Greendowns County to kill the children of Captain John Simes."

He watched the whiskey hit Harry.

Slowly, Harry turned his face to Tommy. "I don't remember using that name."

"You must have," Tommy said. "How else would I know who you're talkin' about?"

Harry wiped his mouth with his hand. He was widening and blinking his eyes. "I thought we were just two old veterans philosophizing."

"I've just been listening," Tommy said.

The man was trying to clear his head. "A kid, last night, at the motel where I'm stayin' . . ."

"Yes?"

"Never mind." Suddenly, the man gave in to drunkenness. His shoulders slumped over the bar. "You wouldn't understand."

"I was there. I've understood so far. Lieutenant John Simes killed your buddies. You're killing his kids."

"Bodyguards."

"What about bodyguards?"

"Outside Lieutenant Simes's house. I went by earlier, this afternoon, two, three times. Two men sitting in a car outside his house."

Tommy put his drink on the bar. "I guess you're harmless enough, for now."

"Yeah," Harry said. "Go away."

Tommy stood up, pulling his artificial leg under him. "You're used to telling that story in bars, aren't you? To other old veterans?"

"I came . . ." Harry's head had dropped forward. "Never mind. Bastard."

"Perhaps we shouldn't be sitting here, Stewart."

"You'd know it's called keeping the pressure on, if you weren't such a dumb slut."

"The woods make me nervous," Carl said.

In the late afternoon, Stewart and Carl had parked their rented red Oldsmobile on a green verge in the shade of a tree across the road from the Simeses' house. Before turning off the motor and the air-conditioning, Stewart opened every window in the car. He left the ignition key in position to leave the radio on, tuned to the local station. Country music played, interspersed with commercials for auto dealerships, furniture stores, and, every half hour, local news. The lead of every news broadcast concerned the Simes family murders and concluded with, "Sought by police is Skylar Whitfield. . . ."

They had placed their jackets neatly on the backseat, loosened their collars and ties, removed and put their shoulder holsters on the floor of the front seat of the car.

Before sundown, when he was sure their presence, and the duration of their presence, had been noticed in the Simeses' house, Stewart, in rolled shirtsleeves, left the car, crossed the road, and strolled to the front door of the house. He rang the bell, waited. He introduced himself vaguely as an insurance detective to a helpful, neighborly wife who opened the door. He asked to see John Simes.

Stewart made sure John Simes knew they were there, and why.

And he made John Simes show him the relevant documents.

Sitting in the car, Stewart and Carl enjoyed watching the sunset together, holding hands in Stewart's crotch.

"The patrol car has been by twice since we've been sitting here," Carl said.

"They're looking for the Whitfield kid. Obviously, we're not the Whitfield kid."

"I don't know." Carl giggled. "You always say I look so young."

"In the mornings," Stewart said. "Some mornings."

"Most mornings."

"We have every legal right to sit here," Stewart said.

"Aren't we making them curious? The police, I mean? I mean, Stewart, this is not exactly the same as sitting in a parked car on John Street, New York."

"Let 'em think what they want."

"If they stop, what do we do with the guns?"

"Oh, Carl! You're such a worrywart. I told the woman who answered the door we're assigned to protect the Simes family."

"You saw the actual documents?" Carl asked.

"I told you that."

"So there's reason for us to wait."

"Keep the pressure on."

"You're sure the documents are real?"

"You think he'd be doing all this if they weren't?" Stewart spoke firmly to his friend. "Carl, what you and your little hitty friends seem to forget is that I have a law degree from Illinois State. Please don't forget that."

"I won't. Listen to the frogs, or whatever they are. 'Rivet! Rivet!' "

"I mean, as long as I came with you . . ."

"I know." Carl moved closer to his friend on the seat of the cooling car. "Jobs like this get so bor-ing. I love it when you wrangle an excuse to come with me."

"Hiya, Sheriff."

"Shut up, Summerhouse."

In the dim corridor night-lights, Pepp had entered the jail cell, taken off his boots, and stretched out on the bunk. He sucked a bruised knuckle.

There had been no particular news when he returned to his office shortly after six P.M. When he returned at a quarter to ten, Special Deputy Marian Wilkinson told him two reports of Skylar Whitfield being seen on a horse had been received by telephone. Each call reported Skylar was in the northwest area of the county, not far from Whitfield Farm and the Simeses' house. Each report said he was being trailed by a small brown dog.

Marian said, "I couldn't raise you on the car radio, Sheriff."

"You mean I had the radio off?" Pepp wiped his nose.

"Must have."

"I'm so damned tired. This cold. Have you talked to the deputies?"

"They're in that area now. There are other men with them."

"Who?"

"You know. Good ol' boys."

Under the fluorescent office lights, Pepp squinted at her.

"They're getting organized," she said. "They want to be deputized."

Pepp said, "Let me sleep on it."

Horse, Pepp thought, letting his eyes roam the jail cell's ceiling. *Why didn't I think of that? That's how that kid has been getting around—by horse. . . .*

Summerhouse yelled. "Oh, God! I been cotched again!"

The brilliant fluorescent lights in the cell block came on in waves.

"What have I done now? Where am I?" The huge man in the next cell rose up from his bunk. "What have I gone and done now to get cotched?" He raised his hands over his head. "For the love of mercy, don't shoot!"

Special Deputy Marian Wilkinson swung open the door of Pepp's cell.

Behind her, in black trousers and an open white shirt, his white hair in disarray, was Judge Hiram Hall.

The judge stopped at the threshold of the cell. "Are you awake, Pepp?"

"What?"

"Are you awake?"

"What time is it?"

The judge glanced at his watch. "About ten-forty-five." He looked at the man in the next cell standing huge-eyed with terror, his hands clasped behind his head, his feet spread. "Come on into your office, Pepp."

The judge turned and went back into the main rooms of the police station.

Marian waited while Pepp pulled on his boots.

When Pepp entered his office, the judge was sitting behind Pepp's desk. The Reverend Baker sat on a wooden chair at the side of the room with his head on his hands. Attorney Frank Murrey, in paint-stained jeans and a tennis shirt, stood near the desk. Dr. Charles Murphy came from behind the door and stood near Pepp.

Special Deputy Marian Wilkinson followed Pepp into his office. She stepped around him, stopped between Pepp and the judge.

"So tell him," the judge said to her.

"Pepp . . . half hour ago we got a call. I sent Chick Hanson to the scene. As soon as he confirmed, I called the judge. . . ." She gestured helplessly at Hiram. "I couldn't tell you myself. He called these others, I guess. . . ." She looked at the faces of the other men in the room for help.

Charles Murphy put his hand around Pepp's elbow.

"Pepp," the judge said. "Martha Jane has been murdered. Tony White spotted her car pulled' up on Standworth Road. Was it Tony White?" the judge asked Marian.

"Tony White," she said. "He's the one who called."

"Is that Bubba White's grandson?" the judge asked.

"Grandnephew," Frank Murrey answered.

"Oh, yeah. Bubba's grandnephew. Apparently, Tony noticed her roof light was on and stopped to see if she needed help. The car's door, driver's side, was open. He found her only a few feet away. From what Deputy Hanson reports, and he ought to be gettin' pretty accurate about such matters, Martha Jane had been dragged out of her car and beaten to death. Is that what Chick said?"

"Yes," Marian answered.

"Obviously, the coroner's got to get out there." The judge looked at Dr. Murphy.

"She had a meeting tonight," Pepp said.

"She would have been on her way home?" Hiram asked conversationally. "Standworth Road?"

"Yes."

The judge swiveled sideways to the desk. He sounded judicial enough as he said, "Pepp, obviously we haven't had the time to think all this through, but I think everyone agrees with me that this is one crime scene you don't need to see."

"I'm going," Pepp said.

"I don't know how we can do it, by law," the judge continued, "but, obviously, you need to be relieved as of right now." He looked at Frank Murrey. "Figure we can borrow a sheriff from some other county? What about Fitz from Saint Albans?"

Frank shrugged. "I don't know."

"He called me," Pepp said.

"Who?" the judge asked.

"Skylar Whitfield. This morning. He called me with some cock-and-bull story about a bushy-haired stranger. I ignored him. Told him he was full of bullshit, trying to create a diversion. I asked him to give himself up, told him I'd go get him myself, wherever he was."

Everyone listened silently to Pepp and remained silent a moment after he stopped speaking.

Pepp extricated his elbow from Dr. Murphy's hand.

"I'm going out." Pepp looked directly at the judge. "You can't relieve me."

"Pepp," the judge asked, "what with one thing and another, the circumstances, you realize you have to be about half-crazy right now?"

"Skylar Whitfield." Pepp went around the desk and opened the big drawer. He took out his wide belt with the holstered gun and strapped it on him. "I'm going after Skylar Whit-field," Pepp said. "And I'll accept all the help I can get."

21

The coroner said, "Pepp, let me take you back to my office. Give you some medication."

"You tryin' to make me laugh?"

"Pepp, can't you understand you have to be in a state of shock? You can't really know what you're doing right now."

Pepp had driven himself to the scene of Martha Jane Culpepper's murder on Standworth Road. He stopped the car, opened the door, put one booted foot on the ground. And remained sitting there.

His nose cold had disappeared entirely.

Between his family car and a patrol car, the body of Martha Jane Culpepper, his wife, was visible to Pepp as a dark bulk on the ground, not much bigger or more shapely than a garbage bag dropped, tipped over, at roadside.

He watched the lights around the scene. There was brilliant moonlight. The headlights and the roof light of the car Martha Jane had been driving, his family car, were fading as the battery died. The headlights and the roof rotating lights of the other police cars had been left on to illuminate and protect the scene, and they were still strong. Deputy Tom Aimes shot flashbulb pictures of the area around the car and Martha Jane's corpse. The coroner and a few others worked over the scene with flashlights. Cars and pickup trucks flooded Standworth Road, all with their lights on. People from these vehicles stood around, silently, none trying to violate the scene, view the corpse, few talking to each other. Their faces were drawn with the sadness not only of death but of life taken from one person by another. Many faces were taut with anger.

Pepp knew there were guns in many of those cars and trucks, that here there were men who were good hunters and knew the fields and woods of Greendowns County as well as Skylar Whitfield.

The people attracted to this scene on Standworth Road in the middle of night were good people who wanted to help, however they could, who meant to be a part of this community effort as they each were of many other community efforts, raising money for the swimming pool, Little League, the rescue squad. . . . Helpful people, who had heard of the new murder, that of Martha Jane Culpepper, on the local radio, who had phoned each other with the news, who had left their television sets or their beds to come to the scene quietly, now waiting to be told what they could do.

Finally, to all these lights were added the headlights of Untermyer's long, black, slow-moving hearse.

After the hearse arrived, Dr. Murphy noticed the way Pepp was sitting half in, half out of his car. He came over to Pepp.

The doctor was crouched, knees bent beside the open door of the sheriff's car. "Chandler will fix you something to eat. I'll give you a sedative. We'll put you to bed at our house."

Pepp asked the coroner, "What's the verdict?"

Dr. Murphy looked between his knees at the ground. "She was beaten to death, Pepp. Like the others."

"Weapon?"

"Fists, I'd say. That's preliminary, of course."

"Preliminary . . ." Pepp's chin lowered to his chest. "Preliminary to a preliminary report to be followed by a report that tells us nothing." He cut his eyes to Dr. Murphy's face. "Isn't that right?"

"That's the way it has been. Never can tell what we might find here."

Pepp reached for his hat on the seat beside him. "We're not going to find anything here." He switched on his car's loud-speaker and lifted the microphone off its dashboard hook. He turned the volume up.

Putting on his hat, standing up, he said to Dr. Murphy, "Excuse me." He indicated the doctor should stand aside so that people could see Pepp as he spoke.

More loudly, into the microphone he had turned on, Pepp said, "Excuse me?"

The people in all those various stripes of light looked at him with faces shocked at the sound of an amplified voice under these circumstances.

"I guess I thank you all for coming out," Pepp drawled. "There's nothing we can do here now." He realized he was addressing the people just as if he were giving a campaign speech. "As you all know, this is the third murder of this type in Greendowns County within a few days. A boy we arrested for the first murder, of Mary Lou Simes, on the basis of pretty good evidence of his guilt, escaped jail." Pepp knew there was a joke to be made here, somewhere, appropriate to a campaign speech, an appeal to the county for funds to finish fixing the jail's roof, but inappropriate here. "The young man's name is Skylar Whitfield, and I guess you all know him. At least, you thought you knew him. Anyway, you all know what he looks like.

"The night Skylar escaped from jail, Mary Lou's brother, Jack Simes, and a couple of his buddies, chased Skylar Whitfield into the quarry and gave him a beating. Of course, they should have called the Sheriff's Department instead, but I guess they know that now.

"A few hours later, Jack Simes was attacked from behind and beaten to death by a baseball bat in the driveway of his family home. . . . Now this."

In the crowd, which had come closer to Pepp as he spoke, Pepp saw Tommy Barker, leaning against a tree, listening to

Pepp, watching him. "Skylar Whitfield telephoned me this morning. He gave me some cock-and-bull story, trying to pull our interest away from him. I told Skylar I would pick him up myself, that he would be safe if he surrendered to me. He swore at me and hung up. Now: this," Pepp repeated.

"The Sheriff's Department, including every special deputy, has been working around the clock since early Saturday morning. Trouble is, that boy knows the woods and back roads of Greendowns County as well as anybody." Pepp hesitated. He considered suggesting that Skylar also clearly had had the help of some of the people of Greendowns County in his evading rearrest. Instead, Pepp said, "We've been real shorthanded. Tommy Barker?" Pepp said, "I'm real glad to see you here." He looked through the crowd, "And you Jimmy Joe, and you, Bobby . . . Ajax . . . I see we've got some of the best hunters in the county here now. Well, I need to ask for your help. I'm askin' Deputy Tom Aimes to organize you into a search party, and I'm deputizing, as of this minute, every one of you. You're looking for a boy named Skylar Whitfield, who has been charged with first-degree murder, who has escaped jail, who can be considered armed and dangerous, and I tell you to take no chances with him. He's proved himself to be the trickiest and most dangerous crittur I expect this county has ever seen. No one will ever blame you men for protecting yourselves, if you know what I mean. Take care of yourselves, but let's get Skylar Whitfield tonight, one way or the other, before he kills again. Deputy Hanson? Can you hear me?"

"Yo!"

"Deputy Hanson, I'm askin' you to stay and finish up here, protect the scene of this newest crime, until it's daylight and the state forensics boys can show up and do their work."

"Yes, sir!"

Pepp thought of asking a few of the ladies to supply Handsome with snacks, to get him through the night. "The rest of you, I ask to go home, and let Doc Murphy and Mr. Untermyer and the others do their work. There's nothing you can do here."

Pepp released his thumb from the microphone's button. Being careful not to knock off his hat, Pepp rehung the microphone on its dashboard hook. He lifted his rifle from its brackets. Deliberately within sight of the people, now milling slowly, some going home, some looking for Deputy Aimes, he checked his shells in their chamber.

Arms across his chest, Dr. Murphy again stood close to Pepp. "What are you going to do?"

Pepp said, "Go huntin'."

The only one in the crowd who had not moved, whose attention had not broken from the sheriff, was Tommy Barker.

"Want some practical medical advice?" Dr. Murphy asked.

"No, sir," Pepp said. "Not at this moment, I don't."

M.L. came into the den where John was sitting.

Slumped in his easy chair, only one leg on a footstool, John Simes had been staring vacantly at the television. A repeat of a documentary on the Amazon rain forest was being shown.

M.L. sat on his footstool, blocking his view of the Amazon rain forest.

She said, "John, I really admire the way you have been able to stop your . . . games, your watching sports, your constant phone calls . . . your gambling during this terrible, terrible time. I know it's an addiction, a disease with you, and from what I've read, such things are apt to get worse when one is under stress." She sobbed. "I just couldn't stand it, now." He did not respond. She said, "Thank you for stopping, John, at least for now, as a kindness to me." She took his hand. "You're shaking." Leaning over, she put her tear-wet cheek against his chest. "This horrible nightmare . . . it must be so much harder on you. . . ."

Still John Simes did not respond.

The telephone rang.

Drying her eyes and nose with her handkerchief, M.L. stood up. "I just want you to know I appreciate it. You see, John, right now I need the hope that sooner or later we can beat this compulsion, this sickness of yours, together. We were beating it the first years we were married. This hope . . . it's all I have left." Trying to control her weeping, M.L. left the room to answer the telephone.

This devastation has been continuing for years. . . .

John did not listen to his wife's side of the telephone conversation she was having in the hall. Since Saturday, well-meaning friends had been telephoning them. John had spoken to none.

In a few moments, M.L. returned to the den. Over her half-lenses, she was looking perplexed at the telephone paper pad in her hand.

Standing between her husband and the television, she asked, "Do you remember that French girl who was with Jack at college all last year—Jacqueline?" Next to the smooth, mechanical tones of the television narrator, M.L.'s voice sounded high, thin.

"Yes."

"What is her last name? I can't remember." M.L. turned and searched her husband's face.

John Simes thought a second. "Martine."

"Martine," M.L. said. "Jacqueline Martine. We met her at Jack's very first football game last fall. She was there every weekend. Jack and Jackie, everybody called them."

"What about her?"

"Well, I never knew Jack was serious about her. I mean, really serious."

John Simes's eyes roamed over the glassed gun cabinet on the other side of the den.

"I mean, he didn't mention her much when he came home from college."

"She went home to France for the summer."

"I know he wrote her," M.L. said. "It's so difficult with young people these days, to know what their real relationships are, whether they are lovers or just pals. . . . It was easier when there was more separation between young men and women, when they had to have dates to see each other, actually decide whether to put things on the romantic plane or not. . . ."

"That was before the Pill," John Simes said. "Television. Permissiveness."

"Did you know Jack had a love life? I mean, did he talk with you about it?"

"Not really. I hope he had a love life."

M.L. looked down at her paper. "He did."

"What's the paper?" John Simes finally asked. "What was that call?"

"A cable."

"From Jacqueline?"

"Yes. From Nîmes, France. Of course, she doesn't know Jack is dead. It was addressed to him." M.L.'s face crinkled to restrain weeping, again. "Oh, dear. It never crossed my mind to notify her. I'm glad I didn't." She raised the glasses on her nose. "I'll read it to you. 'Double citizen son seven pounds two ounces ten thirty A.M. local time. Looks just like you. Send football. We both will be in Greendowns next month. Prepare the way. All very well, happy here. Both love you, Papa.'" M.L. touched the handkerchief she now constantly had in hand to her nose, her cheeks. "It's signed 'Jacqueline.'"

Millions of acres of forest are being destroyed a year. . . .

John Simes asked, "Jack had a child?"

"So it seems." Blinking back tears, M.L. looked at her notepaper. "Within hours of his death. What time would it have been here, ten-thirty in the morning in France?"

"Jack had a child . . . in France." John's eyes fastened on the lock to the gun cabinet. "Jack has a child in France."

"How can we ever tell this girl . . ." M.L. took off her glasses and sobbed into her hands. "I'm so confused!"

John stared across the room at the keyhole of the gun cabinet.

. . . believed essential to the ecology of the whole world . . .

"In France," John Simes said.

When M.L. stood up, her ankle twisted, but she did not notice the twinge of pain. "I've got to go upstairs," she said. She placed her notepaper on the den's desk and read it again. "A hot bath. I'll take one of those pills Dr. Kramer . . . We have to decide about this. She doesn't need to know right away, not tonight. . . ." She turned to her husband. "Are you coming up?"

John Simes did not answer.

"The pills are for you, too, you know. . . . Well . . . We're grandparents. . . ." Without saying more, M.L. left the room.

John Simes listened to his wife slowly climb the stairs.

Then he got up. He took a key from a desk drawer and with it unlocked the gun cabinet. He took down a box of shells from the shelf, and, standing next to the cabinet's open glass door, loaded his father's .270 Winchester.

"Who?" Dan Whitfield asked loudly in his dark bedroom at the knock on the door. "Jonathan?"

"Me," Skylar answered.

"Wait a minute." Dan Whitfield snapped on the bed's reading light.

Monica got out of bed and slipped into her silky robe.

"Okay." It would not disturb Skylar to know his father was naked in bed. "Come in."

The conditioned air in his parents' bedroom slapped Skylar in the face.

Monica hugged her son's neck. "I'm so glad you're all right."

"Figures," Skylar said.

"Are you hungry?" Monica asked.

"I'm okay, for now." Skylar sat on his parents' bed. "I need to talk with you both."

"I guess," Dan said.

Monica closed the bedroom door to keep the cool air in the room.

Propped up on his pillows, Dan Whitfield asked his son, "First, may I call Frank Murrey, ask him to come out, be here while we get you rearrested?"

"Listen to me first," Skylar asked.

"Skylar, we've got to get all this cleared up sometime. Your mother and I are just scared to death, having you running around the woods day and night, with all this goin' on. We haven't slept a wink, or known what to do. . . ."

"Dad, I think I've got all this cleared up. Will you please just listen?"

"Okay."

Monica, too, sat on the bed.

"Dad, you said on the phone to me that Mr. John Simes doesn't have to do all that well, financially, because his family is taken care of."

"That's right."

"Have I got it right," Skylar asked, "that Miz Aggie Church, M.L. Simes's mother, left a lot of money to her grandchildren, Jack, Mary Lou, Andy-Dandy?"

Monica said, "That's right."

"How much is a lot of money, anyway?" Skylar asked.

"A lot," Dan answered. "A whole lot."

"Miz Church didn't leave any to Miz Simes?"

"She left the property," Dan answered. "The family home. A business block in Courthouse Square. John sold that some time ago."

"He has wanted to sell the house, too," Monica said quietly. "M.L. won't let him."

"So if Mr. John Simes desperately needs a lot of money, the only place he can get it is from his own kids, right?"

"What do you mean, 'desperately'?" Dan Whitfield asked his son.

"What I mean, sir, is that if he doesn't get a whole lot of money right quick, Mr. John Simes gets himself killed."

Monica's cheeks flushed. "How could such a thing . . . ?"

"Maybe Mr. John Simes isn't in the real estate development business at all," Skylar said. "Or heavy construction. Maybe business travel is just an excuse for him to go wherever he wants, whenever he wants."

"He must have been making some sort of a living, all these years." Dan was studying his son's face curiously. "He, personally, is not that well off."

Skylar said, "Mostly, you said, he travels to Puerto Rico and the state of Nevada. Jon Than reminds me those are two places noted for their big-time legal gambling. Can't gambling become an uncontrollable, crazy sickness?"

"Yes," Dan said. "But John used to play poker with a few of us. . . ."

"Is he pretty good at it?"

"Better than anyone else around here. Well, he's a little careless, a little wild. Goes for big stakes on short cards. I think everyone around here gave up playing cards with him years go. He must have played a lot in the army."

"He sure did," Skylar said. "Mr. Tommy Barker has been helping me, you see."

Skylar took a deep breath. "The sole surviving member of Mr. John Simes's old platoon suddenly showed up in town last week. At first I suspicioned him, but Tommy says he thinks the man's just sick and confused and really doesn't know what to do. Sounds to Tommy as if the man is just trying to get up the courage to confront Mr. Simes. I'm still not perfectly sure about all that.

"Anyway, this man told Tommy that Mr. Simes owed every man in his platoon thousands of dollars he couldn't pay. His own platoon was going to bring him up on charges. He was coercing, making his men gamble with him. Apparently, any man who refused to gamble with Mr. Simes would be the first sent across minefields or down guerrilla holes until he changed his mind and decided to 'play.' At the least Mr. Simes would have been court-martialed, the way he was doing things, maybe even brought up on murder charges, Tommy says. This man accuses Mr. Simes of eventually trying to arrange to have his whole platoon, except Mr. Simes himself, wiped out. This man, Kelly, survived. A document of charges against Mr. Simes the platoon had prepared had disappeared by the time this Kelly guy made it back to camp."

"Skylar!" Monica's eyes were furious, frightened behind tears. "Tommy Barker is right when he says this man is sick and confused!"

With a tight throat, Dan said, "What Skylar is saying is that John Simes is an advanced compulsive gambler . . . a murderer

. . . that he has been murdering his own kids . . . Mary Lou . . . Jack . . . and that he means to murder Andy. Is that it?''

Skylar nodded. ''To get the money to pay off his gambling debts to save his own skin. Wouldn't most people do nearly anything to save their own lives?''

''Not kill their own children!'' Monica said.

''Why not?'' Skylar asked. ''Isn't history full of people who kill their parents to inherit money?'' Dan studied his son's face. ''Why wouldn't a father, desperate enough, kill off his own kids to inherit?''

Monica said, ''Not beat his own children to death! Skylar, it's unthinkable!''

Skylar shook his head. ''Their being beaten to death is the clever part. Listen to yourself, Mama. For sure, their being beaten to death does a lot to remove their daddy from bein' a suspect, wouldn't you say?''

Reflectively, Dan said, ''John Simes . . . I wouldn't swear to his stability, Monica. I never would.''

''What makes you think his life is in danger anyway?'' Monica demanded.

''Two mobsters have been sitting outside the Simeses' house all afternoon. At one point, one of them entered the house, probably talked with Mr. Simes, then came out again. They're still sitting there.'' Skylar lowered his eyes. ''Probably waiting to see if Andy-Dandy meets his untimely demise tonight so they'll know they're gonna git paid.''

''How do you know this?'' Monica asked. ''I mean, about the two men?''

''Ol' Dufus is in the bushes, watchin' the Simeses' house, too. Because of Andy-Dandy.''

''What makes you think they're mobsters?'' Dan asked.

''They're not from around here. They're wearin' neckties.'' Skylar shrugged. ''Under the circumstances, I doubt they're Jehovah's Witnesses.''

Dan Whitfield said, ''Your theory is John Simes has been killing his own children because he needs to inherit from them, to pay gambling debts, to save his own life?''

''Yes, sir. You got it.''

"If that were so, how could he possibly hope to get away with it?"

"No one 'round here could guess at Mr. John Simes's motive. No one knows he's a real sick, compulsive gambler who's killed before, probably desperate in real bad debt to the mob. We wouldn't know it, either, if this man from his old platoon hadn't showed up."

"You don't know it now," Dan said. "Not really."

"You always could make up a good tale," Monica said. "Is this how you try to justify escaping jail to us, Skylar? That was real stupid of you, you know."

"Maybe. Jack would have been killed anyway, somehow, by now, because I figure Mr. John Simes is dreadful desperate. That would have taken the pressure off me, if my whereabouts were known, that is, if I were bakin' in the county lockup. On the other hand, I don't see that anybody else has been doin' any serious investigatin' but me. Sheriff Pepp doesn't seem all that interested in what he's doin' just now. And I mean to do what I can to save Andy-Dandy's life. Which is why I've come to you. With those two gunmen sittin' outside his house, I think Mr. John Simes's time is about up."

Monica and Dan Whitfield were looking at their son sitting on their bed at beyond midnight as if they had never seen him before.

"There's something that doesn't figure," Dan Whitfield said. "Guess you haven't heard the news."

"What news?"

"There's been a third murder. Tonight. The wife of the sheriff, Martha Jane Culpepper, was dragged out of her car and beaten to death on Standworth Road."

"What?" Skylar shouted.

"Frank Murrey called to tell us," Monica murmured.

"That doesn't make sense," Skylar said.

Dan said, "It doesn't oblige your theory at all. In fact, it knocks just about everything you've said into a cocked hat."

"Who do they think did it?" Skylar asked.

"You."

"Me? Why me? I hardly know the woman to say hidy to."

"Wreak some revenge upon the sheriff," Dan said. "You telephoned him this morning?"

"Yes, sir."

"Tried to divert him?"

"No, sir."

"You didn't tell him some crazy story about a bushy-haired stranger?"

"I told him about Mr. Kelly, the man from Mr. Simes's old platoon."

"He says you swore at him."

"I never did. I did chide him for takin' the Lord's name in vain, but I did allow it was all right for him to swear at me lightly, which he did."

"Now can I call Frank Murrey?" Dan Whitfield asked. "And call the sheriff, ask him to come out?"

"What time tonight did all this happen?"

"Somebody found her body just before ten o'clock."

"Harry Kelly was at the Holler," Skylar said. "I know that. Mr. Simes was at home. I know that. She was killed in the same way as the others?"

Dan nodded. "Beaten to death. Probably with fists, Frank said."

Looking at the floor, Skylar said, "What sense does all this make? I thought someone was killin' just the Simes kids. Sounds like someone is tryin' to divert the sheriff's attention. . . ."

Dan Whitfield reached for his robe. "We've heard you out, Skylar. Never for a hummingbird minute do your mother and I believe you guilty of murdering anybody. But we've got to get this cleared up in the only way we know how, and that's by getting Frank Murrey and Sheriff Pepp out here, right now."

Skylar asked, "What's my motive for all this?"

Dan Whitfield stood up in his robe. "That you've gone crazy, I guess."

"I wouldn't have credited that, either," Monica said, "until you brought home that tale about John Simes killing his own kids. . . ."

22

"Pretty moon." In the front seat of the red Oldsmobile parked across the road from the Simeses's home, the fingers of Carl's left hand were playing with Stewart's right ear. "The moonlight is really lovely falling through the trees that way, don't you think? Landing on the road, the house, the grass."

Stewart glowered at the dark, silent house. "What's keepin' him?"

"He probably can't figure out how to do it—without drawing suspicion to himself, I mean. Andrew is just a little kid, isn't he? How do you murder your own little son in your own house in the middle of the night? Smother him with pillows? Lock him in his room and burn the place down?"

"Son of a bitch."

"Stewart, don't forget: You and I can't have kids at all, no matter how much we screw around. Why should it matter to us what families do to themselves?"

"Maybe we ought to kill the son of a bitch anyway."

"Mama wants her money."

"After the kids' estate is settled, after he pays up, let's come back and kill the son of a bitch. Okay?"

"Murder really ought to be left to professionals." Carl sighed. "You see, if he knew what he was doin', he would have killed the youngest first. This way he's worked himself into sort of a corner."

"Well, he'd better do it. I'm not going to sit outside his house for the rest of my damned life."

"He will. He's gone this far."

"I'm serious, Carl. If I promise to make the trip with you, do you agree to come back and off this son of a bitch? After he's paid off Mama, I mean?"

"Sure."

"I don't like him. Son of a bitch."

"Relax." Carl tweaked Stewart's ear, making his head twitch. "What exactly does the will say?"

Stewart sighed. He knew Carl was just trying to flatter Stewart's legal expertise. " 'Estate to be divided, in each generation, among the issue of Mary Lou Church Simes, and the issue of her issue.' "

"And if there is no issue of Mrs. Simes, the estate reverts to her and John Simes?"

"Right. The will was drawn before Mary Lou Church Simes had any kids. Issue or issue of issue."

"What does that mean?"

"Children or grandchildren."

"Why can't they just say 'grandchildren'? You lawyers. Make everything so bor-ing. Is that side door to the house opening?"

"Trick of the moonlight, I think."

"Maybe I'll buy a country place, Stewart. For you and me. Somewhere in Arizona, maybe. Would you like that? We can sit out like this some nights and watch the moonlight."

"You'll have to do the buying," Stewart said. "You make a lot more than I do. I'm just a lawyer, remember."

"That door did open. Someone is on the side porch."

"Big. Carrying some kind of a stick."

"That's a rifle, Stewart."

"That's John Simes."

"Crossing the lawn to us."

"He's raising the rifle, Carl."

"Does he think we can't see him, in this moonlight?"

"What's he doing?"

"Get down, Stewart!" Carl grabbed his pistol from the car's floor. "He means to shoot at us!"

The rearview mirror of the red Oldsmobile was shot off its support before Stewart and Carl heard the first bang from John Simes's Remington.

"Shit!" On the car floor, Stewart was groping his handgun out of its holster. The rearview mirror fell on his head. "How crazy is that son of a bitch?"

"Out this way!" Holding his pistol, Carl opened the passenger-side door of the car.

Standing in the moonlight on his front lawn, John Simes shot at the car again and again. Lights in the second-story windows of his house behind him went on.

Keeping his head down, Carl scrambled out of the opposite side of the car.

In a less practiced crouch, Stewart followed him.

Once out of the car, Carl and Stewart remained still a moment.

"Son of a bitch!" Stewart fired his pistol into the air. "It works." He popped his head up to look through the car's open back windows. "Did I frighten him?"

"Get down, asshole."

"I've told you not to call me 'asshole.' You're the asshole."

Carl listened to the extraordinary regularity of John Simes's firing. It was if he were pacing his shooting to a metronome.

"What's he doing?" Stewart asked.

"He's getting himself killed, Stewart," Carl said. "He's committing suicide."

Timing himself against John Simes's regular pattern of fire, Carl squinted over the hood of the car. He fired his pistol once.

John Simes's head snapped backward. His arms flung up. His Remington arched in the air before dropping to the ground. His hips and legs rose slightly. His body spun halfway around in midair before he fell.

He twitched on the ground only a moment.

"Did you get him?" Stewart asked.

"Of course."

"Let's get out of here."

Stewart crawled back into the car, still keeping his head somewhat down. He started the motor.

In a more leisurely manner, Carl stepped into the car, sat down, closed the door. He rested his arm on the windowsill.

Stewart glanced out his window at the figure of the big man sprawled on the lawn, his rifle flung beside him.

Stewart put the car in gear and jounced it off the green verge onto the road. He accelerated the car rapidly.

"Shit, Stewart." Carl brushed broken window glass and bits of metal bullets off the seat. "How are we going to explain this to the rent-a-car people?"

"I'll just fix you something to eat." Monica opened the door to her air-conditioned bedroom. "At least you won't go back to jail hungry."

Jon appeared in the shadows at the back of the second-story corridor. "What's happening?"

Skylar looked at his cousin. "You're dressed?"

Jon looked down at himself. Shirtless, he was in jeans and sneakers. "For around here, I guess I'm dressed for the Haymakers' Ball."

"Why are you dressed at this hour?"

In his bedroom, still dressed only in a bathrobe, Dan Whitfield was dialing the telephone.

Suddenly, Skylar said, "Firing!"

Monica stopped halfway down the stairs and looked up at her son.

"Was that a gunshot?" Dan put down the phone.

"Rifle," Skylar said.

"Somebody hunting at this hour?" Jon yawned.

"It's coming from the Simeses's house," Skylar said.

"That was a handgun," Dan said.

Skylar said, "Two guns."

"Somebody's firing pretty regularly," Dan said. "Like target practice."

"Three guns," Skylar said. "One rifle, two different handguns. Shit! They're after Dufus!" He started down the stairs, taking them two at a time. Passing his mother on the stairs, Skylar said, " 'Scuse me, ma'am. Somebody's fixin' to gimp Dufus."

From the bedroom, Dan shouted, "Wait for me! Wait till I put on some clothes! Skylar, you're safer with me!"

Monica looked up the stairs at her nephew. In a low voice, she said, "Jon, go with Skylar."

Jon started walking down the steps. The screen of the front door slammed.

Monica said, "Jonathan, you make me so mad!"

Monica pushed Jon's shoulder, hurrying him down the stairs.

While Skylar was pivoting over a side fence, he saw Jon in the moonlight coming across the lawn after him.

"I know a shortcut," Skylar said. He waited until Jon climbed the fence. "Well, not really a shortcut. It will keep us off the road."

Skylar began jogging uphill toward the woods. "Let's go."

Jon plodded after Skylar.

After running about two hundred meters, Skylar said over his shoulder, "Would you mind movin' your ass a little faster, please, Jon Than? We may have to plug up some new holes Dufus has got himself."

"Screw that," Jon puffed. "Screw Dufus. Why am I even here?"

"Shut up and run," Skylar said.

In a moonlit clearing at the top of the ridge, Jon stopped. He put his hands on his knees and sucked in breath.

"Shoot, Jon Than." Skylar came back to him and paced in a circle around him. "You're just fightin' air, boy."

"I'm sick," Jon gasped. "It's called mononucleosis. Has anyone told you that?"

"I can't leave you here. Why'd you come?"

"I haven't been able to play sports all spring. I can't run. . . ."

"Who was she, anyway? Was she worth it?"

"What the hell are we doing, chasing through the woods crawling with people trying to get a shot at you, in the middle of the damned night, risking ourselves for the son of the town drunk and the county . . ." Jon looked up at Skylar.

Skylar said, "I never said Dufus is the son of Tony Duffy."

"You said Mrs. Duffy is married to the town drunk."

"I said that. Yes."

"So who is Dufus's father?"

In the moonlight, Skylar watched his cousin's face through narrowed eyes. Slowly, softly, he said, "Dufus's daddy is the very same as your own, Jon Than. Mr. Wayne Whitfield."

Jon stood straight in the moonlit clearing. "Like hell." Taking a deep breath, he raised his face. "Like goddamned hell!"

"I'm lookin' out for Dufus because he's my actual cousin, Jon Than. And I do believe you ought to run a little faster, Jon Than, because, you see, Dufus is your actual brother."

"You friggin' bastard!" Jon puffed. "Dufus is no brother of mine!"

"Sure enough, actual fact: He is."

Even in the moonlight, Jon's eyes darkened. There was not much focus in them when he swung at Skylar.

Skylar ducked. "Quit it, Jon Than! We got things to do."

Jon lunged at Skylar. Jon grabbed Skylar around the chest. Digging his sneakers into the ground, Jon pushed Skylar backward.

Their legs tangled, and they fell to the ground.

"Damn it!" Skylar yelled. "Jon Than, this is no time to discuss family history!"

Jon scrambled to his feet. His hands were clenched at his sides, his elbows bent.

On the ground, Skylar said. "Damn! Am I gettin' tired of people hittin' on me, or what!"

Skylar sprang off the ground with all the strength in his legs. His shoulders and back muscles were taut. With his shoulder, he hit Jon just below his rib cage. Jon staggered back a few steps.

Before Jon regained his footing, Skylar hit him in the nose with his left fist. Then he hit Jon's jaw, hard, with his right.

Jon got his balance. With knees bent, left foot ahead of his right, he moved in on Skylar, swinging and connecting with such speed and force Skylar couldn't figure from where all these blows were coming. When he had his forearms over his face, Jon peppered his stomach. When Skylar lowered his arms, Jon hit all sides of Skylar's head at once.

"Damn, Jon Than," Skylar said, drawing back. "I always figured you're no lover! Where'd you learn how to fight?"

Skylar faked with his left and hit Jon's head, hard, with his right. Then, using all his weight, all his strength, he sent his right fist as hard as he could into Jon's stomach.

As Jon's knees buckled, he grabbed Skylar around the neck. He dragged Skylar to the ground with him.

On the ground, tangled around each other, each was drawing whatever arm was free as far back as possible and hitting the other wherever he could.

"Shit!" a voice said. "I didn't know you all were up here! What're you-all doin'?"

Punchy, Skylar and Jon looked up from the ground.

Dufus stood over them.

"We're rescuin' you, Dufus." Skylar spit on the ground. "Can't you tell?"

"Better quit whatever you-all are doin'," Dufus drawled, "and get movin'. 'Fraid I'm leadin' someone."

"Someone chasin' you?" Skylar asked.

Dufus nodded. "The sheriff, I do believe."

Skylar and Jon disentangled from each other.

Looking into the dark woods, Dufus said, "I've got a bit of a lead on him, but not much."

Spitting and snorting on the ground around where he was sitting, Skylar said, "What the hell happened, anyway? What was all that firin' about?"

"Well," Dufus said. "Looked to me like the Simeses were settlin' down for the night. Lights were off everywhere but in the den. I was just settlin' back for a few Z's myself when Mister John Simes came out of the house with his daddy's old Remington and began shootin' apart the car parked across the road. Never for half a second did he try to conceal or protect hisself. Just kept shootin' at that red car. Whoever all was in that car finally took exception to it and blew his brains out."

"Mr. John Simes?" Skylar asked.

"Yes, sir."

"Mr. John Simes is dead?"

"Yes, sir. He surely is. Deader'n a pan-fried rabbit."

Sitting cross-legged on the ground, Jon was touching his jaw gingerly with his fingertips. There was blood around his nose and mouth.

"What did you-all find to fight about, anyway?" Dufus asked.

"Oh," Skylar said. "He's a snotty Yankee."

Looking at Dufus, Jon said nothing.

"Figure one of you won yet?" Dufus asked.

"I just want this boy to go back where he came from," Skylar said.

Jon said, "I'm going home." His pronunciation was not clear.

"Then I won," Skylar asserted.

"Then you won before I ever got here." Jon spit blood on the ground.

"Anyway." Dufus looked back into the woods. "I was just withdrawing through the woods, seein' Mr. Simes was likely to draw police or flies, one. I came out to the road, and who's standin' in the road but the sheriff, with a damned big firing iron. I do believe our surprise at seein' each other was mutual. I did mind my manners and said, 'Oops, 'scuse me,' but you see, by then the red car was done gone, and it crossed my mind the sheriff might think I left Mr. John Simes on his lawn in his present condition. So I hightailed it this way, thinkin' I could get up the hill faster than he could, and I do believe I did, but here you all are, rollin' around on the ground settlin' some private contretemps."

Jon said, "Contretemps?" His correct pronunciation was blurred by a ringing head, blood in his nose and mouth, loose teeth.

"That's French, Jon Than," Skylar said. "It means you're a sombitch." Skylar got to his feet. "We gotta get truckin' here. Each of us will go in a different direction. Right? Dufus, you keep goin' along the ridge. Jon, you go down, toward the sheds. I'll head at an angle near him, down toward the Simeses' house. Everybody make as much noise as possible, to cause confusion. Talk out loud to yourselves. Dufus, you might just try that 'Twinkle, Twinkle Little Star' song they taught you the second year you were in second grade. You sing that right pretty."

Jon wiggled a tooth with his finger. "I am walking back to the farmhouse, quietly."

"Well, Jon Than," Skylar said. "You just do that. But I do suggest you do not sit there for very much longer, holdin' your teeth in!"

"See you all." Waving his left hand at shoulder height, Dufus headed for the edge of the woods.

Jon picked himself up. " 'Contretemps,' " he muttered.

They could hear Dufus talking loudly to himself, and answering in a different voice, as he walked away.

Through the moonlight, Jon looked at his cousin. "Is what you just told me the truth?"

"Sure enough. An actual fact."

"Does my father know it?"

"I hear he's been told."

"Has he ever done anything about it? About Dufus?"

"No."

"Why not, do you suppose?"

"Because Dufus isn't a possession of his? Anything he bought and paid for?"

"You mean, you think I am?"

"I don't know. Are you?"

Jon sniffed. "Do you think my mother knows about it? About Dufus?"

"How would I know that?"

Jon did begin walking slowly back toward Whitfield Farm.

Standing in the middle of the clearing, Skylar watched him go.

After walking a few meters, Jon turned to face Skylar.

He asked, "Do you think my father expected me to find out about Dufus when he sent me down here?"

Skylar said, "You've got just a few more questions than I've got answers, Jon Than."

"Stop right there, Skylar."

Skylar had just slowed his running pace to enter the woods at the edge of the moonlit clearing.

He stopped. "Sheriff?" He could see no one in the woods.

Again, the slow, heavy voice: "Put your hands over your head, Skylar."

"Sheriff Pepp?" Skylar raised his hands well over his head. "How's your cold doin'?"

Pepp, carrying his rifle at his side aimed at Skylar, stepped out of the woods into the moonlight. "Much better, Skylar, thank you for askin'." He walked in a circle around Skylar. "Yes, sir, I think finally I have found a cure for the common cold."

"I'm right glad to hear that, Sheriff. Adrenaline have anything to do with it?"

"You're not even carryin' a knife. Oh, I forgot. We have your knife."

"Actually, now that you mention it, Sheriff, I sure could use it."

"Where's the rifle? What did you do with it?"

"What rifle?"

"The one you used to shoot Mr. John Simes."

"I never shot Mr. John Simes, Sheriff. You know that. Mr. Simes was shot by those two mobsters sittin' in that red car outside his house all day. Has somethin' to do with his gamblin' debts.''

"Gamblin'? Who?''

"Mr. John Simes.'' Skylar exhaled heavily. "Damn all! No criticism intended, Sheriff, but I do declare I suspect I'm the only one who has been payin' full attention to this situation since it started!''

"You got all the answers, have you, Skylar?''

"May I put my arms down, Sheriff? I feel like a moose bein' measured for a wall.''

"Sure.''

Skylar lowered his arms and turned to face Pepp. "Mr. John Simes was murderin' his own children. You do see that, don't you?''

"Sure,'' Pepp said. "And some kind of mobsters murdered John Simes.''

Skylar said, "And you murdered your wife.''

Pepp raised the aim of his rifle to Skylar's chest. "How come, with all your advantages, Skylar, you weren't goin' on to college? You're a real smart boy.''

"Am I right?''

"I don't know who killed the Simes kids,'' Pepp said, slowly. "Or why. I've been a little distracted lately, what with one thing and another.''

"Sheriff Pepp, would you call the murder of your wife a 'copy-cat murder'?''

Pepp said, "I don't know who killed John Simes, either. Driving up the road, I heard the gunfire. Got out of the car. Found John Simes dead on his lawn. Saw someone comin' out of the bushes. It might have been you. . . .''

"The only thing you do know is who murdered your wife.''

Pepp breathed in through his nose. It felt good, having his sinuses clear. "Yeah. I know who killed Martha Jane.''

"You did.''

"Tell you one thing, Skylar. . . .'' Pepp checked to make sure there was a shell in the firing chamber of his rifle. "Having you dead sure will clear the air 'round here.''

"You don't deny it."

"No, sir, I don't."

"With me dead, I get blamed for everything. The only reason you have for killin' me is because you murdered your wife. Am I right?"

"You are exactly right," Pepp said. "That's how I figure it, anyway. I'll probably feel real bad, having killed a bright kid like you. But . . . I really ought to give the people what they'll believe. You always were a bit of an odd duck, Skylar Whitfield."

"Damn all, Sheriff Pepp!" Skylar shouted. "My parents voted for you!"

"Then I'll be fair," Pepp drawled. "Tell you what I'll do . . . I'll give you a chance to escape. Why don't you start runnin' that way. . . ." With his rifle, Pepp indicated Skylar should run across the moonlit clearing.

"And you'll shoot me in the back. You'll tell people it was the only clear shot you had at me."

"Something like that."

"Not goin' to do it," Skylar said. "Your shootin' me straight out and close up will make things harder for you to explain."

"Okay," Pepp said. "I'll back up. Stay right there, if that's what you want." With his rifle aimed at Skylar's midsection, Pepp walked backward.

"Don't trip." Skylar unzipped the fly of his jeans.

"What are you doin', boy?"

Skylar said, "I've never shat my pants yet, and I'm not about to now!"

At a fair distance from Skylar, Pepp raised his rifle.

Skylar said, "I wish I could be around to hear you explain how come you shot someone while he had his donk out pissin'."

Aiming his rifle at the center of Skylar's head, Pepp said, "Jesus, Skylar, you are a wiseass."

"Sheriff, I've mentioned to you before something about takin' the Lord's name in vain."

There was a shot.

Clutching his penis, Skylar fell forward. He landed on his right shoulder and rolled.

He lay on the ground a moment. Then he wriggled forward a couple of meters. He lay silently another moment. He heard movement in the grass. He rolled and wriggled another few meters. Listened again. The sounds he heard were not approaching him.

Finally, he lifted his head.

There was a man standing near where Sheriff Culpepper had been standing. He carried a rifle, aimed at the ground, under his right arm. He was looking down.

He was not Sheriff Culpepper.

"As I live and breathe," Skylar said, getting up. Zipping up his fly, Skylar approached the man. "Ha, Tommy. How're ya doin'?"

Sheriff Culpepper was dead on the ground. Skylar knew Pepp was dead but in the moonlight could not see a bullet hole. He figured the bullet must have gone through the sheriff's chest, from side to side.

"You heard everything?" Skylar asked.

"Enough." Tommy Barker sat down on a nearby log.

Between his knees, Tommy put the butt of his rifle on the ground.

He put the barrel of the rifle in his mouth.

Skylar looked away from the body of Sheriff Culpepper on the grass. Skylar glanced at Tommy Barker sitting on the log. Skylar was about to say something appreciative.

Instead, Skylar shouted, "What are you doin'?"

One of Tommy's fingers was on the rifle's trigger.

Skylar leaped at Tommy Barker. Hands cupped, he lifted and threw Tommy's head back. The rifle fired into the air.

Tommy fell backward over the log.

Standing over him, Skylar said, "What the hell do you think you're doin', anyway?"

Tommy rolled the upper part of his body over, so that his chest was on the ground. His artificial leg was at an unnatural angle to the rest of his body.

Tommy Barker said, "I've been sayin' the next and only man I'd ever shoot again would be myself."

"Well, you were wrong," Skylar said. "Believe me, Mr. Tommy Barker, you'll never hear a word of criticism from me on the matter."

"I don't want to kill other people anymore," Tommy said. "I want to take myself away from the possibility. Do you understand that, Skylar?"

"Mr. Tommy Barker," Skylar said, "I need you as a witness."

After a moment, Tommy said, "Oh. Yeah."

After another moment, he sat up and adjusted his artificial leg. "I forgot that."

Sitting on the ground with his legs straight out before him, his rifle by his side, Tommy Barker said, miserably, "Pepp was a decent man. He loved his kid. What happened to him?"

23

"I'm fixin' to marry up with Jimmy Bob."

Early Thursday morning, Tandy McJane stood in Skylar's bedroom. Her hands were on her hips, and her feet were planted wide.

In his bed, just waking up, Skylar smiled. "You've been scarce'n a hen's teeth 'round here, the last day or two." He flipped one side of his bedsheet back.

"I'm not gettin' in there."

Skylar blinked in the semidark bedroom. The door to the bathroom was open. Beyond that, the door to the guest room was slightly open.

"You've already notified me my face is a mess," Skylar said.

"Your face is a mess. Jon Than's face is a mess." Tandy maintained her front-porch pose. "Skylar, can't you hear what all I'm tellin' you?"

"No. What're you tellin' me?"

"I'm sayin' I'm fixin' to marry up with Jimmy Bob. I already told him so."

Staring at her, Skylar sat up in bed. "You're pullin' my you-know-what."

"Not right now, I'm not."

"Then what are you talkin' about?"

"I told you, Skylar. He's got a job drivin' an eighteen-wheeler."

"So what?"

"I don't see you ever takin' no job drivin' an eighteen-wheeler."

"No. Probably not."

"Skylar Whitfield, you're no homeboy. I always knew that about you."

"You're serious."

"You bet your left testicle I'm serious," Tandy said. "You can risk your right one, too, on that."

"Damned Jon Than." Skylar got out of bed. "Damn his hide."

Tandy's eyes ran down Skylar's naked body. In a softer tone, she said, "You got to get out of here, Skylar. Get yourself educated. You're no good to nobody the way you are now, boy."

Skylar began to put his arms around her. "I'm not?"

She flung his arms aside and stepped back. "What are you goin' to do with yourself? Just tell me that?"

"Tandy? Tandy!"

"Don't you snurl your nose and pooch your lips at me, Skylar Whitfield!"

"Tandy, why're you doin' me this way?"

"I just told you. For your own good."

"You're marryin' Jimmy Bob for my sake? You ever made love to that boy?"

"No. But I expect I will. Isn't that expected in the married state?"

Skylar took a step closer to her. "Tandy, come here."

"No." She put her hand on the bedroom doorknob.

"I've never known you to play this way," Skylar said.

"I'm not playin', Skylar. Playin' is over." She opened the door. "Skylar, you've got to write that Knightsbridge Music College place in Boston, Massachusetts, and tell them you're grateful for their acceptin' your application to go there, and for all the scholarship money they're offerin' you, and never no mind about me. One way and another, you've about driven everyone crazy, 'specially your parents, who think you applied to all those other places you never did, and I'll get along without you just as fine as a dog without either fleas or ticks! You write that letter this mornin'. You do it *rat now!*"

Tandy McJane left Skylar's bedroom.

The overhead bedroom light snapped on.

Jon stood in the bathroom doorway. He was dressed in khaki trousers and a blue buttoned-down dress shirt. In his hands, he carried a folded pair of blue jeans.

"I just heard my hide damned," he said.

Sitting on the edge of his bed, Skylar looked at his cousin. "My face as ugly as yours?"

"Uglier." Jon dropped the jeans on Skylar's desk. "Mrs. McJane washed them for you. They were a real mess."

"You all packed?"

"Yes." Jon sat backward on the desk chair.

"Can't wait to get out of here, can you, Jon Than?" Skylar went into the bathroom, snapped a towel off a rack, and wrapped it around his waist. "Shit."

"My parents have agreed Whitfield Farm is not good for my health."

Coming back into the bedroom, Skylar said, "Well, you got your jaw cracked for you anyway. Your ticket home. I'd say you talk funny, but you always have."

"Even my parents think I talk funny now." Jon was having difficulty using his stiff jaw. "Even they said so, on the phone."

Skylar sat down on the edge of the bed again. "You heard everything?"

"Inadvertently. Not everything."

"Everything Tandy said?"

"Was that Tandy?" Jon smiled. "Why, I thought I was overhearing a quartet of country guitars twanging together most inharmoniously."

Not smiling, Skylar looked at Jon. "Tandy said all that. And she meant it. I guess."

Jon said, "I'm sorry."

"I had everything I could ever want here. Why would I ever want to leave? A horse, a dog, a pickup, good, hard work, friends, decent parents, Tandy . . ."

"To learn more about music?"

"To learn how to write music better, maybe."

"How did you ever hear about Knightsbridge School of Music, anyway?"

Skylar shrugged. "Mrs. Duffy made some inquiries. You'd be surprised at some of the people that woman knows."

"I bet."

"Musicians . . . I mean: besides your father, Jon Than."

"Okay, Skylar. I give."

"I wrote off to that Knightsbridge place. They sent me some forms fussy with questions. So I scribbled down some music —you know, stuff I've found myself playin' up at the Holler?—and sent that off to 'em. I sent them a tape, too, of my playin' some of that Telemann music, you know, you heard me playin'?—and sent that off to 'em, too. Father John got the right equipment and helped me make the tape up at the Holler."

Jon grinned with his cracked lips. "Why, I do declare! That Holler place is a downright cultural institution!"

"You got that right."

"And Knightsbridge accepted you on the basis of what you sent them?"

"I wrote 'em back sayin' I doubted I could afford 'em, seein' I hear you lose a dollar-fifty every time you draw breath up North. So they offered me money to go there."

"You've got a scholarship to Knightsbridge?" Jon laughed. "You sombitch!"

"I've been quiet about it, till I made up my mind." Skylar said, "I guess I haven't been exactly honest with my parents. I never did apply to those other places they expected me to."

"Well?" Jon asked. "You made up your mind yet, Skylar?"

Hands relaxed at his sides on the tumbled bedsheets, Skylar looked around his bedroom. "Guess Tandy's made up her mind, sure enough." Skylar sighed. "She loves me enough to make me go. Guess I'm bein' elected outta here."

"Oh, God," Jon said. "I hear a country song a-comin' on!"

"Jon Than? How many times I have to ask you not to take the Lord's name in vain?"

After watching his cousin a moment, Jon said, "Great. You'll be in Boston. We'll get to see a lot of each other. You'll get to meet my family. Get to know the rest of your family."

"Doubt that," Skylar said. "After Dufus gets through visitin' with your friends and relations up there in Boston, I doubt another southern farm boy will be much welcome."

Jon stood up. "You suppose he's packed yet?"

"He's only got his new clothes to pack. He sure looks funny in that barbershop haircut. Jon Than?" Skylar picked a blister on his hand. "Don't be surprised if Dufus is real scared on that airplane goin' to Boston with you."

Jon stretched his arms over his head. "I expect he might be."

"Don't be surprised if he doesn't like Boston much, and wants to come home right quick."

"I won't be surprised at anything, Skylar. Gotta have style, that right?"

"Same as bein' contrary," Skylar muttered.

Jon said, "Just thought I'd give everybody a chance. . . . My father . . ."

Skylar stood up. "Guess I'm fresh out of things to say, just now."

In mock awe, Jon said, "Lordy, Lordy! And I mean it!"

Skylar picked up his trumpet. Then he remembered his bruised lips. "I can't play this thing."

Jon slid the light chair under Skylar's desk. "And that is only one reason I punched you out."

"Go on home," Skylar said. "Homeboy."